Housecarl

Book 1 in the Aelfraed series

By

Griff Hosker

Housecarl

Published by Griff Hosker 2016
Copyright © Griff Hosker Third Edition

A CIP catalogue record for this title is available from the British Library.
Cover by Design for Writers

Contents

Characters and places in the book

Aedgar-Earl of Mercia
aelfe-Saxon Elf
Aelfraed-Descendant of Alfred the Great's son
Aethelward-Aelfraed's uncle
Alfred-King of Wessex
Branton-Osbert's brother, an archer
byrnie-Armoured coat
Catherick-Catterick North Yorkshire
Cynan Ap Iago-Welsh prince
Danegeld-Bribe paid to Danes by English kings in the 8th -10th centuries
Ealdgyth -Wife of Gruffyd
Eystein Orri-The fiancé of Hardrada's daughter
gammer-Old woman or mother
Gruffyd Ap Llewellyn-King of Wales until 1064
Gruffydd Ap Cynan -The King who succeeded Gruffyd
Gryffydd of Rhuddlan-Welsh housecarl
Gytha-Relative of the Earl of Hereford
Harald Hadrada-King of Norway
Hetaireia-Imperial bodyguard of the Byzantine Emperor
leat- An open stretch of water close to a river
Jorvik-York
Legacaestir-Chester
Maeresea-River Mersey
Malcolm Canmore-King of Scotland
Mara-Delamere forest Cheshire
Medelai-Middleham North Yorkshire
Osbert-Sergeant at arms of Aelfraed
Osgar-Housecarl of the Earl
Oswald-Priest at Topcliffe
Persebrig-Piercebridge
Ridley-Housecarl of the Earl
strategos-A Byzantine general
Sweyn-Leader of the Housecarls
Thingman-Housecarls of the English Royal family until 1051
Ulf-Housecarl
Wight-Spirit

Witenagemot -The council of England who chose the king
Wolf-Housecarl of the Earl
wyrd-fate

Chapter 1

Northumbria 1052 A.D

I cannot remember much about my mother, Aethelgifu. It is said that I was her favourite which might explain why my brothers hated me. I was called the runt, partly because of my small size but mainly because I was born twelve years after my brother Edward. I could understand why my brothers despised me so for my mother had died less than a year after my birth and the two events seemed to be inextricably linked but I could never understand my father's antipathy towards me. It was never the fierce hate and violence of my three brothers but it was, at best, indifference and, at worst, a vague disgust at my existence.

I was largely brought up by my grandmother, Aethelfled, but I always called her Nanna. She loved me as fiercely as my brothers hated me and she protected me as much as my father ignored me. She was a lovely old lady, as round as she was high and the oldest person I knew at that time. She had a wonderful aroma about her which made me feel, somehow, both safe and loved. It seemed to me that her arms were always around me like a warm protective wall. For as long as I could remember I slept in the bed and room with the gentle old lady who would send me to sleep with stories of my ancestors for I was descended, so I was told, from the youngest son of Alfred the King of Wessex who was known as The Great. His grandson, Aethelwine, and his brother were killed at the battle of Brannaburg seemingly without children but Nanna told me that he had had a wife who had born him a son and we were descended from that line. My mother's name and that of my grandmother were the names of the daughters of Alfred and I had indeed been named after that King by my mother. That, perhaps, was another reason why my brothers and father felt the way they did about me for I was the exception. My father was Edwin, my eldest brother, Egbert, my middle brother, Edgar, and my third brother, Edward. I was different. I looked different and I felt different from the rest of the family. When my grandmother was not present my brothers would call me an aelfe, the son of a Wight, as though some spirit had inhabited my mother and I was not of their blood. When they spoke to me that way I hoped that it was true for I felt no affiliation to the cruel brothers who tortured me so.

Nanna taught me to read and that too was a matter of dissension for my brothers could not and they resented that I could do something which they could not. Although we were nobility it was of a rural kind. My father's family had been awarded land when the people of Northumbria

6

finally threw off their Danish shackles and became their own masters. They were called Thegns although before they had fought and defeated the Danish overlords they had been warriors for hire. Given the land of Medelai, they were the guardians of the invasion route from the north and owed their allegiance to Count Gilpatrick. When my father had met my mother, she was living at the court of Edward who became known as The Confessor when he ascended the English throne. In the years before the house of Wessex regained the throne of England Edward's court had been the centre of all things, English and my father had chosen his bride to give himself a little more credibility and a link to the English crown.

All of this was told to me by my grandmother who made sure that I knew of my connection to the ancient royal house of Wessex. She never, for one moment, implied that I might become someone who would rule but she instilled in me a belief that I should do all in my power to support the house of Wessex. Harald Godwinson had even visited his childhood friend, my mother after she had married my father and this too afforded great honour on my family for all knew that Harald was Edward's heir and would become king.

The protection afforded to me by my grandmother was only available within the confines of the wooden hall in which we lived. Father spent much of his time down the road at Jorvik and the court of Northumbria where he could plot and plan with the other Thegns. The farm was managed by Oswin, the family steward, but he walked warily around my brothers, huge warriors who strutted around armed to the teeth whenever father was away; which was most of the time. Once I was outside I was fair game for my brothers. Egbert and Edgar were warriors and, fortunately rarely around but Edward, just twelve years older, more than made up for that. He took great delight in hurting me whenever he could; this was frequently in the form of violence but, perhaps, even worse it was his words that hurt me the most for I grew to shrug off the blows and smacks but the words drove themselves insidiously into my soul. He called me a child of the underworld whose spirit had bewitched and enchanted our mother. Despite my grandmother's assurances that this was nonsense my dreams were haunted by black and evil spirits which woke me with the shrieks and cries which filled my head. I always suffered powerful dreams throughout my life. While Nanna was alive I was comforted by her gentle touch and cooing words but once she died my nightmares terrified me.

One day Edward found me outside where I was playing at being a warrior with a stick. Seeing that I was alone he stalked me and then attacked me from behind. His punches rained into my side and bloodied my nose. When I crawled, tearfully, back to my grandmother I saw from her shocked expression how much he had hurt me. For her, this was the last straw. It was many years later that I found out that my grandmother had then sent for her son, my mother's brother, Aethelward, to be a protector for me. I did not know that she had seen her own imminent death and had done the only thing she could, find someone to look after me as she had, through the love of my mother.

I can still remember the day Aethelward limped into the yard at the farm. I was coming up to seven years old and filling out. My uncle had the world-weary look of someone who has seen life and suffered but who could face any adversity the fates threw at him. He dragged a left leg and used a spear as a walking stick. The round shield at his back and the sword hanging from his side marked him as a warrior and even my brother Edward was impressed by his scars. His face showed that he had been wounded in places other than his leg. The scar running from his mouth to his chin gave him a strange lopsided grin. In another man, it might have given him the look of a fool but the green eyes, which were the same colour as mine and my grandmother's glared out to defy anyone to comment adversely. It was his eyes that made me love him for my eyes were the same colour whilst my father's and brothers were blue; it was another of the many differences between us and had been a cause of many comments. I had begun to fear that Edward was right and I was fey, for Edward had told me that green eyes were the mark of the devil. As soon as I saw my uncle I knew that this was a lie and that was the beginning of my escape from the tyranny of my brothers.

"This is the boy then? This is Aethelgifu's son?"

"Aye, and he needs you."

I was too young then to understand the nuances and subtleties of looks and gestures but I saw a look exchanged between the two of them that I did not recognise. He held me so that he could see my face. He stared intently at me and his eyes widened as he looked beyond my face to my grandmother. She must have made some sort of sign for he nodded, not at me, but her. "Now I am here we will make a man of you. I will make a warrior that will make my sister proud. Aelfraed, you go and play outside." He must have seen the look of terror on my face for any place away from Nanna was a place of danger; Edward and my brothers were about. It was not just those who were the problem now for the servants felt they could treat me with impunity. The only ones who did not bother me were the women and the slaves. For the rest, I was fair game and amusement.

"He feels safe close to me." I did not see my grandmother's face but she must have made a gesture for my uncle left without a word. "You will be safe now, Aelfraed. Your uncle is a mighty warrior who fought for the king. He was a Thingman and singers have written songs about him."

"Why does he walk funny?"

She smiled and held me close to her. "He was wounded and nearly died, my son, but now he is here to look after you."

The footsteps behind me told me that my uncle had returned. "You can play outside now, Aelfraed. No one will harm you and I will not be long. I just need to talk to your grandmother."

Despite his reassuring words when I emerged into the sun I felt as frightened as though I was stepping into an enchanted forest at midnight. The first thing I noticed was that Edward had a red and flustered look. Although he was seventeen, his beard was slow to grow. When it did it would hide the red marks which I now saw. He took one look at me and then fled into the woods. The others who were around made themselves scarce leaving me with the yard to myself. It felt glorious. For the first time in my life, I was unafraid and I had all the buildings to explore.

It was when I was in the stable that I first spoke to Ridley. He was younger than I was and the son of Oswin the Steward. I had seen him before but never had the chance to speak with him. He was the closest in age to myself and the only one with whom I thought I could play. I had never had the chance before but now I boldly approached him. "Do you want to play?"

He shrank back in fear. "You are an aelfe! Do not hurt me!"

"Who told you that? It is a lie!" I impulsively reached down to touch his arm and he recoiled in horror. "See, nothing has happened to you. I am just a boy."

When his hand did not burn and he did not turn into a frog he looked a little closer at me. "You have green eyes."

"So, have my grandmother and my uncle and my mother!"

He considered this information and I could see the thought processes at work. Ridley always had that habit, even as a man, it was as though you could see him thinking. His brothers and sisters had died young and

Oswin did not bother much with him. He stood and walked towards me. He reached up and touched my head running his hand gently down my face. "You seem real but why did your brother tell me you were a Wight?"

I shrugged. "He hates me and I know not why. Can we not be friends and play? I have no friends yet."

He seemed to like that idea. "Can we play chasing? I cannot catch the others but I might catch you." I had never played that game, it was not one of Nanna's but I had seen the other children running around the yard and knew the general idea. "I nodded and touched him. He immediately reached for me but I had leapt away and was screaming into the yard with the squealing Ridley in hot pursuit.

That first game did something to both Ridley and me, it bonded us together. We were evenly matched, for he was the same size as me and, and we both had something we had never had before, a companion. It was the beginning of a friendship that lasted beyond that fateful day at the bridge and the dark days which followed. We soon began to play a whole variety of games as my life changed for the better.

The whole family always ate together in the hall but that first day when the limping warrior returned, the atmosphere changed. The chair at the head of the table, my father's place was left empty as usual but the seat at the other end, the one my mother had used but latterly had been occupied by Nanna was claimed by Aethelward. Egbert and Edgar had returned from hunting and been in congress with Edward so that by the time they arrived for the food the three of us were seated at one end of the table.

Egbert was a brute of a man. He worked on his sword play each day and his arms were like the branches of a tree. He glowered at Aethelward who was picking at one of the two partridge he had taken.

"You! My brother tells me you have warned him to leave the Runt alone. What gives you the right?" Aethelward ignored him and Nanna leaned over to encourage me to eat. As I looked at her she winked. I was somewhat taken aback and picked at my food but kept a surreptitious eye on the proceedings. I could sense violence in the air. "I am talking to you!" In anger, Egbert smashed the pommel of his sword on the table."

Aethelward calmly wiped his hands on his breeks and then looked at the glaring, angry face. His voice was measured and yet threatening at the same time. "Boy! Did my sister and her husband teach you no manners? Have you forgotten the laws of hospitality? Not to mention the sin of bringing and holding a weapon during a meal."

Egbert was taken aback but he suddenly looked foolish with a sword in his hand in his own home. He reluctantly put the sword back in its scabbard and on the adjacent table. He quickly turned around. "It still doesn't answer my question, old man. What gives you the right…?"

My uncle was on his feet in a moment and his hand gripped the throat of my brother. His eyes were narrow and angry and his voice was filled with anger as he pressed his face close to Egbert's. "Firstly, boy, I am Thegn Aethelward of the Thingmen and I am your uncle so do not talk to me about rights. Your father is not here which makes me the senior Thegn and whilst I have overlooked your rudeness before I will tell you this, the next time you raise your voice to me will be your last breath on this earth. That is my right. Is that clear?"

My terrified brother nodded and he was dropped to the floor by my uncle who sat down. He turned to his mother. "I am sorry for my outburst mother. You certainly brought me up better than that but some people needed a lesson in manners. I can see that I have come back just in time."

Edgar sat up as though poked with a stick.

"You are staying?"

"Of course, I am staying." He smiled a wolfish smile, "Why nephew am I not welcome?"

"Well no but…" his answer tailed off and I saw Edward and his brothers all pale. It was now obvious that they had thought they would go back to their cruel ways once he had left but now they were faced with the unpleasant prospect of a guardian angel watching over and protecting their victim. Suddenly the food before me tasted much better and I began to eat heartily. I did not notice the smile exchanged between mother and son but I did feel Nanna's hand pat me gently on the head.

"When your father returns, I will make a proposal to him," he leaned forward. "Make no mistake I am here to stay and," he glanced down at me, "there will be a change in the way this family lives."

That night as I snuggled next to Nanna, Aethelward sat with us. "Nanna has told me of your suffering young Aelfraed and as you heard that will change but your life will change as well. Soon there will be just the two of us."

I looked up at my grandmother, my eyes filling with tears as the import of his words sank in. "No! You cannot leave!"

"I am going nowhere my child but I will be leaving. It is the way of all of us and I will be with your mother soon. I want to tell her that her favourite son is well."

"I was her favourite?" It was the first time that I had been told but I had picked up the idea that I was in some way special. My brother's hatred of me confirmed the fact.

"You were and now that her big brother is here to watch over you and to train you then I can depart happy."

Aethelward put his arm around his mother. "Had I known I would have returned sooner."

"It is wyrd. You are here now."

He looked at me again, "I begin to train you on the morrow, we will make a warrior of you."

I looked up at him, "But men are warriors, Edward is not even old enough to be a warrior yet and he is much older than me."

"He should be a warrior and he should have been trained. My training began when I was younger than you. We will work every day for a time is coming when you will need to fight and defend this land."

I shrank into my grandmother's side. Fighting! My life had been turned upside down in less than a day and I began to feel real fear for the first time. The bullying of my brothers had been predictable and, with Nanna's help, manageable. Now I was going to be thrust into a world where I knew nothing and I was scared.

Nanna's voice was reassuring and gentle, "Fear not, Aelfraed, for you were born to be a warrior. It is in your blood."

"Then I am an aelfe!"

Mother and son looked at each other and then laughed, "No, my child, but you are the son of a great warrior."

Doubt filled my mind for no one had ever said that Edwin of Medelai was a great warrior; perhaps I had misjudged my father.

My three brothers left early the next day. Aethelward grinned from ear to ear as they galloped out of the yard. He looked at me. "It is the small things which are the mark of a man and tell you much about him. I now have the measure of your brothers and believe me I would not wish to stand in a shield wall with them."

"You have stood in a shield wall?"

Everyone knew that only the best of warriors stood in a shield wall. I wondered once again about my father for I knew that he had never stood in a shield wall.

"Aye, for I was a Thingman." I looked up at him sheepishly. I did not know what a Thingman was and had not wanted to ask. He noted my look. "Never be afraid to ask if there is something you do not know. That is how we learn by asking questions. Those who fear to ask questions never learn and soon perish. I see you are puzzled by the word Thingman. The Thingmen were the bodyguard of the king and when we fought the king never lost a battle."

"Is that where you hurt your leg?"

"Aye. We fought some Danes and one of them feigned injury, when I passed him he hamstrung me."

"So, you cannot fight now?"

"Oh, I can fight but not in a shield wall. I have learned to ride a horse."

"But my brothers ride horses."

"Aye, but they do not fight from a horse. I went to the French Northmen and learned there. They are like the Danes but they fight from the backs of horses and use lances. They are a powerful foe. Now that is enough about me for a while. When we have a break, I will tell you of Constantinople and the land of the Romans." My eyes must have shown my excitement for he patted me on my head. "You are my sister's son and more, I can see that. Come, pick up your sword." He had made me a wooden sword. When I lifted it I found it very heavy. "You notice its weight, eh? That is to build up your muscles. Tonight your arms will ache and for the next few weeks but there will come a time when they will not hurt and then you will be ready for a real sword."

I was so young and so desperate for play of any kind that I threw myself into the training. I had spent so many years hiding and making myself as inconspicuous as possible that it was liberating to be having so much enjoyment. I know that it was not meant to be enjoyable and my dour uncle tried to make it hard work but in all honesty, it was not. I had the energy of a child if not the strength and picked up the skills very quickly. It must have impressed my uncle for he stopped after a while to question me. "Have you done this before? Perhaps in play?"

I shook my head. "Until you came I had not played. I play with Ridley. Chasing." I looked embarrassed. Chasing did not sound like a warrior skill.

Surprisingly he nodded. "Chasing is a good game. It speeds up the reflexes and makes you supple." I gave him the confused look with which he was becoming familiar. "Supple." He grabbed me and twisted me. His touch was not rough and tickled and I giggled. He suddenly grabbed me in both arms and held me close to him. I felt tears steam down his face. "That is how Gifu, your mother, looked when she laughed. Gods but you are her twin." He put me down. "Go and find this Ridley, I have an idea."

Ridley was not hard to find for he was watching us from beyond the cow byre. He approached the fierce-looking warrior nervously. "Come child, you need not fear me. I am Aelfraed's uncle and it will save time if you call me uncle too. Will you do that?" Ridley nodded. "Good. Your silence is a good sign that we shall get on. Would you like to learn to fight as Aelfraed does?" Ridley grinned and nodded so hard I thought his head would fall off. "Good. Then wait here while I get you a sword."

And that was how it began. My training became much swifter as I had someone the same height as me to fight. Aethelward could see my posture better and he corrected it. Ridley loved both the training and my uncle. His father, the Steward, was a serious man neither given to play nor conversation and he suddenly found that someone paid him attention. The exotic wounded warrior was an intriguing and exciting grown-up. We spent three days with just our swords and learned to block, thrust and stab to Aethelward's satisfaction. He smiled at our bruises and said they were marks of honour marking our progress and we proudly boasted of them to each other.

Once, when I had turned my back on Ridley and he had struck me I turned angrily around. My uncle restrained me. "No, Aelfraed, the fault lies with you and not your opponent. Always be ready for the unexpected attack." He pointed to his wounded leg with his stick. "I discovered that even those we think are dead can be deadly. Remember too that there will be more than one enemy on a battlefield and not all will be to your front. No do not chastise Ridley, rather thank him for providing a valuable lesson."

We had then practised with Uncle trying to dart in behind our guards when we were engaged with each other. From his nods, I could see that he approved of our progress.

"Tomorrow we shall see about getting you two a shield each."

Our burgeoning and excited questions were halted by the clatter of hooves in the yard as my father and my brothers returned. All four of them stared malevolently at our uncle who turned to us. "You two go and play, I think the Thegn, your father, wants a word with me." I must have looked afraid for he suddenly grinned and gave me a wink. "Fear not. I am going nowhere until I choose."

We watched as he limped over to the hall. It was then I noticed that he always wore his wolf skin cloak about his shoulders and, just peeping from the bottom I could see the tip of the scabbard of his sword, worn across his back. It struck me as odd for I had never noticed them when facing him but now, seen from the back, they showed that the warrior was still wary and still prepared for action. We half-heartedly prodded and poked at each other in the yard but the raised voices from the hall intrigued us and, without words, we ceased our training and ran to the wall to eavesdrop. We knew that we should not and that, if discovered, we would be punished but the angry noise from inside was just too irresistible.

"Are you forgetting, Edwin, the debt you owe me?"

"It is not honourable for you to mention that and the debt will be repaid when I am ready."

"It is not honourable to treat a helpless boy like a thrall and to treat a warrior like a criminal."

There was a silence and I wondered what their faces showed for I had learned to look at the faces of men when they spoke and, more importantly, when they remained silent for they often told you more of their thoughts.

I heard my brother, Egbert, suddenly shout, "What is this debt? We owe this man no debt!"

My uncle's voice was laden with threat. "I think, Edwin, that you stay away from your hall too much. You should be here to teach this pup lessons in manners for if he shouts at me again he will lose more than his tongue."

"Try it old man..."

"Silence!" My father's voice cracked like a whip and I wondered at Egbert's defiance for I remembered how he had been held like a squirming fish by the warrior he called an old man.

Aethelward's voice laughed a reply, "Any time you are ready, Egbert, you can try your blade but, ask your father first, for he knows that you would lose."

Just when it was becoming interesting I felt my ear being tugged and Ridley and I were hauled to our feet by Nanna. "No one hears anything good when they spy on others. Back to the yard and do not let me catch you listening again."

As we trudged back to the yard I could see the pain on my grandmother's face as she coughed blood into a cloth. I felt guilty for I knew that she should be resting. She was right, we had learned nothing from the argument save that my father owed my uncle a debt and Egbert was willing to fight Aethelward. Neither helped me although I secretly wished that my bullying brother would try his blade against that of my uncle for I was certain that he would lose, and he would die. The pagan side of me relished the thought but the Christian side, that of my Nanna, made me feel guilty that I was wishing death on my brother.

That night as I lay in my bed I was desperate to ask Aethelward about the debt but knew that, if I did, he would know that I had disobeyed him and I did not want him to think badly of me. Instead, I asked, "Tell me of Constantinople and the Romans."

He smiled, his eyes half closing at the memory. "I was not much older than your brother Egbert and I was full of myself." His eyes opened and he looked seriously at me. "My first battle was a disaster and I think that it saved my life. Remember, young Aelfraed, that mere belief in oneself will not save you when you are badly led." He pulled the covers up to my ears and his sonorous voice told the tale and I suddenly thought that it sounded like one of the sagas we heard at Yuletide and that my uncle had more skills than merely those of a warrior. "The Emperor was a young man, not unlike Egbert, who thought that he merely had to turn up on a battlefield and he would win. My first battle, the battle of Azaz, showed that he was wrong. We marched into the desert to fight the Arabs and I felt invincible."

"Did you have fine armour?"

"Who is telling this tale, young Aelfraed, you or I?"

"Sorry."

He ruffled my hair, "Never stop the tale for it must be told to the end. Aye, we had fine armour; a long mail shirt and greaves on our legs. We each had a long well-balanced axe and our shields wore the sign of the Raven. Atop our heads, we each wore a sound helmet with a leather cap beneath. Oh, we were well protected but as we headed into the desert the heat was so much that men began to fall. There was little water and then men began to die from diseases. When we were all weakened then the men of the desert, the Arabs, attacked and even though they were not as armoured as we, their attacks killed those who were not as skilled nor as well protected as we were. When they came within range of our axes then they died but they used arrows and spears and learned to keep away from the edges of our weapons. Were it not for the Hetaireia, the Emperor's own bodyguard, who sacrificed themselves then we would not have escaped. It showed me then that men must fight for something in which they believe or a man they can follow. Emperor Romanos was not a man to follow."

His voice fell silent. I used the silence to venture a question. "But you served him still."

"Aye, you show wisdom beyond your years, young warrior, I did but he only lived a short while longer and the ones who followed were neither as foolish nor as reckless with their warrior's lives. Now sleep, like your grandmother."

I looked at Nanna and the tendril of blood that dripped from the corner of her mouth. "Is she dying, uncle?"

He looked at me sadly. "Warriors do not lie to other warriors, even when those warriors are not yet grown. Aye, she is dying and will soon be with your mother. I think she only stayed alive long enough to see me and to pass your protection onto my shoulders."

I turned my face into the covers so that my uncle would not see my tears. I might be training to be a warrior but I was still the child who loved and adored this woman who had always been there for me and protected me from all the threats around me. I knew then that she and my mother had regarded me as special. I knew not why but I determined I would neither let them down nor this mighty warrior who had fought at the ends of the world.

Nanna died seven nights later. My uncle brought me to her. Her eyes were closed and I thought for a moment that she had died already as her skin was grey and there appeared to be no movement. I almost cried out in relief when her rheumy eyes slowly opened and she smiled that comforting smile that had kept me going through the darkest of times. She reached an arthritic hand towards my hand and I felt the cold of approaching death. For the first time in my young life, I was watching and feeling life depart.

"Aelfraed, you have greatness in you. You are descended from kings and you must never forget it. My son has been charged to watch over you and guard you as long as he lives but remember," she paused as she coughed up some more flecks of blood, "that your mother and I will watch over you for eternity." This disquieting message seemed at odds with the devout Christianity of my Nanna but I could feel the passion in the grip of her stiff fingertips. She saw the tears dripping from my eyes.

"Do not weep for me. I have loved you since before you were born and I will continue to do so long after I have passed on. Kiss me and say goodbye."

I dutifully leaned forward and kissed her on the cheek as she kissed me on mine. It seemed for a moment that the rosy glow of her cheeks, which I had always seen, rushed back for the briefest of moments and then she lay back. "Goodbye, Nanna."

Aethelward nodded and gestured for me to leave. He remained with her for a short time and when he came out his face was dark. "Our mother has gone."

Chapter 2

Although the arrival of my uncle had marked a serious change in my life the most momentous meeting came almost ten years after Nanna's death. The Earl of the land of Northumbria for the last few years had been Tostig Godwinson. My uncle did not like him and was disparaging about him when he spoke with me. I had noted, however, that whenever my father and brothers were around Aethelward kept his own counsel. We had become close by then and I asked him about this, apparent, hypocrisy.

He had looked at me carefully and spoke quietly, "Some men like to use information to weaken a warrior, and others can be trusted. I know that you would never betray one of my confidences." I had recognised that there was bad feeling between my uncle and my father but I had not thought that it would be so deeply rooted and I became wary and watched my words.

The training had continued over the intervening years and Ridley and I now met with the approval of Aethelward. By approval, I mean that he did not always shout at us or call us useless clods. Those were heady days indeed. Although we had both filled out and grown Ridley had developed into a giant of a man. He towered over all of us and his father regretted allowing Aethelward to train him. It was an expensive luxury but whatever hold my uncle had over my father it extended to the Steward and his son for Ridley trained every day. My uncle would vary our training diet by taking us on long walks through the hills and moors to hunt and to exercise. When I asked about horses he had snorted. "There will come a time when you can think about a horse but first let us master your feet which still move too slowly."

The day which changed my life began with the arrival of two outriders. They were mailed and armoured with the most magnificent armour I have ever seen. It seemed to gleam as though silver. When I asked Aethelward about that he laughed and told me that good warriors burnish their armour to stop it rusting. I was envious for I only had an old leather byrnie for armour. When I had first been given it I had felt proud like a real warrior but now, having seen fine armour, it paled.

The riders rode straight to my father who had spent more time on the farm since the arrival of my uncle. We were busy exercising but I could see that Aethelward's attention had been aroused. As the two riders left my father looked towards us and then gestured for us to approach. That in itself was a matter of note for I had been avoided by my whole family since Nanna's death. Leaving Ridley to take the weapons away we drew closer to my father and brothers.

"Make yourselves presentable, Earl Tostig approaches and his brother Earl Harold."

My uncle's face lit up into a smile when he heard the name of Earl Harold and as we went to clean up he told me why. "I will be interested young Aelfraed in your assessment of these two brothers for they are the most powerful men in the whole land."

"More powerful than the King?"

"The King is more concerned with matters of the soul and the Church for he is a holy man. Harold is the next in line to be king, although the Witenagemot would have to choose, Harold, is the one they would choose."

"You like him." It was a statement, not a question for I had learned to listen to the way my uncle spoke as well as the words.

"Aye. He is a noble warrior and a man you can trust. Your mother and I knew him when we were children and I feel about him the way you feel about Ridley. I would trust him with my life and the life of my family." There was something he had not said but I could not discern it. "Today is an important one for you Aelfraed. Watch your tongue and watch others. Do not attempt to flatter or ingratiate yourself. Others will do that and will become lesser men for their falsehoods."

As soon as I saw Earls Tostig and Harold I could see that they were brothers but I could also see that they were different. Perhaps my uncle's words coloured my judgement but I disliked Earl Tostig the moment I saw him and fell under the thrall of Harold. They had a small but very well armed retinue and I could see, at a glance that they were all hardened warriors. They were the elite, the Housecarls.

My father had tried his best to belittle both Aethelward and myself by standing with my brothers on the steps to the hall leaving me and Aethelward at a lower level. It was a snub and meant to demean us. I must have shown my irritation for I felt a hand on my shoulder and a small, quiet voice spoke in my ear. "It is not where you stand but how you behave which marks you as a man and a warrior."

As Tostig and Harold dismounted his Housecarls watched all of us, their mailed and veiled faces seeking any sign of treachery. Knowing that Aethelward had been one such warrior raised him even higher in my estimation and made me wonder again about the claim that I was descended from a great warrior. In the years since I had heard the words, I had looked for a sign but Edwin of Medelai showed no attributes of a great warrior, if anything he appeared less now than he had, more of a greedy merchant than a fighter.

I saw my brothers fawn and fuss over Tostig who appeared to enjoy the flattery. Harold, by contrast, appeared ill at ease and embarrassed by the whole thing. He turned and caught sight of my uncle.

"Aethelward! I hoped that you were still alive." He and my uncle embraced like old friends. A scowl appeared on the faces of Tostig and the rest of my family who appeared unhappy that the attention had moved from them to someone else.

"No, my lord, I survived, a little punctured here and there but alive nonetheless."

Harold laughed and turned to Tostig. "Brother, why did you not tell me that this mighty warrior resided here? I would have made this visit long ago." Tostig shrugged as though it wasn't important and my father shepherded the Earl into the hall. Harold looked at me. "And who is this? Your son?"

Aethelward laughed. "Not my son my lord but my nephew. This is Aethelgifu's son, Aelfraed."

A strange look came over the Earl's face; he and my uncle exchanged a knowing look and he unexpectedly embraced me. "Your mother was one of my oldest friends and I was sorry to hear of her death." He released me and held me at arm's length. "But I can see that she would be proud of you. You are powerfully tall. A warrior eh?"

I blushed and grinned, "I hope to be."

Aethelward snorted. "That is some time off nephew."

"This is wyrd, old friend, for I have a task I need help with and I could not think who could perform it. Now I can see that this was not an accident. It was meant to be."

Both of us were intrigued but Harold shook his finger playfully and said, "After the feast, we will talk and there is another old friend with whom we shall speak."

All the way through the feast I was reminded of Aethelward's comments and felt sick at the sight of my father and brothers ingratiating themselves into the favour of the Earl. The final straw came when my three brothers were invited to be Housecarls in the retinue of the Earl. I did not wish to serve the Earl but I felt slighted that I had not been included. I was as big, now, as Edward and I knew that I was a better warrior. It irked me that the three of them would be the rich and well-armed warriors guarding the Earl while I would have to remain on the estate. It did not seem fair but as I came to discover as I grew older, life was not fair.

The announcement appeared to have the same effect on my uncle and Earl Harold for they both moved away from the noisy table to the door of the hall. I did not know what to do and felt foolish sat alone; Harold was a few paces away and he turned to me, "Come Aelfraed. Join us."

I think that was the proudest moment in my life up to that point and I eagerly followed them. When we were outside Harold walked towards the fire of the Housecarls who were still guarding their Earl. Harold halted us and then approached the group who all stood to attention. Harold waved them down and then said, "Ulf." A huge bear of a man disengaged himself from his fellows and came towards us.

My uncle recognised him and shouted, "Ulf you old dog! I thought you would have been with some rich widow enjoying telling lies about your prowess!"

"And I thought you would have been chained to some Byzantine galley."

As Harold and Aethelward had done earlier the two men embraced and slapped each other's backs. Aethelward looked sharply at Harold, "Wyrd? An accident? You bring one of my oldest friends here as though it is not planned. My lord, I did not think you would have your brother's slippery tongue."

"You do me a disservice old friend. Ulf here would have performed the task alone had I not met you but your participation would ensure that the result was a happy one."

"The Earl is right. I was to leave on my mission after we had returned to Jorvik." He looked at Harold and grinning, shook his head, "This is still the same man we fought alongside in the Thingmen."

"I am sorry my lord. I have been around my brother in law too much. Perhaps Aelfraed should…"

"No Aethelward, for I see a role in this for your nephew, unless you think he is not up to it."

"As I do not know what it is I cannot answer. Perhaps if you tell your tale I can decide."

Harold led us to the empty blacksmith's hut where the glow from the fire still remained. "Four years ago, Gruffyd Ap Llewellyn destroyed the garrison at Glastonbury and he has now united all of the Welsh kingdoms through conquest. They are a threat to our safety."

"With due respect my lord they are a threat to Wessex. Here the bigger threat is the Scots."

Harold laughed and looked at me. "That is what I have always liked about your uncle, his honesty. Unlike others I could name. You are right Aethelward but if we can secure our Western border then it will make it easier for us to shift troops north and face the Scots. We cannot fight both at the same time and if we move our men north then the Welsh will pour into the heartland of our country. The Dyke cannot hold them back."

My uncle nodded. "I must teach you chess young Aelfraed. Harold here is the best player I know. Suppose I agree with you what then? You want me to invade the Welsh with a youth?"

Harold laughed again and it made me smile. When people ask why so many were willing to die on the forsaken hill with the erstwhile King of England I tell them it was his laugh. He had a ready smile and a laugh that made everything seem safer somehow. "No, I need you to go with Ulf and young Aelfraed and spy on the Welsh."

"You do not ask much my lord. What makes you think that I could spy for you? A lame old scarred warrior and an untried youth."

I have to say that I did not like being referred to as an untried youth but I knew that my uncle meant no disrespect. He was doing as Harold said he did, he was speaking the truth.

"And that is the perfection of the plan and why I say it is wyrd. Who would suspect you two?"

"Then why send Ulf? He is no lame warrior and he is certainly tried. Would the Welsh not suspect him?"

"They would and he will remain in hiding. It is you two who will go into the settlements. Ulf is there for your protection."

"And if you had not discovered us?"

Ulf spoke for the first time, his deep languid voice evoking sadness even with cheerful words. "Then I would have gone alone and I would probably have died amongst the sheep shaggers and my lord would not have discovered the intent of this King of the Welsh."

"You make it hard to say no, knowing that I owe this man a life."

"As I owe you a life, Aethelward, and I will make good my debt. As for your debt consider that it is paid with your agreement."

"And Aelfraed?"

"He need not go."

"But I want to!" The words burst out of me. I would not be left behind. I was no longer afraid of my brothers but I was afraid of not having the chance to be a warrior.

"It seems he is going."

"And Ridley?"

Harold looked nonplussed for the first time. Later, as we travelled south Ulf and my uncle told me of the complex mind that was Harold Godwinson. He liked to plan to the most minute detail and he had not considered that anyone would add to his ideas. "Ridley?"

"Aelfraed's training partner. He is a sound warrior and would be handy in a fight. It would give us two protectors."

Harold clasped Aethelward's arm. "Then he goes." He looked seriously at me. "It goes without saying son of Aethelgifu, that this stays between us here."

"I swear." I put my hands on my testicles to show that I meant it.

Harold looked wryly at my uncle. "I will take your word that there is something there to swear on." The three men laughed at my blushes. "I am only teasing Aelfraed. You are your father's son and you will not let me down."

I wondered at the look which Aethelward flashed at the Earl but thought no more about it. I was going to be a warrior. "We will leave when your party has left tomorrow."

Harold nodded, "It will take some months to find this out. When you have discovered his plans then you will come to the King's court. Secrecy will no longer be needed at that point." He drew me close to him and I saw, for the first time, how tall he was. He leaned close to me. "When you return, we will see what we can do for you. You would be a warrior?"

I nodded vigorously. "It is all that I wish."

"You will continue to train with Ulf and your Uncle when you are on the road and then I will make you part of my plans for I can see that you are sharp as well as courageous." He looked over to my uncle. "If that is what you wish old friend?"

"Aye, it is." Aethelward looked almost relieved. "Had this not come along then I would have had to take him to the Irish to get some experience."

"I thank God that you did not have to go down that route for the Irish are as unpredictable as the weather."

And so, the next day as my brothers left with Earl Tostig, their superior looks telling all the world of their honour and my disgrace I smiled to myself. Uncle had been right it was not what the world knew that was important it was what a man carried in his heart that counted. Ridley was delighted to be included with us and his father, the Steward, somewhat relieved to have his son taken away by Aethelward for a trip to the capital. My father was the most relieved man for in one fell swoop he was rid of the son he hated and the brother in law who flouted his rule with every breath he took. He gladly gave the three of us horses, no doubt anticipating a profit from his other sons who would be the highly paid Housecarls of the voracious and greedy Tostig. It was said that he could get taxes from the very stones he walked upon.

As we rode down the old Roman road which led south I suddenly realised that I had spent my whole life on the farm, never leaving the valley and now I was going to a different country. I thanked God again for the message my Nanna had sent to my uncle. I hated to think what my life would have been like had he not returned.

Ulf had a spare horse with him for his armour and he rode, as we did, in just a leather byrnie. Ridley looked ridiculously large on his horse and his feet almost touched the ground. That, in itself, suited Ridley who was not the most confident of riders. I too preferred the ground beneath my feet but we all knew that we had to make all possible speed to accomplish our task. I was just excited to be part of something bigger than the life on a busy farm. I had no idea what we would see or what we would have to do but I trusted in my uncle. I did not know Ulf yet but the dour man seemed dependable and, most importantly, my uncle trusted him.

Ridley and I followed the two men who discussed their plans ahead of us. I was desperate to be a part of the discussion but Aethelward's words, 'untried youth' kept ringing in my ears and I remained stubbornly silent. I could feel Ridley's glances towards me as we rode and knew that he was desperate to speak. Eventually, as we left Ripon and began climbing the road across the back of the country, I regretted my silence which was, in any case, unnatural and turned to speak to my companion, "Well Ridley how does it feel to be away from our valley?"

The relief of speech caused his words to pour out in a torrent. "Well, master I am excited but nervous too. This place we are going to, Wales. I have heard that they have dragons there."

I had heard of Welsh dragons but assumed that it was just a story. I scoffed at Ridley's naivety. "I don't think there are dragons in Wales Ridley. That sounds like a story to me."

My uncle turned. "Do not mock what you do not know nephew. There are stories that the dragons were imprisoned in the mountains through which we will be travelling and the flag of the Welsh king, Gruffyd, is a red dragon."

Ridley's face beamed with a smile. "See master. I was right." The smile left his face as the import of the words sank in. "Are they still buried?"

Ulf laughed, "They are lad and that is good although it would be good to be a Beowulf and fight one. Then men would tell the tale of Ulf and the Red Dragon around their fires."

Everyone knew the tale of Beowulf and Grendel but this was the first time I had even thought that we might meet one. "And we pass through the burial place of the dragons?"

"Aye. Dinas Emrys is the mountain which covers them and we are heading for a pilgrimage site which is hard by."

"Pilgrimage?"

"Yes, we are heading for the monastery of St Asaph. It is a holy place and will explain why we are travelling. When we next pass a stand of ash trees we will cut a stave each to add to the illusion."

Ulf nodded. "We can then travel south-east through Wales and people will think that we are heading home rather than spying on our enemies."

"Is this not a lie uncle? For you said that warriors do not lie."

"True nephew. Warriors do not lie to warriors and we will visit the holy place and we will not be lying. When we leave, we will be heading home for our new home will be with Earl Godwin."

"You mean we are not going back to Medelai?"

"No Ridley. We may visit again but Master Aelfraed is to be a warrior and will be part of the Earl's army. The two of you will have to train to be part of the shield wall."

Ridley and I exchanged the excited look of young men who have dreamt of such training. We were almost men in terms of our bodies but our minds were still innocent and like that of a child. At that time, we believed that the shield wall was noble and showed the honour of warriors. We had to learn that to stand in that killing ground had little honour and even less nobility. It was a savage place where only the fittest and most ruthless would survive, but that was in the future. As we climbed the high road we just talked of standing shoulder to shoulder with other warriors defending the honour of our liege lord.

The road we took was a lonely and empty one; built by the Romans it was in need of repair but it was the swiftest way to cross the high country. Although we had plenty of dried meat and there were enough streams for water we all pined for the eggs and fresh foods of the farm. Ridley enjoyed his food and he longed to go hunting to catch a rabbit or two. Aethelward shook his head as Ridley begged for the opportunity to hunt. "This is not a game Ridley. This is what a warrior does. Not for him the life at court with fine food and ale. He goes without. Ulf and I have stood in a shield wall for the better part of a day before now with neither food nor drink."

"Aye, I remember that day. Those Danes were hard men but they left before we did."

"You are right Ulf. We showed that we were the better warriors. Remember this nephew we are different from the Danes because we fight for our lord and our country. The Danes fight for a leader and for plunder. When you fight the Danes, you kill the leader and then they flee."

"And the Welsh?"

"Ah, now they are different. They are cunning. Their land is rocky and does not suit the shield wall. They like to use arrows and let you waste your strength in useless attacks. This is why Earl Harold needs to know their plans and their strength so that we can attack them at places which suit us."

Ulf snorted. "The whole country is one big rock. I doubt that there is anywhere which suits us."

My uncle shrugged. "That is why we have been sent. To discover that which we do not yet know."

Ulf inclined his head towards Aethelward. "And that is why the Earl sent your uncle for he is the cleverest warrior I ever knew. You would do well to copy him."

My uncle laughed. "You need not worry about Aelfraed, Ulf, for he is already capable of out-thinking me."

Ridley looked at me in awe as I blushed with the compliment. I did not know that I was held in such regard. I now understood why my uncle had taught me chess and played each night. I had thought it was a pastime, now I knew that he was both training and assessing me and my skills.

The walled town of Frodsham was the last safe place we travelled through. It seemed solid and safe and the town watch looked to be alert and wary. It was a frontier town and enemy land lay ahead of us. When we finally crossed the Maeresea we could see, in the misty distance, the mountains rising high into the sky. We would not seer the tops for they were wreathed in threatening clouds. Ridley leaned over to me. "That looks like dragon fire to me."

I did not want to appear as gullible as Ridley and I shook my head. "No that looks like a cloud to me."

"Do we have to climb those mountains?"

Ulf answered over his shoulder. "No, the monastery is at the foot of the hills. We only have a short distance to travel. Once we have passed Wat's Dyke we will be in Wales."

My uncle reined in his horse. "Be on your guard for after we have travelled through the forest ahead we will be in dangerous country. Both of you are doughty fighters but up to now, it has been play. The next time you draw your weapons you will be drawing blood. Think on that. Keep your swords handy and, Ridley, place your bow on the pommel horn ready to string should it be needed."

Ridley looked to be pleased to have something to do and he took out his bow from its case and notched the string around one end. I held his reins as he fiddled with his quiver and slung it over his shoulder. I was glad that we had brought my friend for he was a reliable archer and I had the feeling that we would need him.

The Forest of Mara loomed ahead of us stretching east and west as far as the eye could see. It appeared to be a solid barrier, a wall marking the end of England and the start of Wales. I saw Ulf and my uncle don their leather helmets. They had not ordered us to do the same but Ridley and I were still learning our trade and we quickly put ours on too. I wished that mine looked as well used as those of Ulf and Aethelward but those we wore were newly made. Stronger, no doubt, than the older ones worn by the two warriors but they marked us out as apprentices as did our shiny leather byrnies. We had long left the Roman roads and were now on cart tracks. The grass on our present road and lack of tracks showed that it was not a well-used way.

Ulf kicked his horse on and rode a little ahead of us. My uncle called to me. "Aelfraed come here." I rode Raven, my horse, next to him. He handed me the reins of the packhorse which Ulf had given to him. "Here watch the spare." My face must have shown my disappointment for he smiled and added. "We need Ridley's bow and if we meet trouble then we will need my weapons and Ulf's to defend us. Your time will come." He turned to Ridley. "You watch our rear; from here onwards we will always be close to danger."

The track seemed to turn from day to night as we trotted beneath its leafy canopy. The branches looked to be threatening and suddenly sinister as they moved above us in the gentle breeze. There was a total silence, broken only by the clip-clop of the hooves on the forest floor. I almost jumped when Raven snorted and I heard Ridley stifle a giggle behind me. It was with some relief that I saw a clearing and Ulf and my uncle dismounting. "We will camp here. There is water nearby and it is not as gloomy as the other parts through which we have passed."

My uncle might have thought it a pleasant spot but I still found it overpoweringly dark and malevolent. We dismounted and led the horses to the stream to drink. As they were drinking we took off their saddles and used them to mark the boundaries of the camp.

Ulf's voice barked, "You two go into the forest and find some dead, dry wood for the fire."

The last place I wanted to go was into the forest although I was shamed into doing so by Ridley's cheerful whistling as he wandered off into the undergrowth. I was torn between performing my task and watching for whatever was in the forest which might hurt me. My uncle said that I was a thinker and perhaps I overthought things for my imagination provided ghosts, ghouls and phantoms not to mention aelfes and hobs. I steeled myself to look for wood and soon found my arms laden with a bundle.

By the time I returned to the camp it looked half organised with Ulf chipping away with his flint to light the kindling and uncle hobbling the horses. Ridley had reached the camp before me and was handing his timber to Ulf. I almost breathed a sigh of relief that I had reached the camp safely. Once the fire was going the forest seemed less intimidating and I felt foolish for worrying about nothing.

"Cut up some of the dried meat and put it into the pan, we might as well have some hot food. Ridley, go into the forest again and see if you can find any herbs and roots."

"I could take my bow in case I see a rabbit."

Ridley was keen to show Ulf his prowess and surprisingly Aethelward grinned as he said, "Make sure you get the herbs first!"

While I used my knife to cut the tough dried meat into manageable chunks I watched, intrigued as Ulf and my uncle took lengths of thin cord and crouched close to the trails. When they had finished whatever they were doing and they seemed satisfied they returned to the camp where they lay down, their heads resting on their saddles. The meat was now in the water and I took some of the precious salt we had with us and put some in with the meat. I suddenly spied a bush next to the stream and I went to recover some of the elderberries which had escaped the attention of the birds. It would add to the flavour.

As I stirred I ventured the question which had been in my mind for the past few moments. "What were you doing with the cord uncle?"

"Good. I wondered how long it would take you to ask. Remember always ask better to feel foolish than dead. They are alarms to warn us of any predator, human or animal which ventures close to our camp this night."

I looked around fearfully. I had thought of supernatural terrors, not human ones. "There are men in the woods?"

"There may be and if there are then they will be living outside the law and so be dangerous. The Welsh are not the only enemies we will face."

Ridley's cheerful whistling made us turn to see him enter the camp. He was beaming from ear to ear with a rabbit in one hand and a bunch of herbs in the other. "Supper!"

Ulf laughed. "You have done well and your boast was not an idle one. Skin it and Aelfraed can joint it. We eat well tonight. Now if we only had some ale then we would have a fine feast."

That night as we lay around the embers of the fire I felt companionship such as I had never felt before. There was a comfortable silence that punctuated the tales Ulf and Aethelward told of battles past and comrades they had known. The deaths were not seen as sad events but momentous and worthy of praise. I could see that death in battle would not be unwelcome to Ulf and Aethelward who had outlived most of their friends and comrades. We also learned more about Harold and his half brother Tostig. Although both were renowned warriors it was obvious that Harold was seen by both men as the exemplary and iconic leader. Tostig seemed too concerned with himself and how he could profit from any given situation. I allowed myself a half-smile realising that I had chosen the worthier of the brothers and that would be reflected in the honour which I would gain. Ridley sat up and paid particularly close attention when the two men spoke of the Housecarls and their mighty shield wall.

In one of the silences, his small voice ventured a question, "Do you have to be noble-born to be a housecarl?"

Ulf's laugh seemed to echo through the forest. "Gods no! There would be but Aethelward left if that were the case. The only rule is that you are a mighty warrior who can stand with his comrades even when all else have fled and give your life for your liege lord." He looked curiously, almost paternally at Ridley. "Why lad, would you be a housecarl?" In answer, he lowered his head shyly and nodded. "Well you could do worse and you have the size already. When we have the chance, I will see what your arm is like. Now I feel it is time for rest for tomorrow we will need our wits about us. Tomorrow we meet the Welsh."

In the event, we needed our wits a little earlier. I was woken by a hiss from the side of my head, it was my uncle. "Wake Ridley, we have company. Get your weapons but move slowly."

I thanked the spirits of my ancestors that I had the wit to think calmly. I slid my sword from its scabbard and then rolled to the side to speak with Ridley. I touched his shoulder. "Be calm. There are enemies close. Get a weapon and then be ready."

I peered, from my prone position to see if I could discern anything but all I saw was the darkness. Then, as my eyes adjusted to the dark I saw the leaves move unnaturally and when I stared I could see that there was a lightness that appeared to be a man. There were outlaws approaching. I was afraid but also excited. The tales we had heard around the fire had convinced me that Ulf and Aethelward could deal with any problem which arose. The hardest part was not moving as I saw the armed men approach. I trusted in my uncle and Ulf, they would know the moment to move, and I just prayed that I would not let them down.

When the word came, I was ready but it still took me by surprise. With a roar and an unnervingly quick turn of speed, Aethelward shouted, "Now! And leapt at the first shocked outlaw. His sword took him in the throat. I was on my feet looking for the shape I had seen coming from the forest. The man was a huge bear with a helmet, shield and war axe. As I raced towards him I wondered if my first fight might be my last. I tried to remember all that I had been taught and one idea stuck in my mind; use my speed of blade for I could see that he was a lumbering brute who would not be able to move as swiftly as me. I feinted to his right and as he moved his shield to block me I rolled to his left and hacked at his unprotected legs. I felt the blade jar into his shins and then sensed his axe as it sliced above my head. A hand span lower and I would have had no head. It was a harsh lesson. I rolled forwards and backslashed my blade at his unprotected back. Again, the blade struck flesh and his blood spurted down the edge of my sword. He roared with pain and swung his axe at me. Had I had a shield I would have deflected the blow but I only had my sword and I fell backwards over the body of the man my uncle had slain. He thought he had me and lumbered forwards but I had no intention of lying there to be meekly split and I rolled towards the woods. I was on my feet in an instant to face him once again. He hissed at me in some barbaric language but I focussed on his weaknesses; I could see that he had to favour his left side because of the wound to his leg and his back. I swung my sword at his right, aiming for the hand which held the axe. He was tiring and the parry was weak. Again, I feinted to the right and as he moved the shield to cover my attack I saw a gap and stabbed forwards. To my everlasting amazement, he did not block the blow and the sword found the weakened link in the rusty mail and slowly sank in through his layers of fat. He looked down in surprise and then roared; he opened his arms and grabbed me to pull me in towards him. I had not expected that move and the breath from his stinking mouth filled my face. I was terrified. I suddenly remembered that I had a dagger and I reached around to my belt to try to reach it as his arms tightened around me in a bear hug which threatened to kill me. I extricated the dagger and squeezing it up through his grip stabbed upwards into his throat and into his skull. Suddenly I saw the life leave his eyes as his arms dropped to the side and he slowly slid to the floor, he was dead, I had killed my first man.

Chapter 3

I spun around to look for another attack and saw, instead, that the other five had been despatched by my three comrades. It looked as though the fat warrior I had killed had been the better-armed of the bandits for the others lacked helms and armour but they lay dead nonetheless. Ulf grinned at me. "I worried, young Aelfraed that he had taken to you and wished you for his bed. Had I known you were fighting him I would have stepped in to help."

Aethelward saw the shock on my face and came over, his arm around my shoulder. "You did well nephew for he knew how to fight and next time you will not make the same mistakes."

Mistakes? I had thought that I had fought him well. "Are there others?"

"We will find out. You two strip any armour from the bodies and see what they have that we might use. We will search the forests."

Dawn was just breaking when the two warriors returned. It had been a grisly task removing armour and valuables from the dead. It had taken two of us to strip the mail armour from my opponent. The bodies yielded a few coins, the fat one had a purse with a gold piece and two silver ones while the others had a couple of swords and daggers between them. We had laid the bodies in a line, more to stop us from falling over them rather than from any sense of honouring the dead for they had tried to kill us in our sleep and were not worthy of any respect. The horse they brought with them looked to be bigger than ours and I deduced that their leader had been its rider.

"Well, Ridley you may have done well from this attack for I venture the horse will suit you and unless I miss my guess the armour and helmet will fit you better than Aelfraed."

Ridley looked at me for approval. I had no desire to wear the rusty armour but it would have been good had the helmet fitted me. I would have to continue to wear my leather one. "You may have them Ridley but the armour will need work for it is rusty and has links missing."

"For which you should be grateful nephew for if he had looked after it your blade would not have penetrated." He picked up the axe. "This is cared for and is a good weapon. You were lucky that he did not catch you with it for the edge is like a razor."

He handed me the axe which seemed well balanced and I hefted it in my hand. Ulf nodded. "When the opportunity presents itself, I will show you how to use it."

"Ulf is one of the best axemen you will ever meet. Now we must ride for we need to reach our destination by nightfall. I would not risk another night in these bandit filled forests."

The monastery was a huge complex of buildings nestled on a hillside in the Clwyd Valley. My uncle halted us in the woods on the southern side of the valley. As we peered down at the cluster of buildings I was amazed. I had only seen Jorvik which was a bigger place but this was in the middle of nowhere. Ulf grunted. "There are a thousand men down there."

"All monks?"

"Most are monks but they have others who work the land. There is much profit in the Church."

I knew that many warriors, despite the pressure from the King, still favoured the old dark religions which did not have priests but allowed a man to choose his own god. I suspected that Ulf was once such a warrior.

"Now keep in mind we need them to remember us. Aelfraed and I will go down to meet with the abbot while you two keep watch here."

Laying aside most of our weapons and keeping just a sword the two of us rode along the ridge to join the trackway which led first to the monastery and thence to the coast. I was smiling as I did so, not because I was not afraid, I was but Ridley had been petrified to be at the foot of the mountain which contained the red Welsh dragon. I suspected that Ulf would tease him mercilessly.

The land around the monastery of Elvae was well cultivated and terraced, using every part of the hillside to maximise their crops. It was not yet dark and we could see hooded monks toiling in the fields. A few looked up as we passed but, seeing but a man and a boy they returned to their work. We were not a threat. The ash staffs we held were there to mark us as pilgrims but I was not convinced that it would fool anyone. We found ourselves on a wide roadway which was obviously the main entrance. We could see the gates in the palisade were still open but there was a gaggle of monks gathered there, obviously to greet us. We both dismounted when we were thirty paces away and approached on foot. I stood slightly behind my uncle so that I could emulate and copy his actions. He bowed his head and I followed.

"I am Aethelward of Medelai and this is my nephew Aelfraed."

"I am Brother Aidan. What brings you to our monastery?"

There appeared to be no suspicion in his voice but his eyes darted from our faces to our weapons and back. My uncle spread his hands. "We are here to seek the shrine of St Asaph for I would have my nephew to be graced by the Saint's beneficence."

The monk seemed to see the ash staffs for the first time and looked at me. "And your nephew, why would he need the Saint's grace? You are a wounded warrior I can see that but the boy looks hale and hearty."

The monk's sharp eyes had missed nothing but Aethelward had been prepared for such questions. "I suffered my wound fighting the Norsemen when I defended the land of Bede against the invader." By invoking the name of that venerable man of the church Aethelward was trying to get the sympathy of the monk. "Had I visited a shrine before I fought then perhaps I would have been protected. I would like my nephew to be protected before he fights the Danes."

It seemed that Brother Aidan saw me for the first time. "You would fight the Danes? You would fight the enemies of the church?"

His eyes seemed to burn into me to discern if there was a lie within. I felt grateful that I would not need to lie for I would happily fight the Danes although I was not totally committed to the Christian ideal. "I would."

"Then perhaps you should meet with the King and serve him."

My uncle's voice appeared innocent but I knew the weight of his words. "He is at his court?" The court of the King was but a few miles away from St Asaph at Rhuddlan as Gwynedd was the heart of his kingdom.

"No. He is with his army in the south. Perhaps if you travel that way you may meet him."

"I should like that Brother Aidan for I have never met a King before."

The monk smiled and nodded at the passion of my simple assertion. He touched my head with his hands. "I will give you my blessing and then I will direct you to the shrine." I was not prepared for the feeling which washed over me as the old man placed his bony hands upon my head. It seemed that I was warmed and I felt a glow spread through my body. I suddenly felt calmer and more at ease but I knew not why. "May the grace of God protect you in your fight against the Northmen."

I impulsively kissed the back of his hands as he withdrew them and mumbled, "Thank you."

Again, he smiled and pointed down towards the river. "If you go towards the river you will see the shrine."

"How will we know?"

Again, Brother Aidan smiled, "If you know the story of St Asaph then you will know."

As we walked back to our horses my uncle murmured, "That was well done Aelfraed but I think Brother Aidan is still testing us."

I had no idea who St Asaph was. I just knew that he had been a saint who had been with Saint Mungo but I had no idea of his story. I assumed, and hoped, that my uncle would. As we walked along the well-worn track we saw a glow from a building at the end. My uncle just said, "Of course" and continued walking.

We reached a small wooden building and before it was a stone circle containing a fire. Next to the fire were lumps of charcoal and coal and above it was a beautifully carved wooden cross. Aethelward knelt and I copied him. He placed a lump of coal on the fire as I did. "Tonight, we will sleep here." I did not argue with him but I did wonder why.

We fed and tethered our horses and then made our camp. Night had fallen as we chewed on the dried meat. A light appeared down the path. I began to fear that it was something ethereal until I saw that it was two younger monks. They had in their hand's pots. "Brother Aidan cannot invite you into the monastery for it is a closed order but he sent you food. Here is some freshly brewed ale, some of our honey, bread and cheese." He looked up at the cross, "May St Asaph watch over you. If you leave the pots here were will remove them in the morning and," he leaned in confidentially, "the saint smiles on those who protect his fire."

After we had eaten I asked uncle what he had meant. "Saint Asaph famously brought hot coals to Saint Mungo and carried them in his apron. That is why they keep the fire burning as a reminder of the Saint and his deed. We brought the ash staff as that is the sign of the saint much as the cockleshell is the sign of St. James."

I did not care for the reason as the bread, honey and cheese were delicious and a welcome change from the diet of dried meats we had endured. The beer was not small beer it was a potent brew and soon I was asleep. I slept better that night than any other night on the road. I know that Ulf would have said it was the ale but I believe that we were being protected. That night I dreamed of warriors and dragons. I suddenly found myself facing a mighty warrior and behind him was the prow of a dragon ship. I was being beaten back and my sword was struggling to defend me, I fell and saw the mighty axe descending to my head. All that I had to stop was my sword which suddenly changed to an ash staff and then the warrior disappeared and I awoke sweating and breathing heavily. What did my dream portend? I had not had as many bad dreams since the arrival of my uncle. Perhaps it was the mixture of powerful ale and cheese.

The fire was still burning the following morning and I made sure that it was fed before we left. I looked up at the cross before we departed and it made me feel better. I gripped the staff and wondered about my vision. Was it the ale that had made my thoughts drift that way or was it something more? As we rode in silence towards the head of the valley Aethelward rode his mount next to mine. "You had a vision?"

I stared at him. Was he a Wight? How did he know? "I had a dream… it was the ale."

"I do not ask you to tell me your vision for that is yours; it is the mark of a warrior. I ask you to think on your vision and to interpret it for all visions and dreams have meanings."

"How did you know that I dreamt?"

"I heard you speaking and you moved in your sleep. I have seen it before. Harold had such a dream many years ago when he was but a young man. I recognised the signs but, pray, do not ignore it. Think on it and use it."

I nodded and looked at the ash staff. "Uncle, would this staff make a good spear?"

He took it from my hand and turned it. He looked down its length and then hefted it above his shoulder. "Aye, it would. We will use one of the swords we took from the bandits and make a spearhead the next time we find a smith." He smiled. "It was wyrd that we came here Aelfraed and I can see your mother's hand in this."

Ridley and Ulf had been busy since we had left them; the mail armour had been cleaned and scrubbed with the river sand and now looked as it should have done. Ridley's face beamed as we rode into the camp. "See master. It is almost like new and Ulf says that we can repair the broken links when we find a smithy."

I looked quickly at Aethelward who just said, "Wyrd."

"Did it go well?"

"Aye Ulf and my nephew helped to carry it off. The monks believe that we are pilgrims and I gave my name so that we should be remembered."

"I still do not know why the monks are important."

"The King of Wales needs credibility. He has only ruled this land of Wales for a short time and needs the support of the church. This is the largest and most important monastery in this heartland of Wales, in the shadow of the dragon." I smiled as Ridley involuntarily shivered. "The court of the King is at Rhuddlan and I know that men from the court will visit the monastery before too long. The Welsh king will keep patrols travelling along this road and they will bring news to their king."

"Which is why we will need to avoid the road." I saw the plan clearly.

"Precisely young Aelfraed and we will head southeastwards towards the frontier towns. It would not do to be seen as a party of four."

With the packhorses loaded we set off, Ulf, as usual, was at the front while Ridley took the rear. He did not mind the packhorse for it carried his precious armour and, hung from the pommel, was his helmet now scrubbed and polished. I was a little envious. He was already well on to the way to becoming a warrior and he was well-armed. I absent-mindedly stroked the smooth shaft of the ash staff. Ridley might have his armour but I had had my vision and I would get armour that I knew.

"Well, we know that he is to the south of us. That means he will be with his army."

"You are right Ulf for he has only recently conquered that land. We will head for Morgannwg which borders the lands of Wessex. We can watch for signs of war as we travel south."

We had been on the road for seven days when we crossed the trail of the warriors. Ulf's sharp eyes picked up the signs and we halted. With the combined attention of the two warriors, we ascertained that at least a hundred warriors had travelled south, in the same direction as we. It was the first indication we had of warlike intentions.

"Well, we can go to Earl Harold now and tell him that there are warriors gathering on the borders."

Ulf laughed. "Would that it was that simple. These warriors may be heading for the newly conquered lands in the south of the country and there are but a hundred. No, it is a sign but we need to find out what it means."

I looked at Aethelward. "Then how do we find out?"

"We visit the next town and ask."

"As simple as that?"

"No not that simple. We will visit the town and listen for people talk and a hundred warriors passing through will be an event worthy of retelling. You, nephew, can tell of our visit to the monastery and Brother Aidan. They will enjoy that news."

The next town was in Maelienydd. I could not begin to pronounce it but it was a prosperous-looking place with a wooden wall and armed guards at the gates. When my uncle explained that we had been on a pilgrimage we were allowed to enter but I could see that the guards viewed us with suspicion until we dismounted and they saw my uncle's injury. It made them less suspicious. We headed for the hut which had a crudely painted picture of an ear of barley outside. Aethelward nodded towards it, "An alehouse. A good place to begin. You need to listen although if they speak Welsh then neither of us will understand them."

Fortunately for us, the woman who owned the alehouse could speak easily with us. Our coins were welcomed by her and made us even more welcome. There was no one else in the hut and we struck up a conversation. Aethelward asked her if she had rooms and flourished a silver coin. Her eager eyes lit up and she told us we could sleep with the horses in her stable at the rear. I suspected that we had paid too much for what would be basic accommodation but I knew that we would be better off and warmer than Ulf and Ridley camped beyond the town in the woods.

By the time other drinkers had entered the woman, Morag was talking with us as though we were old friends and we were accepted as such by the locals who enjoyed the chance to talk with strangers from beyond their borders. Aethelward was correct and my tale of Brother Aidan and his blessing added truth to the story for he was well known by all. It was Morag who inadvertently gave us our first intelligence. "If you are heading back to the land of the Angles then do not go south for there are many warriors there and I think you will find neither rooms nor food."

"Oh, many warriors eh? Thank you. It is kind of you to warn us."

"Well, we have had them travelling through here for the past month." She leaned over to speak confidentially to Aethelward, "They do not like to pay either. I was glad to see the back of them. At least when the new king came through here he paid."

"He was not with his army then?"

"He travelled with his guards a week before them."

"Then it was a mighty host?"

"He must have emptied the lands of Gwynedd."

"Mighty indeed and timely advice. You are a gracious hostess and I will tell other travellers of your hospitality."

She reached over to pat the back of his hand with a lascivious look in her eye and I suspected that had I not been there then Aethelward would have had the company of the widow's bed that night.

When we met Ulf and Ridley I wondered if we would be heading to Earl Harold but my uncle showed that he knew me better than I knew myself and he explained why we would not be following that particular course of action.

"There is little point in returning to our lord with such scant information. What kind of troops does he have? Who are their leaders? What is their state?"

"But uncle how do we find that out?"

"Simple. We visit their camp and see them."

I could not think of an answer but it seemed most hazardous to me that we would risk all by visiting the camp of our enemy. I did not see the wry smile Ulf gave my uncle for, once again, my uncle was several moves ahead of me on this particular chessboard.

We eventually found the Welsh army just across the Severn from Hereford. It was a mighty host although I had not seen more than fifty men together before then and perhaps my judgement was coloured. The army filled a number of fields and seemed to be mainly archers but the warriors who were armed with spears and shields looked formidable enough. My uncle led the two of us into the heart of the camp. I was terrified. I expected to be slaughtered at every juncture although no one showed us the slightest interest. We were just two would be warriors riding through the camp. Aethelward had donned his mail armour and carried his shield at his side. He told me to hang my axe from my pommel, wear my helmet and sport my shield across my back. I suppose it all added to the illusion that we were volunteers although I knew the moment I opened my mouth they would know that I was English. What terrified me the most was that he headed directly for the tent which sported the flag of the Welsh dragon; he was taking us to their king Gruffyd Ap Llewellyn. I wondered if he had become mad during our journey through Wales.

When we reached the tent, we were confronted by two axemen. Both wore shining armour and had high helmets topped with white feathers. The swords and axes at their side left me in no doubt that these were two of the King's bodyguards. Aethelward nodded for me to dismount which I did with some difficulty for my knees were shaking uncontrollably. My uncle seemed totally at ease and said to the guard, "Tell the king that Aethelward the Saxon is here."

This was it, I thought. I would end my life killed in the camp of the Welsh army. I had killed a bandit but that would be the extent of my feats for these two guards before us could destroy me in an instant. Aethelward smiled down at me as though to reassure me but I still thought him mad. If I could have done so I would have fled from the camp but I knew that my body would have been plucked from my saddle by many arrows.

The guard returned and nodded to my uncle who waited. The flap of the tent opened and there stood the king. I assumed he was the king because he wore a small crown but he could have been anyone. His armour was scale armour and shone like burnished gold. He looked sternly at me and then at Aethelward and then, suddenly his face burst into a grin and he embraced my uncle. I was astounded. "Aethelward! What in God's name brings you here?"

He gave a small bow and said, "Your majesty, my nephew and I were at the shrine of Saint Asaph and we heard you were in the south of the country. My nephew said he had never met a king. As you are the only king I know I thought we could journey here on our way south."

It was then that I knew how clever my uncle was. He had used the little truth we had in our story and used it to provide a plausible excuse for our presence. I followed and bowed my head.

"And your nephew's name?"

"Aelfraed."

"Welcome Aelfraed. to my kingdom. Come, the two of you, join me in some wine and then I can catch up with your life." He noticed the limp and nodded. "I can see that it has been eventful, come."

I was too stunned to even think about speaking and I sat there as the two men reminisced. It turned out that my uncle had fought as a mercenary against Earl Leofric of Mercia for Gruffyd and earned the respect of the king. The men were of an age and it explained why my uncle had been chosen for this task.

Later as the evening grew darker and the alcohol flowed freer the King began to ask questions of Aethelward that would have worried me had I been the one being questioned.

"So, old friend, what do you do now?"

"Now? I escort my nephew back home."

"Ah and is home the court of King Edward?"

I suddenly realised that this was warrior speaking to warrior and Aethelward could not in all honour lie. "Our home is now in Northumbria at Medelai."

"Ah. Not the court of Earl Harold, your friend."

"I have many friends, your majesty. That is what comes of fighting for so long but as you can see," he tapped his leg, "I fight no more."

The King seemed relieved. He turned to me, "And Aelfraed, I see that you have trained; would you be a warrior and stand in the shield wall as your uncle did?"

"I would your majesty."

"Would you stand in my shield wall?"

This was a trick question and had I had more alcohol I might have answered with a lie but I saw the quick flick of my uncle's eyes and deflected the question. "Your majesty would not want an untried youth in his ranks. When I have trained as a warrior then you can ask me again."

"I will, young Saxon, for you have a look about you which reminds me of your uncle when he was about your age. He is a famous warrior, the Varangian Guard who fought against the Mercians and helped this Prince of Wales gain his kingdom."

As we drank into the night I noticed a sulky looking warrior in the corner. As my uncle was busily pumping the king for information I wandered around the tent trying to find out who he was. Eventually, I discovered that he was Cynan Ap Iago; the son of a king whom Gruffyd had killed to attain his kingdom. As Iago had been but four when the tragedy occurred he had been brought up by the king as a young noble of the court. There was something about him that disturbed me for he seemed to be staring at my uncle. I took him to be a little older than I was but he had not filled out his body and looked, to my eyes, a little weak. Perhaps I had been used to facing Ridley and that coloured my judgement but I found myself now weighing up warriors as potential opponents. My one victory had been so slender that I was determined not to lose the next time I fought. I managed to position myself in the shadows behind Cynan and his small coterie. They were speaking Welsh but some words did make sense to me especially when I heard Iago almost spit out my uncle's name. When they all left, I returned to my uncle's side wondering what this Cynan had against my uncle.

The next morning it seemed that everyone except me was suffering from the celebration the previous night. My uncle's tales had amused everyone except for the sulky Cynan it seemed and the king was reluctant to let us leave. "Stay Aethelward and be my adviser. You were the cleverest warrior I ever knew and you could aid us."

Aethelward then showed me his true nobility for he faced the king and clasped his hands. "I could not do so majesty for you will be fighting my people, the English. I know that you are now allied to Aedgar of Mercia and, having fought his father, I could not be an ally to his son."

The king nodded, "Many men would not accept that answer but I know that you are honourable and I would not wish you to fight against your own people." His face became colder and his voice harsher as he added," Leave my kingdom in safety but, Aethelward the Saxon, if you return, I will view you and your nephew as enemies. Last night was for remembrance; the future begins today and I will embrace you as a comrade and say goodbye."

The two men embraced and I sensed a sadness felt by both men for the times they had shared and the deeds they had done. "Aelfraed, I believe you will be a fine warrior and I hope never to face you in war but if I do then all of the last day will be forgotten."

"I understand your majesty and I thank you and your people for their hospitality."

With that, we rode east towards England. We kept to the rough road which headed east. I knew that Ulf and Ridley were waiting for us in the woods above the trackway and was surprised when we did not ride up to them. I was even more surprised when we stopped and Aethelward dismounted to examine his mount's hooves. I had been following and I had seen nothing untoward but I had learned to trust my uncle and his decisions. As he knelt down he spoke to me. "I cannot see them but I believe we are being followed."

"That is why you did not head up to Ulf."

"Aye. We will continue along here but keep your ears open."

As we trotted eastwards I felt I ought to tell him about the young man and his friends. "There was a group of men who did not sound like they liked you last night."

Aethelward laughed. "That is not surprising as I am English and the Welsh have no love for us."

"No, this one was a young man and he seemed to glare at you all night. I heard some of their words but they were in Welsh."

"Do you have a name?"

"I think the young man was something, Ap Iago."

"Ah that makes sense then, I fought against his father and helped take his kingdom for Gruffyd."

I somehow felt relieved that I had not been imagining the event but then I became worried. If this Ap Iago did wish harm to come to my uncle, then it would not be as bandits for his companions were well-armed warriors. I suddenly realised the danger we were in for the king had made it obvious that, once we left his court then we would be fair game. I kept glancing over my shoulder until Aethelward snorted, "You will only give yourself a stiff neck doing that. Listen for the sound of hooves. This is why we are on the road and not in the woods. It will be easier for us to hear them this way."

I was quite surprised when I heard the bush talking to my uncle until I discovered that it was the voice of Ulf. My uncle did not stop, he merely slowed a little.

"You are being followed."

"I know. How many?"

"Ten of them."

"That makes it difficult. Is there anywhere ahead which we can use?"

"Aye there is a turn and the road drops a little it will be slow going for horses."

"Good, then we turn and face them there. Let them pass us and then take them in the rear. Use Ridley and his bow it will disguise our numbers."

Ulf spat out, "Will you be teaching your grandmother to suck eggs yet?"

Then there was silence. I had not even seen the huge man and wondered at how he had hidden himself. I had little time to speculate for Aethelward placed his helmet on his head and said to me, "Arm up nephew for today you will have to face warriors. Use your sword for we have had no time to teach you to use the axe and these warriors will be skilful."

"Could we not outrun them?"

"We could but we would have to face them again. At least this way we know where they are."

"But they outnumber us."

"You will find nephew that numbers are not always the deciding factor. We have surprise on our side for they know not of Ulf and Ridley. That may yet turn the tide. But whatever happens, we must get our news through to the king."

"What did we discover? I thought he was subduing his own people."

"That is the illusion but he intends to attack with the Mercians now his allies and his left flank well protected. He will pour into the heartland of Wessex when his men are all gathered."

The turn and the drop seemed to come remarkably quickly. With surprising speed, my uncle dismounted and led his horse to a tree where he was tethered. I did the same and then took my shield and stood to stand side by side with Aethelward. I suddenly regretted the lack of a symbol or sign on my shield. How would they know who they were fighting? I resolved to paint something on it should we survive the day although with odds of greater than two to one I was not confident that we would emerge unscathed.

The silence seemed unbearable. "Why did we not remain mounted?"

"We fight better on foot. We are not the Normans who are well trained on the backs of horses. We need space to swing and the firm earth beneath our feet. If they try to attack on the backs of their horses, then go for the mounts." I looked in horror at my uncle and thought of my own mount. "If the horse is hurt then so will the warrior ." I noticed then that he had his spear poised to strike and felt unprepared with my sword alone. At least I had a sharp edge upon it. The battle with the bandits had shown me the need for that.

The rumble of hooves warned us that they were approaching and the first three men crested the road. They seemed surprised to see us. I did not know if we would parley but the first three men decided the action themselves and they charged at us. Aethelward hissed, "Stand firm and the horses will miss us."

He drew back his arm and hurled his spear, which struck the lead warrior in his throat, plucking him from his saddle and making his mount veer left. The warrior next to him had no option but to jerk his mount away from us and as the beast turned I stabbed into its neck. It was unprotected and the lifeblood gushed out like a fountain. Its head dropped and the rider flew over its mane. I turned to follow the flight, ready to fight the warrior when he rose. In the event, the bole of the tree behind me ended the man's life and I turned to watch the others. The seven warriors halted at the crest and I saw their leader, Cynan Ap Iago, order them to dismount. He looked around in shock as the man next to him fell from his horse with an arrow in his back. He stared at us looking for a bow and then dropped from his saddle as another man was hit by the hidden Ridley.

"Now we attack!" With a roar, my uncle leapt forward as quickly as his leg would allow. I noticed then the other dead warrior, killed by my uncle's blade. As we lurched up the bank I saw another of Iago's men hit by an arrow and then heard the roar of Ulf as he joined in the attack. It was too much for Iago who had obviously expected an easy victory and he and his remaining two men fled on their horses. Even then they did not escape the attention of Ridley who managed to strike one of the departing horses on the rump.

Two of the would-be attackers were still alive when we reached them. One of them had an arrow sticking in his back but it had not penetrated far and he would live. The other was gurgling blood from his mouth and his pleading eyes stared at Aethelward. He placed the man's sword in his hand and then plunged his sword into the man's neck, mercifully ending his suffering. "Go to your god with honour."

Ulf and Ridley had reached us and they looked at the last man who lay there expecting to be despatched himself.

Aethelward broke the arrow off and lifted the warrior to his feet. Ulf wrapped a crude bandage around the wound. "Aelfraed, get him a horse."

I had no time for a question and I sought an unwounded horse. When I returned Aethelward was speaking to the warrior. "You are a brave man but tell your leader, this Cynan Ap Iago, that I have let you live and I did not pursue him as I could have done but the next time I see him or you then you will die. Do you understand my words?"

The man's eyes were angry and showed his pain but he nodded.

"Very well, we will leave the bodies here and you can bury them with honour for they died for their lord, their foolish lord, who thought that because he had a lame old man and a boy he could make a name for himself. Tell him that you gain a name by fighting on a battlefield and not skulking in an ambush. Now go."

The warrior struggled onto the back of his horse and Ulf slapped its hindquarters to speed it on its way. Two of the men's horses remained. The others were either dead or fled. Aethelward grasped Ridley's arm. "That was well done Ridley, your prowess with your weapon has saved us this day." He turned to me. "And you have surprised me, Aelfraed, for it takes courage to face a charging horse and not to flinch. Now let us see what the bodies yield."

These men were better armed and armoured than the bandits and I found not only a helmet but a mail byrnie which fitted. Ridley grasped the axe which lay on the floor and grinned at me. "Now we both look like warriors."

Ulf laughed. "Aye but that does not mean you are warriors yet."

"Come let us ride, for this Cynan Ap Iago may have more fellows who wish to end my life and now they know our numbers. As we rode away I looked over my shoulder and saw that the ravens, crows and magpies were already feasting on the dead and I found myself hoping that the companions of the dead would return soon to bury them. I shuddered. It was one thing to die gloriously on a battlefield but another to fall on some forgotten road and become carrion for the birds.

Chapter 4

Winchester was a disappointment to me. It was a huge bustling town with a fine church but, after the solidly reassuring stone walls of Jorvik, it felt like a new town something which could be blown over in a strong wind or the rush of Welsh spears. There was a wall but it was not as high as Jorvik's and had wooden palisades on top of the stone base. Ulf and Aethelward, however, visibly relaxed as we rode through the main gates; the guards acknowledging them as old friends. Ridley and I rode side by side taking in the bustle of the first real town we had seen since leaving home many months earlier. I glanced at Ridley. He had grown in every way; he was bigger, stronger but he also had an ease about him he had not had before. Certainly, the two previous fights had given him confidence and Ulf had taken him under his wing, replacing the indifferent Oswin as a father figure. Whilst we had been scouting they had been in the woods training and I wondered if Ridley would be more skilful than I when we began to prepare to be warriors.

Our martial appearance did not appear to attract undue attention perhaps because of the proximity of the Welsh but I thought that we looked like seasoned warriors. Two combats had not yet made me a Beowulf but I felt that I was on the way to becoming a warrior and I could not wait to begin training in earnest. Ulf headed directly for the quarters of Earl Harold. As the leading warrior in the kingdom, he had his own hall for his retinue. It was close to that of the king although we could see from the lack of royal guards that he was not in residence. Aethelward had told me that he divided his time between London and Winchester. I had hoped to meet him if only to compare him to the Welsh king. Uncle had intimated that I would be disappointed with the comparison for Edward was a pious man and not in the least warlike whilst Gruffyd had been every inch the warrior. Aethelward felt ambivalent about the king, he owed him his loyalty but he could not forgive the disbanding of the Thingmen; the royal force which ensured the safety of the land. As he had said, whilst riding along the roads, the safety of the land was now in the hands of the Earls and their armies. Harold was reliable but Aedgar of Mercia and Tostig were less than dependable, both men having aspirations of their own. Aedgar was close to the Welsh king and it was said that Tostig had a close alliance with the King of Scotland. I was glad to be serving an honourable man.

When we reached the hall, Ulf and Aethelward were greeted by a greybeard who stood at the door of the hall sharpening an axe. I later found out his name, it was Sweyn the leader of Harold's Housecarls. He was the most important man in the household and I immediately recognised that from the deference shown to him by both my uncle and Ulf.

"You old warhorse. I heard that you were back in harness." He laid down the axe reverently on the bench which lay outside the main doors of the hall. He clasped my uncle's arm and then Ulf's. Their heads close he asked, "Did you discover all that the Earl asked?"

Aethelward, "Aye."

Sweyn held up his hand, "Then tell the Earl when he returns from the hunt." He seemed to see Ridley and me. "Two new warriors Aethelward?"

"They would be. This is my nephew Aelfraed, Aethelgifu's son." Sweyn and Aethelward exchanged a quick glance and I noticed my uncle nodding. My mother seemed to be as famous as my uncle.

"And the young giant lurking below."

"That is Ridley, a doughty warrior, my nephew's training partner and shield-bearer. They would both be warriors."

"Aye, the Earl said something about that. Put your mounts in the stable and your belongings in the hall and we will talk."

There was a large barrel of ale in the corner of the hall and the five of us sat around a long table drinking while Ulf and Aethelward found out about the politics of the town. Ridley and I sat in awe just listening to the three senior warriors for it was obvious that these three were very important men and we could learn much.

"The Earl has his work cut out trying to stop the King giving too much freedom to these Normans. There are four of them at court and they stride around as though they own the kingdom"

"Perhaps they are preparing for when Duke William comes over." I quickly glanced at Ridley as I took in the import of the words.

Aethelward looked sharply at me. "You two remember my words on the road." We nodded and I felt affronted that my fidelity and silence was being questioned.

"It is the churchmen though who have the biggest voice and as they control the rich abbeys and monasteries then they have the money and the power. Your news will be important to the Earl for it will determine what he does."

"Any news of the North?"

"The Earl's brother is up to his usual tricks and he has raised the taxes again. The man doesn't seem to understand that there is a limit to the money that can be raised. Northumbria is rich but not that rich."

He looked down at me. "You two are Northumbrian?"

"Yes sir," Ridley, tongue-tied, just nodded.

"You could have trained there why come all the way down here."

I just blurted out, "I preferred Earl Harold."

The three warriors burst out laughing and Sweyn said, "You will have to watch that tongue of yours but it is good to hear a man who believes so passionately."

I beamed; I had been called a man. I suppose that if I had had a mirror and seen myself I would have seen what they meant for I had a beard and I was as tall as the warriors I sat amongst. My body had filled out but I thought there was still some growing in me which surprised me for my brothers and my father were all shorter men than I was. I put it down to my mother for Aethelward was also a tall man.

Ridley leaned forwards and said something quietly in Ulf's ear. Ulf smiled. "Sweyn, is there a smithy nearby?"

"Aye just at the back of the hall. Why?"

"Young Ridley has some mail but he needs to repair some links and Aelfraed there would forge a spearhead."

Rather than laughing at us Sweyn showed his respect by nodding. "Would that other young warriors felt that way about their weapons. Too many of them want any sword that they can get their hands on. They do not know that a good weapon has a soul. You do well Aelfraed to forge your own for that way you know you can rely on the blade. Come it will pass the time until the Earl returns."

I gathered my ash staff and the blade I would be melting. Ridley carried his mail shirt and I noticed the ease with which he did so. He was a strong warrior and I thought back to my uncle's words, shield-bearer. Perhaps Ridley would not be content to carry my shield, perhaps he would be in the forefront of the shield wall.

The blacksmith was almost dwarf-like in his height but his shoulders were so broad that I wondered how he managed to get through most doors. "Gurt we would use your fire for a while. Go and have a wet in the hall." The gap-toothed blacksmith grinned and happily left.

Sweyn picked up the discarded apron and threw it to me. "I hope you have some skill in smithing Aelfraed?"

I too hoped I had. I had watched and helped the smith at Medelai who had been one of the few men who had shown me kindness and I knew the basics. "Ridley, pump the fire."

Ridley worked the bellows happily and soon the flames were the correct colour. I put the metal into the cauldron and watched as it began to melt, slowly at first and then suddenly it was liquid. It suddenly occurred to me that I had not seen a mould for the head. Aethelward clipped me sharply on the back of the head as he handed me the clay mould. "Think and plan young Aelfraed. Not just in combat but in all things."

I checked to see that the metal was the correct consistency and was about to reach for the tongs when Sweyn stopped me. "This blade will be part of you Aelfraed and so you must become part of it."

I looked in confusion at the others and Aethelward said quietly. "It needs your blood to make it stronger and to make you brothers."

I suddenly understood and I took my dagger, already sharpened and drew it across my palm. The flesh opened like a piece of ripe fruit and I watched as the blood dropped hissing into the metal. I took the tongs and poured the metal into the mould.

"That was well done and now it is time for you to work for your comrade. I took off the apron and handed it to Ridley. It was only when I began to pump the bellows that I understood Ridley's strength for my arms ached within moments of starting but I knew that I had to keep going as he had done. Fortunately, it was a simple task to make the mail rings and then hammer them into place. Ridley stood back to admire his handiwork and Ulf picked up another handful of the precious rings.

"You are strong and you can carry more weight. I would add some more about your shoulders and your neck."

Although I mentally cursed the additional labour it would require, Ridley happily continued until he had a mail shirt with a double row of links on the shoulders and the neck.

"The fire is still hot, go fetch your shields."

Ridley and I happily ran for our shields. They had had the least work and the least attention but I remembered the fight with the bandit and now knew that it was as much a weapon as a sword. They were both simple round shields and neither had any metalwork.

Sweyn shook his head. "These would last but two blows in a shield wall. You need metal around the rim and on the front."

"Will that not make them heavy?"

Ulf laughed. "You think that you are strong enough yet Aelfraed to be a warrior? There is still a long way to go. The two of you will need to be much stronger before you can stand and fight in a shield wall. A heavy shield will give you much protection."

We spent the next hour adding metal to the shields. The metal around the edge was easy as there were hoops laid by for barrels and they fitted well. Then we found some circles of metal. The two of us took turns to beat the metal disks until they were flat and then hammered them across the surface. When we thought we had finished Sweyn handed us some iron nails. "Now finish it off by embedding nails on the surface so that a blade striking your shield will strike metal no matter where it hits. You want to blunt the edge of your enemy's weapon as much as you can. Try to make the pattern regular, it looks better and protects you better."

We had just finished when we heard the clattering of hooves. "There is the Earl. Get cleaned up and we will go to meet him." Gurt had returned, the happy smile showing that he had enjoyed his ale break. "Gurt, watch the spearhead and the shields until the morrow."

By the time we had tidied our equipment and left the smithy, the hunting party had dismounted and were greeting each other. I looked at Ridley and he had the same expression as I did, what were we to do? We just waited out of earshot while the hunters stared at us making us even more self-conscious. People said of Earl Harold that he thought too much of himself; I never saw that side of him. I saw self-confidence and a belief in himself but I also saw someone who was aware of all those around him, no matter how lowly a position they held.

As soon as he spied the two of us he turned and opened his arms. "Ah, my two young warriors. Come and join us. I have been hearing good things of you."

We approached the large group of men and I saw Aethelward's smile reflected in that of Ulf. Harold looked at Ridley who appeared to be taller than the tall Earl. "By heavens, boy, you have grown since I last saw you. I think you could be a shield wall all on your own." Known for his jests and ready wit the men all laughed and Ulf slapped the blushing Ridley on the back. "And I hear young Aelfraed that you have killed your first man, a warrior no less."

I felt embarrassed as I remembered the fat old bandit. "He was fat my lord and not young."

This time everyone, Ridley included, laughed. "Fortunately, Aelfraed we do not always get to fight brave young warriors. You take your victories where you can. I am proud of you as I know your uncle is." I wondered if my head would burst at all the praise from the greatest warriors in the land. "Now then come with me for I need a detailed account of the Welsh and you two young men are important for you may have seen things that others have not."

We were taken to a fine home, that of Earl Godwinson, and there were just the four of us with Sweyn and the Earl, it all added to my sense of awe that Ridley and I were now moving in such exalted circles. Two warriors guarded the door and the Earl's attention was focussed on our every word.

"So, Aethelward, you say that he is going to attack?"

"Without a shadow of a doubt although not this year. His newly conquered subjects are causing him some trouble."

"And would you advise an attack from us?"

"You have a problem there my lord for it appears that Aedgar of Mercia is his ally; it would invite an attack from the rear."

"This Cynan Ap Iago, I find it hard to believe that he would countenance supporting the man who killed his father."

"He was an angry young man my lord." Aethelward gave a wry grin. "Perhaps more with me than anyone for my part in defeating his father. I think he is looking for an opportunity to regain his throne and the king keeps him close to watch him."

"Keep your friends close and your enemies closer still eh?"

"Yes, my lord."

"We cannot have this sword of Damocles hanging over us Aethelward. Come now you have a mind which sees things others do not. What is fermenting in that fertile brain of yours?"

I now know that I had come to understand my uncle as well as any man for I knew that he had formulated a plan already and I found that parts of it had been in my mind also. Perhaps the games of chess we had played had helped.

He walked over to the chessboard and asked, "What is the aim of a game of chess?"

Ulf snorted his impatience, "Why to win of course. Even I know that old friend."

"And you win how?"

Harold stood next to my uncle and picked up the black king. "You take the king."

"Exactly. Now we could go through all his warriors, his pawns and I believe we would defeat him."

"But we would lose many men in doing so."

Aethelward nodded at Sweyn, "Precisely! So how would it be if we didn't fight his army but just captured the king."

Ulf and Ridley looked confused but I could see where he was going and I leapt to my feet. "By going to Rhuddlan and his court. There he only has his guards!"

Harold slapped me on the back. "You are right Aethelward he does have a sharp mind. So, we go by sea. And attack him where he feels safest."

"It would be simple enough to march north, through Mercia, as though going to visit your brother and then head up to the Dee and make the short crossing to Rhuddlan."

"We would need boats."

"There are plenty on the south coast. They could sail around the coast to meet us. Remember, we have almost a year to plan and put our pieces in position. It is too late in the season for an attack this year and we could fortify the frontier forts in case he strikes early."

"I like it. We can train the warriors over the next few weeks and strike early next year." He hugged my uncle and then looked at me. "And we will have time to see if we can make this cub into a true wolf."

The next few months were amongst the best in my life. Ulf was given the task of training us as Aethelward spent most of the time closeted with the Earl planning strategy. We did not mind. Ulf had told us that we had to wear our mail shirts and armour each time we practised. At first, we thought it was enjoyable but we soon tired when it increased the length of time we had to spend cleaning and repairing it not to mention the weight of wearing it. We did notice that we were becoming stronger and knew that Ulf was a wise warrior.

When we began the training for the shield wall Ulf took us away from the other warriors. "When you are in a shield wall you are not fighting alone, you are with your brothers and you are one. You are one mind and one body. There is a place of honour in the shield wall and that is to the right for the warrior on the extreme right is in the most danger. The men at the rear also have to be able to push hard to allow those at the front to fight and kill their enemies." He looked at Ridley. "You will stand to the right and behind Aelfraed. The two of you will be in the rear rank."

I felt somehow cheated and I wanted to be in the front rank. I was going to say something when I saw that Ridley just nodded and accepted the decision and it made me realise that I had killed one fat bandit and I thought I could take on King Gruffyd. I almost laughed aloud but instead, I nodded.

"Now we will rejoin the others for Sweyn has decided that we need to work as one unit from now on and he asked me to tell you your positions. You will need to get to know the warriors around you and work with them."

As we returned I gripped my spear. I was immensely proud of that weapon for I had made it and bound the head to the haft. It had a fine balance to it and was sharp enough to shave with. I never minded sharpening my weapons for I knew their value in combat. I was even more pleased that I had painted my shield, for my enemies, and my friends would know who I was. I had taken the emblem of the Earl, a white horse and married it to that of Gruffyd whom I admired and I had a red horse painted on my shield. Ridley had the same but while my horse's head was raised, his was lowered. I had been worried about choosing an emblem so closely associated with the Earl until Sweyn made a comment. He nodded to the house where Aethelward spoke with the Earl. "Your Uncle has connections with the King and the Earl you have chosen wisely, Aelfraed, perhaps even more than you know."

The others in the shield wall had fought together before and we were amongst the replacements for those lost in the last fight against the Danes who had raided the previous year. We could see the gap in the rear rank and knew that our places had been allocated. I was to the left of Ridley and to my left was a man not much older than we, he was called Wolf. He nodded at me as I stood next to him and the chess player in me deduced that the newer ones would be in the middle where they could do the least damage to the integrity of the wall. The warrior to Ridley's right was an older man with a long scar running down his left cheek. "I am Osgar and you have been given much honour."

I looked to my left and right and realised that we were but six men from the right, As Ulf had said, the wing for the better warriors. It showed the confidence that Sweyn had in us.

The field on which we found ourselves was outside Winchester and, although largely flat had plenty of rocks underfoot. We quickly found out that we had to listen to Sweyn's words for he did not repeat them. "Walk!"

If you have never tried to walk in armour, carrying a shield and a spear, making sure that you are touching both men on either side of you then you have no concept of what it is like to fight in a shield wall. We were in the wedge formation with Sweyn at the front and then Ulf and another seasoned warrior, then four men and so on back to us the sixteen men at the rear. I could not believe how hard it was to walk. It was only when Osgar said quietly, "Use the same foot as the man next to you."

Ridley glanced down and used, as Osgar did, his right foot. I copied him and nudged Wolf so that we were all in step. It struck me that had we been told this then life would have been easier but once we were in the rhythm it was easy. They say that pride comes before a fall and so it was with us. The command, "Run!" brought an increase in pace and, as I looked down to the right to check which foot I should use I tripped on the spear butt of the man ahead. Had I fallen alone it would have been bad enough but I brought down Ridley and Wolf as I crashed to the ground in an ungainly heap. "Halt!"

Before we could struggle to our feet the grinning warriors around us had split into two groups and made a passage for Sweyn to walk down. He towered over us as we shamefacedly stood to face him. "I am sorry sir, it was my fault."

Sweyn just shook his head. "The three of you are at fault and we have a punishment." I glanced over to see Osgar sadly shake his head. I noticed that the rest of the warriors had reversed their spears and that the passage was now but two paces wide. Sweyn pointed to Ulf at the other end of the passage of spear butts. "You have to run down the passage to Ulf." The grin on his face told me that it would be painful.

I turned to Wolf and Ridley. "I am sorry. I will make it up to you." In answer, Ridley set off roaring as he raced down the passage his shield held high and his head tucked in. He took me and the warriors by surprise and he was halfway down before the first blow struck. Wolf immediately followed and he was five paces down the alley of spear butts before he was hit. I knew, even as I started running, that they would be ready for me. I did as Ridley had done and also I wrapped the end of my cloak around my knuckles; this was partly to protect my hand but also to stop me from tripping over the garment. My comrades did not hold back and I was eternally grateful for the helmet and leather cap which dulled the blows. Some of the warriors were quite vicious and one stabbed his butt at my nose and I felt something crack.

By the time I reached Ulf, I could barely walk and I could feel the blood dripping from numerous wounds. Ulf leaned over and said quietly, "It is a mistake most men only do once. Next time don't fall."

As I took my place in the rear rank I saw Ridley smiling at me; he looked to have only suffered a couple of bruises. Wolf on the other side had a gash in his cheek but he did not look angry. I vowed to be more careful the next time. When I heard, "Run!" I was ready and I did not look anywhere but ahead. I felt proud of myself until I heard, "Charge!" and we went even faster. All those games of chasing came into play as Ridley and I kept pace for pace with each other. Suddenly I felt Wolf lurch towards me and his hand gripped my shield for balance. I was terrified that I would fall and I lifted the shield higher. Miraculously it helped him to regain his balance and then we heard, "Stop!" Fortunately, the three of us managed to stop in time but two unfortunates ran into the backs of the warriors in front of them who stabbed their spear butts down onto their feet. Obviously, that was a lesser crime than falling.

The afternoon was filled with more of these exercises. I noticed that Sweyn and Ulf took it in turns to lead and when not leading they would stand in the rank behind us. I later discovered this was part of the strategy for it gave a leader before and behind and that way we could react to events not visible to the front rank.

After a short rest, we were divided into two smaller wedges. Ulf led ours and Sweyn the other. We faced each other a hundred paces apart and then Ulf roared, "Walk!" After a few paces he shouted, "Run!" and finally roared, "Charge!"

The two wedges met in an almighty crash. That was not the end however, that was the beginning for Ulf shouted, "Push!"

Osgar turned to us. "Push your shield into the back of the man in front of you and dig your spear butts into the ground."

We did so and I felt the man in front start to move backwards onto me. I gritted my teeth and pushed down with my doughty ash staff and flexed my legs to take the pressure. I felt sure that we would be pushed back and wondered what punishment that would entail and then I felt Ridley's shield move forwards and I pushed a little harder too. Suddenly Wolf was pushing with me and I heard Osgar shout, "That's it, keep going! We have them!" Soon we were walking forwards again and then just as suddenly we were running for we had broken them."

It must have been a momentous event for there was much backslapping, especially of the three new ones. "Why are they so happy?"

"Sweyn had the best warriors against us. That is the first time he has lost."

Ridley looked terrified, "We won't be punished, will we?"

In answer, Sweyn strode up to us. "Well done! Perhaps I should make all my warriors run the gauntlet. Do that in battle and you will soon be in the front rank."

As we walked back to the hall every bruise and cut was forgotten as the three of us relived every push and shove of the afternoon and, more importantly, we listened to our new comrades striding alongside us as fellow warriors. The trip, the fall and the gauntlet were forgotten for we had shown them that we could be warriors.

The next morning Harold took most of the Housecarls with him to visit the King in London. As uncle was not with him I assumed it was to tell the king of his impending attack on the Welsh for the Earl could not act without the king's permission and we all knew that King Edward did not like a war of any kind. Harold was the most charismatic and charming of men and if anyone could bring off that feat then it would be him. The newer members of the Housecarls were left with Ulf to continue their training and Aethelward came to watch. When we were told to bring our axes, I was excited. Ever since I had acquired my weapon I had been desperate to use it.

There were just six of us who were new but I only knew Wolf and Ridley. As I looked down the line I felt a sense of pride for my axe was the most beautiful one on show. The others looked to be useful and functional but mine had delicate filigree etchings along the blade and the haft had runes carved upon it. Ulf had told me that the weapon had come from a Dane and the tunes were pagan symbols. I did not care about the pagan runes for it was a most beautiful weapon.

"You may have handled an axe before." He looked mockingly at Ridley, "Probably cut down the odd tree or two." Everyone laughed, Ridley included; he took Ulf's mocking as he knew that the warrior had his best interests at heart. Ridley now modelled himself on the older warrior emulating the way he walked, sat and even drank. A tiny part of me was resentful that I was no longer the object of Ridley's attention but I knew that we were now part of a whole. "The thing about a tree is it doesn't move and it doesn't try to kill you. When you cut down a tree you are alone and have room to swing. You will be in a shield wall and there will be men all around you. The enemy will be doing their best to kill you. Sling your shield around your back and take your axe in your right hand and hold it to the side." We found we had to move to avoid touching the man next to us. "For this particular part of the training, we will ignore the shield wall until you have perfected the technique." When he was satisfied with our positioning he faced us and took his axe in two hands. One hand was halfway along the axe whilst the other held the end. He began to swing and spoke as he did so. "You need to build up a rhythm and swing the axe in loops before your face. Just begin to swing to get the feeling of the axe. As you swing, slide your hand until they are both at the end and use the full extent of your arms."

He came to look down the line and we continued to swing. It felt remarkably easy and I waited for him to tell us to stop. He didn't and I began to feel my arms tire. Ridley and I knew Ulf and his looks. We both recognised the sardonic smile which was Ulf's cruel side. He would not tell us to stop; he would wait until we tired and then make some disparaging comment. As the muscles in my arms burned I shut my mind to the pain and continued to swing. I sensed, rather than saw, the others lower their weapons until only two of us were left swinging our weapons. The astounding thing was we were both in time and the blades hummed along together, sweeping the air before us. Even with the pain, I could see that it would take a brave man to advance towards me. At the same time, my mind saw the weakness, if I had my spear which I had named Dragon Tamer in honour of the Welsh dragon, I could have stabbed through the swing and killed the axeman. I stored that information away for some future battle.

Eventually, Ulf smiled, nodded to us and said, "Halt!" He came to pat the two of us on our shoulders. "Four of you would now be dead and these two would be the sole survivors of the shield wall. You stop swinging when your enemies are dead or fled."

Wolf gasped, "But my arms ached!"

Aethelward's laugh came from behind us. "Then you need to build up your muscles so that they ache less and fight through the pain." He stood next to me. "Did your arms burn?"

"Like dragon's fire."

"And yet you continued. Why?"

"We had not been told to stop." He shrugged and walked away.

Ulf faced us again. "Notice that Aclfraed and Ridley swung their axes together. That is our next exercise." The others groaned but Ridley and I gritted our teeth. We wanted to be Housecarls and if that means some pain then so be it. We would not let our mentors down.

By the time night fell we were exhausted but we could stand in line, shoulder to shoulder and swing our axes in perfect unison. I did wonder about the differences we would have in the real shield wall for although Wolf and Ridley stood next to me they had others next to them who were different heights with weapons of different lengths.

That evening after we had cleaned and polished our weapons and armour, we sat in the empty hall with Ulf and Aethelward asking them questions of the battles they had fought and the role of the shield wall. I asked about the wedge formation. "That is the one you have trained for the most. It is the one we use when we go for a victory. If it is the whole army then you would be in the seventh rank and behind you would be the other warriors, the ones who are not Housecarls. When we fight like that we normally face another wedge and it is a killing ground. Most of the time you will be in two ranks for defence. You six are newer warriors and you will be in the second rank. When the others return, we will have to practise that tactic."

One of the other recruits snorted, "That sounds much easier just standing behind a man."

Ulf shook his head, "I said we would fight in two ranks but you, in the second rank, use your shield to protect you and the man in the front rank for when we are in two ranks the enemy will use his arrows and javelins. Your shield has to protect the two of you. When we are in two ranks, the enemy may use a wedge. Suppose you are in the second rank when the point of the wedge comes to you. Sixty men trying to get beyond you and into the fyrd. What then?" The fyrd were the peasants who would be armed with whatever they could get their hands on. They would be useful when clearing a field but we knew that it was we the warriors who would win or lose the day.

There was a silence as we drank our ale and watched the flames of the fire dance red and blue. When uncle spoke, even though his voice was quiet we jumped. "And then there is the boar's snout."

I had never heard this before. "Boar's snout."

"Aye Aelfraed. It is a Danish tactic. They have two wedges together so that they look like the snout of a boar. They wrap around a shield wall. The middle gets sucked in and before you know it you are surrounded and cut to pieces. The shield wall only works when it is solid. If it is breached or not continuous then it breaks. It is the contact of the warriors and their shields and continuity of the line which sees us through. You may have to fight and stand although wounded. I have seen dead men supported in a shield wall, doing their duty beyond death."

With that sobering thought in our heads, we found our beds but my night was filled with dreams. Since Saint Asaph, I had dreamt each night. I did not understand the dreams but knew that they had a meaning. That night I dreamt we were in a shield wall and a dragon attacked us. His flames destroyed the rank in front of me and it was left to Wolf, Ridley and me to fight it. I awoke just before I was consumed by his fiery teeth. I wondered if I should speak of this to Aethelward but I did not want to feel foolish. Since our arrival in Winchester, I had seen how important he was and my strange dreams were not.

By the time the Earl arrived with the rest of the Housecarls, the six new recruits felt a bond and strength through having worked together so ardently. We looked forwards to the return of our comrades for we were keen to impress. However, training ceased when the Earl returned for we had news from Northumbria. King Malcolm had begun raiding the borderlands near the Tweed and there was much debate about the action we ought to take. It was then that I saw the wisdom of Harold for many of the Thegns urged him to join his brother and fight Malcolm who had been supported by King Edward when he was in exile. The Housecarls felt that the Scottish king had shown treachery to bite the hand which had protected him. Harold had let them shout their arguments and counter-arguments and then stood. He was afforded total silence.

"If we march north, through the winter and join our brother then that will lay open all of our heartlands to the avaricious and treacherous Welsh. We know that Aedgar of Mercia supports Gruffyd and we could defeat the Scots only to find our land in the south has been taken from us. I have confidence in my brother Tostig and the doughty Northumbrians." He looked at me and nodded and I felt like a giant. This was also the first time that the Housecarls had a real intimation of the campaign in the spring. I knew the details of course but the rest now wondered when we would go north and the debate now began about Aedgar of Mercia and his treachery.

Harold came over to join Aethelward, Sweyn, Ulf and myself. I did not wonder then why I was included and allowed to be with such important men. I would discover that much later. Ridley and Wolf were with some of the other younger warriors engaged in drinking and arm-wrestling contests. Not for them debate and discussion, they yearned for action.

"The King will be here for Christmas and he will tell me then if he will support our campaign."

"The longer we debate the more likelihood there is that Gruffyd will learn of our plan and forestall us with a premature attack."

"That is why I have decided to send you two with half my Housecarls north to the crossing of the Severn to watch for him. You can also keep an eye on Aedgar."

I could barely contain my excitement. I was to be in the vanguard of the army. My uncle poured cold water on that excitement. "With thirty warriors, we can do little but hold them up for a short time. It would be a waste of fine Housecarls."

"You will not only have merely Housecarls. I am giving you fifty horsemen and fifty archers. You will have a formidable force."

Aethelward considered this. "And who will command?"

"Why you of course!"

"Aethelward the lame eh?"

"Do not put yourself down, old friend. You are not there as a warrior but a general and there is no one better suited is that not right Ulf?"

Sweyn answered for him. "Aethelward I would follow you as would any of the Housecarls. Your reputation speaks for you."

He shook his head and looked at me. "This is how flattery works nephew. They send you to freeze your arse off in the borderlands and make you think they have done you a favour!" The others laughed at this and slapped him on the back; he had, of course, accepted the role.

I could not, of course, tell the others what I knew. I was in a privileged position and I did not wish to put that in jeopardy but I was bursting to tell them. What I did do was to use my first pay as a Housecarl to buy things that I knew I would need. I went to the markets and bought some oil, it was expensive but I knew that in the damp borderland my armour would need protection from rust. I also bought a wolf-skin which, again, cost me much money but which would protect me from the cold. I also spent money buying pieces of leather of varying sizes for I knew that there would be no farrier to repair any damage to my gear. I was desperate to ask Aethelward more but he was busy for the next few days with Harold planning and meeting with his leaders.

All preparations ceased when the King and his retinue arrived. We had been told to present ourselves fully armed for his arrival and I could not wait. My armour and helmet gleamed. My shield shone and with my spear and my axe, I felt like Beowulf himself. We were lined up in two ranks before the cathedral with Earl Harold and Sweyn at our head. Aethelward was not there and I wondered at his omission. The King was disappointing. He wore neither armour nor crown. He looked more like Brother Aidan than Gruffyd. I was, however, impressed by his retinue for they were ten Norman knights. Each one had mail covering their whole body, including their legs. They each had a kite shield and a pointed helmet with a nasal. The effect was chilling as no human features could be discerned. There was no flesh to be seen; it was as though they had been made by some blacksmith. Lastly, their lances seemed much longer than the spears we had and I wondered how one would fight them. When Ap Iago had chased us they had neither spear nor lance and were easily despatched. These warriors would need a different approach. I determined to ask Aethelward what his thoughts were but at that moment I stood proudly with my peers hoping that we were making the same impression on the Normans as they had made on me.

The King totally ignored all of us and walked, with his knights into the cathedral. I don't know about the others but I felt that we had been snubbed. I looked at Ridley and Wolf and they appeared to be unaware of any problem. As I looked at the reddening ears of the Earl I knew that I had been offended because my leader had been snubbed and everyone in the kingdom knew that the only thing keeping Edward on the throne was Earl Harold Godwinson.

We stood there for most of the morning and then when the king and his party did emerge, they went directly to the King's hall. The Earl spoke to Sweyn and then followed them. Sweyn turned to us and I think I could detect subdued anger about his face. I had come to know the man and recognise his idiosyncrasies. He was like me, unhappy that our Earl had been treated thus. "You may stand down. The Earl is proud of you and the display you made."

As we went back to the hall I felt empty. I was fighting for a man I could not respect. Even worse I would be fighting a man I did respect, Gruffyd. And then, like a dream-like vision, it struck me. I was not Edward's man I was Harold's man and that made all the difference for my leader was a man of honour and a man worth following. Edward was merely a symbol of England but Harold was England.

Chapter 5

Winchester 1062

The Normans spoiled my Christmas. They arrogantly prowled around the crowded streets, always armoured and often mounted. We recruits could not understand their words but some of the older men told us that they spoke disparagingly about our ancient weapons, armour and tactics. We considered it the height of bad manners to behave so martially in the peaceful town of Winchester, especially at Christmas. There would have been trouble had not Sweyn and Ulf passed on Harold's admonition to bite our tongues. I knew that he did not wish to jeopardise his attempt to persuade Edward to go to war with the Welsh and offending the Normans would do just that. There was one young Norman, a knight not much older than me who seemed to enjoy intimidating the ordinary folk of the city. He was Guy of Evreux and was even more arrogant than his fellows. Matters came to a head on St. Stephen's Day when I had emerged from the small church we used. I had gone to pray for my mother and Nanna. As I came out I saw the Norman knight riding through the street. That was not unusual but he was not riding slowly as one would expect in a busy town. Instead, he was riding as though across an open field, galloping. I saw an old woman and her son crossing ahead of me towards the cathedral and I could see that Guy of Evreux could ride them down. Impulsively, and remembering dear Nanna, I hurried to their side and took her arm for the ground was muddy and churned up. "Here, Mother, let me take your arm."

She looked up at me in surprise and then smiled. "Thank you, young sir. That is very Christian of you." I understood her comment for many of the Housecarls were not Christian and she was surprised that one behaved in so thoughtful a manner. Rather than slowing up when he spied us Guy accelerated and I could just see the grin on his face. I would not move and I made sure that I was on his side of the couple. I was not afraid for I remembered the attack in Wales. The horse would veer away, even if the warrior tried to run us down. I would not give him the pleasure of seeing us run. I was also ready with my right hand to ward off any blow and I kept my eye on the horse. The knight was aiming at us and, although the horse was trying to avoid us I could see that the reins were jerking his head to strike me. I knew that he would crash into us and I did the only thing I could think of, I punched the horse as it drew close. It immediately reared and veered away throwing the young knight to the floor. I escorted the shocked couple to the cathedral and noticed some of my comrades smiling at me.

"Well done young Aelfraed. An interesting approach." Osgar was leaning on the cathedral wall but keeping an eye on the knight. I saw him nod his head and I turned to see the angry young man storming towards me, sword in hand.

"You Saxon dog! How dare you strike my steed. Defend yourself." I had not known he could speak our language until then.

I was, to my own surprise, calmness personified and I spread my hands. "With what Norman cur? Unlike you, we do not ride armed in a peaceful town at this holy time of year."

A crowd had gathered and I heard the clatter of hooves as other Normans approached. Seeing them emboldened the young knight. "Well go and get a weapon and then I will teach you a lesson."

"And why would you need to do that Guy of Evreux?" The man who spoke was the leader of the knights, Odo of Mortain. A powerful baron and a confidante of Duke William we had heard.

"He struck my horse and I fell."

One of the other knights laughed. "And you want to kill him because you are a poor horseman?"

He reddened at that and pointed his sword at me, "He has insulted me and I demand satisfaction."

Odo's voice was chillingly threatening. "Sheath your sword. This is a holy day and we will not spill blood." He seemed to see me for the first time. "Housecarl what have you to say?"

"I was escorting the gammer," I pointed to the terrified old lady and her grandson, "to the cathedral and he rode in too fast. Had I not struck the horse then we would have been hit ourselves."

Odo flashed his eyes at Guy, "Is this true?"

"I was in charge of my horse."

"Were you young Guy of Evreux? So much so that you were close enough for this man to hit your horse. Go back to the quarters and I will deal with you later." As Guy rode away I could see the look which he gave me and knew that this was not over. "You have courage to stand and face a charging horse but I would advise you to move a little quicker the next time." With that, he turned and rode away his companions clanking after him.

I turned to see ten Housecarls advancing on me, all of them cheering. "Well, that is a Christmas gift and no mistake. Come Aelfraed, this

Stephen's day you do not buy ale for we are all delighted that the Norman was humbled so."

"You are a fool!"

My uncle's words sobered me up in an instant. The day had been a blur of praise and banter from my comrades. When I had returned to the hall my uncle's glowering face had warned me of a storm. The drink had made me bold. "Should I have let him knock down the old lady?"

"You should have bitten back the pride that rose in your throat and hurried across the street. You deliberately provoked the knight."

I became angry. "So, we are to bow down and kiss their arses, are we?"

In answer, Aethelward slapped me backhanded across the face, "Do not speak to me like that ever or you shall be sent back to Medelai in disgrace."

I stammered my reply, "You cannot do that I am one of Earl Harold's Housecarls."

"You are a housecarl because I say so. Now you will not leave the hall again until we leave for the borderlands."

I thought about arguing but behind his back I saw Ulf and Ridley their pleading faces willing me to accept my punishment. I nodded. Ridley came over to me. He could always hold his ale better than I could and he put his arm around me. "Come along master let's get you to bed."

Ulf's voice came from behind me. "Give him some well water to drink."

As I swallowed the icy cold water Ridley began to undress me. "You made your uncle angry. He was going to send you home until Ulf intervened and said that you should be given another chance."

As I began to sober up I realised that I had almost lost my place in the shield wall; all because of an arrogant Norman. Uncle was right I could have avoided the conflict but I wanted him to charge me so that I could show him I was a better warrior. It had been foolish and I would apologise the next time I saw Aethelward.

Perhaps my foolish action precipitated our early departure or perhaps it had always been decided that we leave during the first week of January but whatever the reason I was glad to be away from the confines of the hall. The archers and mounted men arrived the day after St Stephen's Day led by Magnus of Wallingford the horseman and Edwin the Archer. Both had enough scars about them to suggest that they were no strangers to the battlefield. Ridley and I were lucky that we had our own horses for our gear. Most of the men had to throw their arms and armour in the back of a wagon. I had hoped that, as we had a number of horses, we would be allowed to ride but Ulf had put his foot down. "We are the Housecarls and we all suffer the same privations as well as the same glory. We walk." Ridley threw me a look that told me that he thought I had been foolish to bring it up and perhaps he was right. I had allowed my combats and the training to make me feel more important than I was and I still bridled at the arrogant Norman. Perhaps walking would be good for my humility.

As we left, in the early hours I saw the Normans watching us; it irked me that they did so but it made me march a little straighter and with a little more pride. Soon, however, I realised that this would not be a glorious march. We used the remains of the Roman roads whenever we could and for the most part, made good time but sometimes we came across stretches where the locals had decided to use the cobbles for their buildings and then we squidged through mud which sucked at our feet. We were heading northwestwards, towards the frontier town of Worcester. Hereford would have been closer to the Welsh but it was still garrisoned by Aedgar's Mercians. Most nights we were able to sleep in a walled town for which we were grateful. At other times, we froze on the ground. I was glad that I had brought my wolf skin for it kept me dry and protected me from the cold. I felt guilty that I had not told Ridley to buy one and I tried to make it up to him by sharing on the really cold nights.

"No master, it is not right for you are noble and I am not."

"But Ridley we are brothers in arms. We fight and die together."

"Aye and that is a good thing but it is my own fault that I did not use my pay wisely as you did. Fear not, master I am tough and I will survive."

As we passed through many of the Roman settlements I was amazed that they had been built in stone all those years ago, and yet now, hundreds of years later we still built in wood. They had indeed been a wondrous people who could build such roads and such buildings. When we reached the old town of Aqua Sulis I took Wolf and Ridley to explore the deserted baths. "They went in water? They deliberately made themselves wet?"

"Aye Wolf, although from what I was told the water was hot as were the rooms."

He shook his head. "Do not mock me Aelfraed. How could they make the rooms hot? I can see no fires."

I pointed to the floor. "They heated air and warmed the floor."

The two of them could not comprehend just what the ancient Romans had achieved. The broken aqueducts were just one of the many things which were alien to them.

It was a relief to reach Worcester which had fine ramparts, a garrison and, most importantly, a warrior hall so that we would be warm at night. I went with Ridley to find stabling for our horses and to see what damage had accrued over the long journey. Fortunately, my oil had protected mine and, after we had cleaned Ridley's I gave him some of the precious liquid to protect his. Aethelward did not waste any time in discovering what lay beyond the frontier. He and Magnus of Wallingford led the mounted men each day, first north and south and then gradually west. Ulf drilled the archers and the Housecarls so that we could fight as a unit. Once again, we were left in no doubt that our role in a two line shield wall was to protect the archers but for once I didn't mind. I remembered how effective Ridley had been when attacked on the road and anything which whittled down the enemy before we met was fine by me. When we were in wedge I found that we were still in the rear rank but that was now the sixth rank. We would be much closer to the fore in any fight. Whenever we could we practised with spear and axe to hone and perfect our skills.

After three weeks of training, I was becoming bored and yearned for action. I envied the horsemen who rode out each day and returned empty handed. At least they had been doing something more productive than practising endlessly. When action did come, it came not from the west but from the east and it was not the Welsh but it was the Mercians. Whilst we had been in Worcester we had gained the friendship of the garrison there. Largely Mercian they were the retinue of the son of the Earl, Edwin. Edwin was not like his father and distrusted the Welsh. Harold and Aethelward must have had some inkling of the discord otherwise we would have been sent to Longtown or closer to Hereford. It seems that Aedgar had aspirations on the English crown but Harold's power meant that could never be. Edwin on the other hand was content to be in Mercia and saw the advantage of a strong England and a weak Wales. I did not know what messages had passed from one to the other but it seems, looking at it now, that there must have been an agreement from Edwin to use his fort.

One morning in early March, Aethelward did not lead out the horsemen instead Magnus took half of them and the rest were gathered, along with the archers at the gate. We wondered if we were to be left behind again when Ulf addressed us. "We march."

It was to the point but it took some by surprise and they had to race back into the hall to gather their weapons. We marched behind the horsemen, who were spread out before us as scouts and ahead of the archers. I had thought that we would have crossed the river and headed west but, instead, we headed north. Although we were the largest host I had ever marched with I knew that the one hundred and five of us were but a small band of warriors and I wondered, as we headed up the old Roman road, what was the purpose of this march. We headed north up the Stour valley. I had a little idea of what lay ahead and my only worry was the Mercians. Were we going to ally with them? It would have made sense. The garrison had told us that few men supported the idea of an alliance with the Welsh, Gruffyd's ambitions were well known. When our scouts galloped back to tell us of the approach of a Mercian standard we relaxed. When Ulf roared, "Wedge!" we were stunned although our training took over and I found myself in the middle of the rear rank of the thirty Housecarls. Behind me, I could hear the archers stringing their bows and, ahead of us Aethelward and his scouts moved steadily forwards.

We were at the top of a rise and below us, we could see a hundred mounted warriors under the banner of the Earl of Mercia. Aedgar himself was there! I saw my uncle ride forward alone and speak with the Earl. There appeared to be an argument and suddenly one of the warriors behind the Earl hurled a spear at Aethelward who deflected it with his shield and then raced back to our lines, the mounted men shooting arrows at the Mercians. As he galloped up I could see he was grinning. Ulf too was laughing and he said, "Well I see you upset him then?"

"Aye, it seems he is not yet ready to desert the Welsh. Horsemen to the flanks. Housecarls today you will face horsemen. Show them what Saxons can do."

We all roared and banged our shields with our spears. I was just glad that, although the Mercians were mounted as the Normans were and wore armour, it did not extend to their legs and they did not have lances, merely spears such as we, even so, I was grateful that we had archers with us. "Lock shields!"

It felt comforting to feel Ridley's shield and Wolf's touching mine. Our spears were held easily over the top so that any enemy attacking from the front would have to face a hedgehog of spear points. Of course, unless they were particularly foolish they would attack our right flank where Osgar stood. I could see them clearly for we were still at the top of the rise. They would have to negotiate the slight incline. It would slow them up but the land on either side was open and the only obstacle between the Mercians and our flanks were the unarmoured horsemen armed with shields and javelins. Unless the horsemen were incompetent they would sweep through them and be upon us. I felt glad that it was my uncle who was leading us. We would survive for he had planned all of this.

Their cavalry galloped up and loosed a volley of javelins at both us and the horsemen. We fared better for we all protected each other with our shields. My uncle had told me that the Romans had used such a tactic but even more effectively so that the whole of their force was covered on each side by shields. We all survived but the light cavalry did not and I saw three or four empty saddles. Then the enemy were around the sides of the wedge. I heard Edwin, the archer, shout, "Loose!" and saw the fifty arrows arc over our heads and into the cavalry. They had round shields but they proved quite effective and I only saw one warrior and one horse injured. Edwin's voice sounded calm as he repeated the order and soon flight after flight was flying towards the enemy. On our flank, they had seen the lack of shields and they wheeled in. We could not turn to face the enemy or we would have exposed our rear to their cavalry. I heard my uncle shout an order but the words were lost and besides I was too busy defending the line to the right. Ridley and I turned our spears so that they were above Osgar's head and Ridley had angled his shield to protect his head. Behind me, Wolf had his spear along our backs ready to strike anyone who tried to attack from the rear.

Osgar appeared calm as he stabbed forwards with his spear. I noticed that he had crouched slightly and as his spear took the horse in the throat I could see why. The warrior flew over his head and crashed into Ridley knocking him to the ground. My friend wasted no time in rolling him over and spearing him in the throat but that had allowed another horseman to urge his horse at Osgar whilst another came at his unprotected back. Our training took over and I stepped over Ridley and stabbed at the horseman feeling the reassuring pressure of Wolf's spear at my back. Dragon Tamer went into the horse and stuck. As it was wrenched from my grip I drew my sword. This was no place for an axe for we were tightly packed. The warrior whose horse I had killed struck down at me, as his horse fell, with his spear. He was a brave man for he was falling towards me. I deflected the spear and, seeing the gap under his arm, stabbed through the space in the mail. The blade transfixed his body and came out under his other arm. I used his own momentum to throw the body behind us and looked to my next enemy.

When I looked up all that I could see was a sea of men and horses, what I could not see was that it was a thin line for we had cut down many. My uncle, from his lofty position, must have seen that the moment was right for I heard him shout, "Charge!" I knew that it was not intended for us, that was Ulf's job and I concentrated on watching Osgar's side. I suddenly felt Ridley at my side and we walked next to Osgar protecting his right side. I daresay we broke formation but there were so many horses facing Osgar that to retain our line would have resulted in his death. The sudden appearance of an extra spear and a sword forced the horsemen back and, as the horses turned, the men with spears found vulnerable spots in both the warriors and the horses. Almost as soon as they had come they had gone and all that was left before us were the bodies of the horses and the ten men we had killed on our side of the fight.

As we reformed the archers slipped amongst the bodies making sure that all were dead. One archer grinned as he returned Dragon Tamer to me. "Next time watch where you throw your bodies, you nearly hit me!"

That was my first battle. It was over so quickly that I barely had time to draw breath. At the front of the wedge lay the body of Aedgar slain by Ulf and around him the bodies of his oathsworn warriors. We had lost two warriors and both were from the second rank, the oathsworn had done their duty. With the eight horsemen and two archers, it had been a small price to pay for now Edwin would be Earl and he was an ally of Harold.

That evening as we retold the tales of the day and the warriors we had killed I thought of the moments in the short battle when it could have changed my destiny. Ridley's fall, the loss of Dragon Tamer, the man falling towards me. I could have planned for none of it and yet I had survived. Osgar, Wolf and Ridley were soon drunk but I sat with Aethelward and Ulf.

"You did well nephew."

"Aye but next time do not break formation." Ulf could not resist admonishing me and my fellows.

"You saw?"

"I saw."

"What else could I have done? Osgar would have had three enemies had we not done so."

"Aye well, you were lucky." He looked at my uncle. "We were all lucky, or were we?"

Aethelward was quiet and then, when he spoke, it was in a quiet voice. "It was planned. It was the reason we were sent here. Edwin had let the Earl know that he wished to support Edward. It means that Edward will now sanction the invasion as Gruffyd will never be weaker. We will invade in the spring."

I did not mind that I had been kept in the dark; after all, I was a lowly Housecarl. But I liked this knowledge for I saw the bigger picture and was beginning to see the politics of the kingdom. Ridley was right I was noble and that meant I thought differently to him and to Wolf but I would never take for granted that loyalty which he gave me.

When we returned to Worcester it was to a mixed reception. Many of the garrison were overjoyed that Mercia was back in the English fold but some did not like the way it appeared to have been engineered. There were fights and arguments between Mercian and Mercian as well as Mercian and Saxon. It was not until the arrival of Edwin, Earl of Mercia that things calmed down. It also coincided with the arrival of Harold and the two Earls greeted each other like long lost brothers. Having the insight of my uncle I knew that this meant the border with Wales was secured and my uncle's plan to invade the north of the country could begin.

As we marched north along the border country I saw the new Housecarls who were junior to us. It felt good to have been bloodied and the story of the flying Mercian was told around the campfires. I would be lying if I said I did not enjoy the notoriety and fame for I did but it made me more determined than ever to be a good warrior who would move his way forward in the shield wall. We had all been promoted to the penultimate rank, this was partly due to deaths and wounds but also because of injuries incurred on the march. I didn't mind but it could be claustrophobic to be surrounded by warriors in a wedge. I knew that I would need to get used to it.

There were many advantages to being one of the Earl's Housecarls, we got to march at the head of the column. On a wet March morning that meant that the roads were not as churned up for us as they would be for the ones at the rear. The horsemen we had brought with us under Magnus were the only horsemen we possessed. The Mercian horse had been cut up rather badly by our blades and the Earl of Mercia left them at home to recover their numbers and get over their humiliation. There were other Housecarls belonging to the other Earls but we knew, as we trudged along at the head of the line, that we were the elite. Harold was the richest man in England, richer even than the King, and he could afford to pay his warriors well. He expected them to use that on their armour and weapons and Sweyn saw to it that none let him down.

We felt safer now that the Mercians were allies but we still kept a wary eye on the hills which rolled away westwards. The archers of the Welsh were known to make sudden raids on their enemies, loosing flights of arrows and then disappearing into the mists of the mountains. Our mounted men were there to prevent that and we were happy that we could not see them for that meant they were doing their job. Ridley and I were able to tell Osgar and Wolf of the land we would see for we had crossed it ourselves. Although we had not seen Rhuddlan itself, we had passed within a few miles of it. Ridley told them of the legend of the Welsh Dragon. Wolf looked as fearful as Ridley had done but Osgar shook his head, "I have fought the length of this land and I have yet to see a sign of a dragon besides, young Ridley, I think that if it is buried beneath a mountain then we are safe."

I liked Osgar who spoke the truth and did not suffer fools gladly. He was the rock at the rear of the line and all of us respected his courage and his calmness. When we fought, it was reassuring knowing that the man on the right would do nothing foolish. When we stood in a two line shield wall it was even more important for it was Osgar who anchored our right flank. If Ulf and Sweyn fell it was Osgar who would lead the wedge and I felt proud to have him as my friend.

We headed for Legacaestir which was held by Harold's brother Tostig for it was a Northumbrian town. It was like Jorvik with a sound Roman wall and a garrison of doughty warriors watching the Dee and the Welsh. It was still a powerful fort and even the Irish raiders avoided it. I was pleased that we would be resting there for it meant more comfort, for at least one night. When we left its secure walls, we would be in Welsh land close to the Welsh King's army. I knew, from our scouting mission, that many of the king's men would be on the borders towards the south but his elite would be guarding his lands in the northwest for this was his original kingdom. His men would know the land better than we did but Harold and my uncle had devised a bold stroke. If we could kill or capture Gruffyd then the head of the snake would be ours. I had learned, through my discussions with my uncle, that Gruffyd had only unified Wales recently and there were many men whom he had displaced, men who resented his action. Aethelward had suggested to Harold that, with Gruffyd out of the way the country would fall in upon itself and return to petty internal border disputes. I had had an insight into the bigger picture and it made it easier for me to march through the mud. My fellows did it because they were loyal to Harold, they were his men. I felt guilty because I still thought of myself as a Northumbrian who had loyalty to Aethelward. I kept hoping that I would feel like my peers but, so far, it had not happened.

The forest did not seem so intimidating as we passed through it, although we were such a mighty host that I thought that any bandits who remained would have fled before us. This time it hid us from prying eyes and scouts. Aethelward sent Magnus and his men ahead of us to scout the defences at Rhuddlan but we knew that they would not be like the walls of Legacaestir or Jorvik and would be wooden. They were there to deter opportunist raiders, not a well-armed army. When we reached the walls either Gruffyd would fight us or he would flee; even Osgar knew that. He was confident that, if we met them in the field we would prevail.

"The only weapon they have which worries me is the bow for they are fearsome archers. Luckily their spearmen are not worth shit and we have our own archers and horsemen to deter them." He pointed over to the mountains and crags in the distance. "I am just glad that his fortress is not up there for we would never take it."

Wolf looked surprised. "It could withstand an assault by us?" He gestured at the formidable force which looked terrifying even without armour.

"The ground is not even and there are rocky crags. If I were King Gruffyd I would have built a fortress there where his archers could shoot with impunity and we could not keep a straight line. I just hope that the land is flat near Rhuddlan." He looked at me for an answer.

I shrugged. "Saint Asaph's monastery is in a valley but the sides are not steep and Rhuddlan, which we saw in the distance, is close to the coast and on a flat area next to a river."

He seemed content. "Good, then we will soon whip this Welsh dragon and be back in Winchester for the May celebrations." Wolf and Ridley both looked involuntarily at the mountains when he spoke. They still feared the real dragon. That night we camped in the forest and Magnus conferred with the leaders. Now that we were on the march it did not seem appropriate for me to be a party to these conferences but I yearned to find out what we were doing. The Earl and my uncle seemed satisfied and the next day we veered towards the west and I could tell that we were avoiding Saint Asaph and approaching the fort from the northwest. The going was much easier once we were out of the forest and we made good time. The sun was high in the sky when we emerged from a small wooded area to stand on a ridge overlooking the fort of Rhuddlan, the court of King Gruffyd. It was a substantial fort but it was only raised a little from the land around. The river ran along one side and there was a wood to the east. We could see the men in the fort and when they saw us it was as though we had disturbed a hive of wasps for they ran hither and thither.

Sweyn ordered us armoured and ready on the ridge. We would have to walk down to the fort to offer battle but it was a little over a mile and we would not be unduly tired. When we marched down we were in two lines of Housecarls. The archers guarded our left flank, the one next to the river and the woods whilst the horsemen watched our right. The fyrd and the unarmoured spearmen were placed behind us and we had the place of honour in the middle. To our right were two more bands of Housecarls; they numbered sixty the same as we whilst to our right were two more bands totalling about fifty. The white horse banner flew proudly above us and Earl Harold led us down to the Welsh who had emerged from their walls and were hurriedly preparing to meet us in battle.

I felt a nervous excitement; this was not training nor was it a skirmish this would be a battle. I could see that our numbers were evenly matched although they appeared to have more archers than we did and fewer armoured men. The Welsh Dragon flew proudly above their king whom I could see was behind his front rank mounted on a fine white horse. Earl Harold was dressed as we were and was afoot. He would stand in the middle of the line but if we adopted the wedge formation then he would withdraw behind us to enable him to see the way the battle was unfolding. Uncle Aethelward was mounted behind the Housecarls and before the fyrd. He would make the decisions during the heat of the battle.

We halted about six hundred paces from our foes. They were slightly above us but I did not think that would make a difference. King Gruffyd rode from his men escorted by his standard-bearer and Earl Harold and Sweyn went forward from our lines. Maddeningly we could not hear the words but their faces did not display any anger and they seemed to be discussing rather than arguing. Eventually, they returned and we watched as Sweyn took his place at the front of the wedge and the Earl walked behind us. Osgar said, to no one in particular, "Well, we attack then."

Sweyn confirmed this when he shouted, "Wedge! And we formed into a wedge. I noticed that the Housecarls to our left and right did the same and we formed five points. As we moved into position I could see that his formation would allow us to puncture their line more effectively. There was no doubt that as the largest wedge we would penetrate the furthest but our comrades would have their flanks protected by archers and horses. I could see my uncle's handiwork in this.

We were silent until we heard my uncle shout, "Forward!"

As we walked we began to chant, "Harold! Harold!" whilst beating our shields. To me, in its midst, it seemed a terrifying sound and I wondered what it would do to our enemies. We knew that we would have to run the gauntlet of missiles but that did not worry us. The command came, "Run!" and we picked up the pace. Gone was the fear of tripping on a spear butt and I gripped Dragon Tamer, ready to thrust and end the life of an unknown Welsh warrior.

Aethelward could see beyond the line and when he shouted, "Shields!" we all raised them ready for the arrows which rained upon us. I was glad that Sweyn had insisted on so many nails and pieces of metal on my shield for only two arrows penetrated it, the rest bounced off. I knew that at least one of the enemy arrows had struck home when I hurdled the body of Thorin who had been two rows ahead of me.

I could now see the sea of shields waiting for us and the prickly points of their spears. I had no time to worry for Sweyn roared, "Charge!" and our front rank hit them. It must have been like being trampled by a bull for those men in the front rank and we moved swiftly. They must have halted Sweyn for the men before me, stopped. We knew then that it was our turn. While Osgar and Ridley fended off and despatched those warriors at our side the rest of us pushed hard with our shields on the men before us. I felt the pressure from the shields behind and suddenly we were moving forwards. I saw a terrified face beneath my feet and I stabbed down on his throat. There were more men fighting at our side now and I wondered if I should turn and fight them. Luckily, I remembered the admonition of my uncle and restrained myself. Just then I heard his voice shout, "Shield Wall!"

Our training took over and we all moved slightly to our right to enable the warriors at the front to join our line. Now I was in the front line and knew that soon it would be axe work. The Welsh saw Sweyn and the others fall back and thought they had won. As they rushed forward we readied our spears and thrust them into the faces of the Welsh elite. Dragon Tamer went straight through the open mouth of a surprised warrior and continued up through his skull. As I felt the haft loosen in my hand I let go, swinging my shield to my back and I took my axe in both hands. This was the first time I had faced an enemy with no shield but I trusted my training and began to swing my axe. I felt, rather than saw the axes of those alongside me also swinging and we were soon in a rhythm. The first man I killed had thought he could dip below the whirling blade but he was wrong; even his helmet did not afford him any protection and it was cracked, along with his skull like an egg. Their archers were busily showering us with arrows and I watched as one hit my gauntlet only to flick off a rivet. I was glad that I had bought the best gauntlets I could.

Our line had now advanced beyond the others and I could see, clearly the face of Gruffyd. He recognised me and smiled and then said something to the men with him. Suddenly the line in front of us vanished like fog on a summer's morning and a wedge of Welsh Housecarls hurtled towards us and the point was aiming for me! The warrior at the front was well-armed and his spear was aimed at me. I felt time slow down and saw that his shield was that of a Welsh dragon; he was of the royal bodyguard and would be a fearsome opponent. Luck was with me as my axe struck his shield and bounced up to hit the head of his spear; the sharp edge sliced through the wood leaving him with a staff. Wolf's axe struck his arm and the man looked down in horror at the stump which remained. I wasted no time in lifting my axe to split his skull and helmet in two. Next to me, Ridley had smashed the shield of his opponent and Osgar had finished him. We were now lapping around the left side of their wedge which was their stronger side while Sweyn on their weaker side had also made inroads so that our line had surrounded their wedge. They stood no chance against over fifty well-trained warriors and soon they were fighting back to back. There were two axes to every warrior and no warrior could fight two foes. Soon there was a bloody mass of bodies before us and I looked up to see Gruffyd and his horsemen flee. Even though I knew that it meant we had won, I felt disappointed, for I had hoped that he would have fought for his honour and his crown.

With the king fled, the army before us disintegrated and the fyrd and the spearmen cheerfully chased after them along with the archers and the horsemen. We were spent. Once we had ascertained that the field was ours we wandered the body strewn hillside dispatching the wounded and retrieving weapons. I felt better when I found that Dragon Tamer was unharmed. I looked for my Uncle and the Earl but they had mounted and followed Gruffyd. I realised that the Earl had more noble and kinglike qualities than the Welsh king who had shown himself to be a craven coward by his actions on the battlefield. His men had died for him and he had deserted them. This was my first battle but I could see that the Welsh could have fought longer for, as we toured the battlefield, we could see that more men had fled than died.

As we drank from the water skins brought by the boys Sweyn sought me out. "You did well Northumbrian. It must have been wyrd that made them attack you. You have killed a famous warrior, he was Gryffydd of Rhuddlan and was a Welsh champion." He picked up my axe. "I name this blade Death Bringer."

All around me my comrades roared. It was a special moment when a blade was named and to have it named by the worthiest warrior in our army made me proud. I could not wait to tell my uncle when he returned.

Chapter 6

When they returned Aethelward told us that Gruffyd had been warned of our approach and had a ship waiting at the coast and he had fled. I felt disappointment for the snake or was it dragon still had a head. We made ourselves comfortable in the fort although the court of King Gruffyd Ap Llewellyn was not a gloriously apportioned palace. Still, we revelled in the glory and in the booty. To the victors went the spoils and, as with us, Gruffyd's Housecarls had carried their treasure with them on their person. Gryffydd of Rhuddlan had been a rich man and I took a healthily heavy purse as well as his arms and armour. His helmet, although finer than mine was too badly damaged to be of use and I sold it to the blacksmith for a small purse of coins. His mail coat was fine and needed little repair. I decided to keep it as a spare. His shield was not as good as mine and I gave it to Osgar whose own had been shattered during the fight. His gauntlets I gave to Ridley whose own lacked rivets. I thought back to the arrow which could have disabled me and gladly gave them to my friend. The other men I killed I let Wolf and Osgar share the bounty for they had helped me to kill my enemies. The booty was welcome but more welcome was the attention of my peers who all came to look at Death Bringer. It had been admired when I had first used it but now it was a weapon of legend having killed a Welsh hero. I felt slightly guilty about their praise for I had done little enough and luck had been on my side.

When I confided this to Osgar he had laughed, "A warrior who does not have luck is a dead warrior. I take all the luck I can get for without it no amount of skill with a blade will keep you alive."

It was towards evening when the monks arrived. Brother Aidan led them across the fields towards us. Despite the fact that they were holy men we kept our wits and our weapons at the ready for monks had been known to fight. This time, however, they came in peace to bury the dead Welsh. The Brother did not seem surprised to see me and approached me. "Well, Aelfraed of Medelai I can see now that you are a warrior and have turned Saint Asaph's ash into a weapon of war."

I looked at the spear in my hand. "Do you disapprove?"

He shook his head. "No, for you are a warrior. I knew that when I spoke with you. I hoped that you would fight for our king for I saw in you nobility which belied your years." He shrugged. "It was not to be but you did make an impression on our king."

As he left with the monks and the bodies I was astounded. I had not known any of that. Perhaps that was the reason he had unleashed his warriors at me for he feared me. I did not know why he would do that for I was just a Housecarl.

The next day we all awoke with thick heads for the one thing the fort possessed was ale and we consumed vast quantities of it. Uncle Aethelward shook his head in disapproval as he awoke me, Ridley, Wolf and Osgar. As we trudged behind him to the Earl's quarters I wondered why we had been summoned. The arrogant, prideful side of me thought it might be to praise me for my actions but the presence of the others militated against that. The alcohol had certainly fogged my brain. Ulf and Sweyn were with him; the two older warriors had a wry smile on their faces which showed less disapproval than my uncle.

"You all fought well yesterday. Sweyn here tells me that it was the turning point of the battle. Well done but that is not the reason I have summoned you. I need to visit with my brother in Jorvik. I need to travel swiftly and yet have protection. Lord Aethelward has enough horses for all of you and with five others we will travel this morning. Sweyn will watch your gear for I want us to be swift. Prepare yourselves."

It had all happened in a blur. Ridley and I led our friends to our horses. The spare would carry our mail. We each gathered their belongings; Wolf found a chest which he emptied and we placed in it our spare arms and armour. By the time we had completed that task Earl Harold and Uncle were waiting impatiently for us. Slinging our shields upon our backs and tying our spears to the pommels we mounted. Our comrades engaged in good-humoured banter as we left.

"Kill one warrior and they become knights!"

"Too good for us now!"

"I'll bet they are off to a whore house."

Thankfully Sweyn silenced them with a roar, "Right ladies let's make this castle inhabitable."

The journey North was totally different from the one when the four of us had travelled south. For one thing, we were not hiding and secondly, we rode quickly and hard. I was desperate to find the reason for the urgency but the Earl and Aethelward rode at the fore with Ulf between us and them. We could neither speak with them nor hear a word. At night when we camped, it did not seem appropriate to bring it up and I hoped that they would reveal their plans in conversation, but they did not. They did speak of the battle and, like me, were surprised at Gruffyd's apparent cowardice. My uncle, of course, had an explanation. "I am not sure he can count on his allies. He has upset too many people." He pointed at me, "When Aelfraed spied on his court he saw much dissension and discord. I think he fears for his position and now that Aedgar is dead he has no major ally. I do not think that he will invade England. That is certain."

"Still I would like to be rid of this particular thorn. Perhaps after we talk with my brother…"

Enigmatically that was all that was said and the four of us were left to discuss and deduce what would occur. I say four of us but in reality, it was three for Osgar saw no point in speculation. "We will find out what we need when the Earl tells us. You are like the village gossips making sagas out of accidents."

When we rode into Jorvik I was excited. I had only visited the place on a few occasions for my brothers and father preferred to leave me at home with Nanna but I knew that it was one of the most important cities in the land and I was eager to show it off to my friends. Ridley too was excited but that was because the Earl had promised us that we could visit Medelai once we had met his brother. I wondered at that for I had assumed that we had been the escort of the Earl on the road for his safety and that, once in Jorvik, then he would have been safe with his brother. I did not speculate with the others for I had had enough of Osgar's scorn but it did make me keep my eyes and ears open when I did view the meeting.

The people in Jorvik did not look as prosperous as the inhabitants of Winchester. They all had the lean and hungry look of an oppressed people and yet we Northumbrians had freed them from the tyranny of the Danes; it seemed strange to me. In contrast, the Earl's quarters were magnificently furnished with fine tapestries and well-made furniture. His guards and Thegns all looked to be well fed and prosperous. I kept looking for my brothers but I could not see them. Part of me was glad for I knew they would mock me in some way but in another, I was disappointed for I wished them to see the warrior I had become.

Earl Tostig still looked sly except now he was a more corpulent figure. I was relieved that he was pleased to see his brother and they embraced. He gave a curt nod to Aethelward and Ulf and I gathered that there was little love lost between them. He glanced at us. "Is this all the guard you brought? I would have expected your retinue."

"Why brother do I need the protection of my retinue in your court?"

Earl Tostig rapidly shook his head, always the mark of a liar. "No brother it is just that the road twixt here and Winchester is fraught with danger."

"I came not from Winchester but Wales and I needed no more than these for these are the warriors who helped me to defeat Gruffyd of Wales."

Tostig's eyes filled with greed and excitement. "You have defeated him. He is captured? Dead perhaps?" It is said of Earl Tostig that the main difference between him and his half brother was their attitude towards gold, for Tostig loved it; for my part, I disagree. There was naught that was similar in the two half brothers.

"No, for he escaped but we have his court and we have his crown. He left rather rapidly."

Tostig nodded and greedily licked his lips as though his half brother had actually given him the crown. He gestured to us. "Come warriors drink with me and I will celebrate your success." He poured us goblets of wine and I noticed that the goblets were made of fine metal. He looked at me with a curious look. "Don't I know you?"

Aethelward spoke for the first time. "It is Aelfraed, the son of Aethelgifu, my nephew."

I caught the sharp look he threw at Harold and wondered why he never said the son of Edwin of Medelai, for he never did. "Ah, I remember. Your brothers are my warriors now. They will be returning soon from a campaign against the Scots."

"Is Malcolm Canmore still being ungrateful, brother?"

"He is. Since the proposed marriage to Margaret broke down he has forgotten the refuge he had with King Edward and last year raided Lindisfarne. My warriors have been ejecting him from the north. Now you will need quarters."

"Four of my warriors wish to visit Medelai, we will only require rooms for three of us and then we can discuss my plans."

"Ah! Ever the thinker eh Harold and will it be profitable?"

Harold wrinkled his nose as though the thought was distasteful but, as the largest landowner in England, he could hardly be surprised. "I think you may well profit from it."

I felt relieved to be heading north with my three friends. Aethelward had pulled me to one side. "Be careful what you say and do when you are at Medelai."

"Why uncle what could I say that would cause a problem?"

"Aelfraed have you not yet learned to listen more than you speak. You have a tongue which runs away with itself and you are privy to more knowledge than others, just think on that."

As I had left him I knew that he was angry but I could not, at the time work out why. It was pleasant, however, to be riding through the Vale of Jorvik on that fine autumn day. We had left the spare horse in the stables and carried only our swords and shields. The last thing we wished was for people to think we were raiders. The farm looked small as we trotted into the courtyard. Ridley's father, as Steward came to greet us. I think he was genuinely touched by the change in his son for he began to weep as he hugged him. He bowed slightly to me, "Welcome Master Aelfraed."

Uncle Aethelward was always annoyed at the lack of respect shown to me by the Steward but, as I had told him, he got that from the way I was treated by my father and brothers. Now, however, I was no longer a boy, I was a man grown and a warrior. "Thank you, Oswin. We are staying in Jorvik for a while with Earl Tostig but Earl Harold has given us four days off to visit here." I scrutinised his face. "That will not be a problem, will it?"

"Oh no," he quickly answered, "Your brothers are serving the earl and your father is… well he is away on business."

I had learned since I had been away to recognise deception and obfuscation and I heard both in Oswin's words but I decided to ignore it for the while.

"Where is mother?"

Oswin's voice darkened at his son's words. "She died last winter of a fever."

Ridley looked as though someone had struck him with an axe haft. He almost fell and Osgar put what Oswin should have done, a paternal arm around his shoulder. "Why did you not tell your son?"

"He was not here to tell." Oswin almost spat the words out and I could feel the source of his annoyance. I had taken his son away and not left him to carry on his father's work. The fact that Ridley had been ignored as a child and was a born warrior appeared irrelevant.

"You could have written."

"He does not read."

"No, but I do." I went closer to Oswin and lowered my voice, "This was badly done, Steward. Where is she buried?"

He looked shaken for I had deliberately towered over him and he was afraid, "In the churchyard."

"We will visit the grave. When we return, I will expect food and for our quarters to be made ready. See to the horses."

"Yes, my lord."

I turned and dismissed him with my back. Wolf looked at me as though anew. "I did not know you were a lord, Aelfraed."

"I am not a lord, Wolf. I am a Housecarl. I am one of you."

After we had visited the grave Ridley felt better and actually smiled. "Well master, I do not know about you but I have now finished with Medelai. There is nothing more for me here."

The others were surprised for it was the longest statement they had heard him make. It was one of those moments in life where you feel as close to someone as it is possible for I felt the same. I had not known that Ridley had suffered as I had because we did not conform to the expectations placed upon us. His mother had been like my grandmother, my Nanna and she had been his only connection to our home. I suddenly realised that I had no connection with it either. Once we left this time we would never return. When we entered the hall Oswin had ensured that we could not find fault with anything. I think he resented having to defer to his son but I was in no mood for any signs of irritation. We ate and drank well.

The next morning I decided that we would go hunting and then return to Jorvik the following day. It had been made quite clear by Oswin that we were not particularly welcome but I would not make life easy for him by leaving prematurely. The forests near my home were teeming with deer and wild boar and the four of us were excited. We rode to the forest to the west and hobbled our horses. I had mocked Ridley when he had insisted upon taking a spare horse for the kills. He took it in good part because that day was unlike any others; it was four friends enjoying life. The battle of Rhuddlan had shown us all how close we were to death when we fought in the shield wall.

There was a stream that cut through the forest and Ridley and I had often watched the animals gather to drink. The small waterfall also afforded cover and gave us the best chance of success. I took Dragon Tamer with me, mainly because I was not a good shot with arrows but my companions took their bows. I do not think any of us were bothered about success on that day; it just felt good to be out in the woods enjoying banter and not worrying about anything.

Ridley's sharp eyes picked out the herd of deer which were moving down through the trees towards the stream. The wind drifted from the stream bringing the sound of the waterfall and the musky scent of the herd. Wolf and Osgar went to his left and right while I waited behind Ridley. I always admired Ridley for he was a consummate hunter; he had far more patience than I did. He moved agonizingly slowly towards the deer and the others followed his lead. I watched as he carefully placed each foot on the ground before moving forwards. The arrow was already notched, enabling him to take a snatch shot should they be spooked. He drew to within twenty paces and then drew back the arrow. He had chosen a magnificent buck. I could not see the other's targets but I prepared Dragon Tamer in case he fled towards us. Ridley's arrow was followed in swift succession by the other two. Osgar had aimed at the buck while Wolf had chosen a small hind. The herd panicked and galloped off in all directions. The stag staggered for a few paces but Ridley's arrow had struck it behind the eye. Wolf's blundered off in the undergrowth and I heard him cursing.

"Now we will have to wander through the forest looking for your poor hind."

"She moved, just at the last moment."

Ridley shook his head and admonished Wolf. "A good hunter allows for that." They had already removed the arrows and so I cut them a stout branch to help them carry the enormous beast. They ran the sharpened wooden stake through his body and hefted it onto their shoulders. They were both strong men but it took some lifting. Wolf and I then followed the blood trail to find his injured animal. It did not do to leave an animal wounded. The trail moved erratically from left to right suggesting that the deer still had enough energy to avoid the hunters. It meant we moved far from the river. Eventually, we smelled the animal and Wolf found where it had expired. He went to cut down a branch and I turned to call the others.

"Halloo! Halloo! We have found it."

I heard their voices in distance. "We are coming."

Just then I heard snorting and saw the bushes closer to Wolf move. I saw immediately that it was a wild boar and knew that it would go straight for Wolf. He had obviously disturbed it when cutting his sapling. His bow was next to the deer and he only had a dagger with which to protect himself. I roared a challenge and then raced towards the snorting, angry beast. It turned remarkably quickly to face the new threat and I saw its tusks and its teeth. It was a male and it was angry. I took Dragon Tamer and regretted not fitting a bar behind the head. Other Housecarls had done so as it prevented the spear from becoming stuck in a body. In this situation, it stopped the boar from eating your spear. I had seen enough hunts to know that it would try to eviscerate me with his sharp tusks and I knew he would be quick. I would have one chance to spear him before he was upon me. As he neared me I dropped to one knee and rammed the butt of my spear into the bole of a nearby tree. It tried to turn its head from the wicked spearhead and when it did so I plunged the spear into the side of its neck. It squealed in pain but still turned its head to try to reach me. As it pushed the butt slid back to the bole of the tree and it was stuck. Wolf had dragged his dagger out and he leapt astride the stricken animal and slit its throat. As it lay, pumping its lifeblood onto the ground I nodded to Wolf. "Thank you. That was good timing."

Wolf shook his head. "No, thank you Aelfraed for I would have been dead but for your intervention. That was bravely done to face a charging boar."

The other two had heard the commotion and dropped their deer. Racing towards us they had seen the culmination of the struggle. Osgar cocked his head to one side. "I think the gods have a better name for your spear, Aelfraed. I think it is Boar Splitter."

When Ridley and Wolf nodded their assent, I spoke. Dragon Tamer sounded grand but I had not tamed a dragon. The gods of the hunt and the gods of combat were wiser than I. "Boar Splitter it is." From that day forth Boar Splitter never let me down. The haft never broke, the head never moved. That day in the woods, above Medelai, made me just that little bit better as a warrior.

Ridley gave me a knowing look as we slung the boar and the stag on the spare horse and I nodded, "Yes Ridley you were right and I was wrong, we did need a spare mount."

He turned to the others, "Make a note of that. It is the first time that Master Aelfraed has admitted to a mistake. This is indeed a glorious moment."

I could not get Ridley out of the habit of calling me master but Wolf and Osgar did not seem to notice. Wolf slung his small hind over the neck of his mount and we headed east. As we had more weight on the horses I took us directly east to strike the old Roman road from the north. The legions, apparently, had marched north to tame the wild Scots and that was the way Tostig's Housecarls would have travelled after the sacking of Lindisfarne. It was a longer route but easier to travel, especially for Wolf. As we crested the rise above the road I saw three riders coming from the north and judged that they would be abreast of us when we reached the road. It would be good to hear news from the borders for I had the feeling that at some time we would have to fight Malcolm and his Scots. As we closed I saw, to my surprise that the lead rider was my father. I wondered what business he had had in the north for he did no business but loved the politics of power. I halted our group to await him.

"Good afternoon father."

He looked up as though I had slapped him and I saw him hurriedly look at the two companions, neither of whom I recognised. From their dress, they were not locals but they looked like warriors. They also looked as though they wished we had not chanced upon them and both of them furtively scanned the woods behind us as though we were part of some trap. "Aelfraed. I did not know you were home. What brings you here?"

The suspicion in his voice made me cautious in my reply. I suspected that he was up to something but I had learned from Aethelward that you gained more intelligence by listening than by shouting. "Oh, we were given some time off by Earl Harold and we went hunting." I waved an expansive hand at our kills. "Successfully as you can see. This is Wolf and Osgar two Housecarls and Ridley you know."

Good manners would have dictated that my father introduce his companions but he did not instead he exchanged a secretive look with his companions and then asked, "The Earl, is he in Jorvik?"

Ridley blurted out the answer before I could stop him, "Aye my lord. He is meeting with his brother Earl Tostig."

My father looked at his companions. "I will leave you, gentlemen, here and return to my home with my son. Thank you for your company. I felt much safer on the road."

They just grunted and then rode east towards the forest. It struck me as strange for if they had been heading south-east they would have taken the fork which was further up the road. It convinced me that my father was up to something. We turned our horses south. "Who were those men father? They are not locals, are they?"

"No, they are travellers I met at the Roman Bridge."

I played the innocent. "I am surprised that you did not take a couple of warriors with you for the road to the north is dangerous."

He laughed uneasily. "I forgot, for it is some time since I travelled the road. Next time…" He hurriedly changed the subject. Since his companions had left he had regained his composure. "You have had a good hunt. We will eat well tonight. Did Oswin care for you?"

"Aye, he looked after us as though you were there."

"And when do you return?"

"On the morrow for it is a brief visit." I noticed that he had no interest in my life or what I had been doing. His only concern was with what the Earl was doing. It merely confirmed my decision to leave Medelai and never return.

Oswin looked relieved when my father, the Thegn returned. I could see that they were desperate for conference. I did not think I would gain any more information and so the four of us took the dead animals to the kitchen to be butchered. Mara the cook was a lovely woman who seemed to be made of rolls of fat. She had been the only servant who had been kind to me. I discovered the main reason was she had been my mother's servant and Nanna had kept her on after mother's death. She threw her arms around me and slobbered wet kisses on my cheeks, much to the amusement of my companions. "Master Aelfraed, my you have grown but it does my heart good to see you back." She held me at arm's length. "By but you are the image of your mother." She shook her head. "What a shame that fine lady is dead but she would be so proud of you. Ridley's father said that you are one of Earl Harold's Housecarls. She would have loved that." She seemed to see the animals for the first time. "Well look at that. I have never seen such a successful hunt in all my time here. It is good to have hunters in the house again. "She kissed Ridley on the cheek. "You shall have a fine feast tonight and I will get one of the servants to make sure that tight-fisted father of yours has not hidden the good wine and ale, for this meat should be served with good ale." She spoke like this all the time, like a river in spate, in torrents.

I felt much better having spoken to Mara. There was none of the reserve and the deceit of my father and the Steward. She was as close as I would get again to Nanna and her unreserved love.

Mara was as good as her word and the food was magnificent. Much to my father's annoyance, she kept popping into the hall to make sure that our platters were full. It was obvious that he was irritated but Mara was her own woman. If the Thegn had chastised her then she would have left. There were many lords in Northumbria who would have employed her as a cook and she knew it. She only stayed at the hall in memory of my mother and grandmother. His irritation only served to fuel my appetite and I ate more than I had in many a moon. Once the food had finished and we were in our cups I asked about my brothers.

"Oh, they are with the Earl's army," he said vaguely. "I have not seen them for some months."

I wondered why he had lied to me. I knew that they had been in Jorvik a short time ago and my father was frequently at court there so why the lie? I would have to broach the subject with Aethelward. He was the only man with whom I could confide my suspicions and he was also the only man who might be able to unravel this particular ball of wool.

As we mounted our horses the next day Oswin and my father came to see us off. "You must come and stay again. You and your friends are always welcome." The words were inviting but the look in my father's eyes was not.

"We will and it was good to be in the bosom of my family again." Ridley shot me a sharp look but I cared not, if my father could be a hypocrite then so should I. We turned our mounts and headed away from Medelai. "Well, Ridley did you find out anything about my father?"

Ridley had spent some time with the other servants listening for snippets of information. He had always been a quiet child and the servants were used to his silence. He had not enjoyed being a spy but I had pointed out that he was Earl Harold's Housecarl now and that entailed a different loyalty.

"He has been north of the Tyne."

"Scotland eh? I wonder why he was so close-mouthed and I wonder who those men were?"

I heard Osgar snort behind me. "There you go again, thinking. It will do you no good Aelfraed."

I turned in my saddle. "This time it might Osgar. The Scots have been raiding Northumbria and my father meets with them."

"It could be a peace mission."

"It could. Wolf but in that case why travel alone and why not mention it? That is not a bad thing and would be something worth boasting of to one's son. No, I will be happy when we have shared this information with the Earl and my uncle."

I spent the rest of the journey to Jorvik running over all the possibilities in my mind. Eventually, I decided that it was too big a problem for me and older, wiser minds could wrestle with it. On reflection, I was pleased that I had visited my home; firstly, it confirmed the low esteem in which I was held by my father and secondly, more importantly, the hunt had bonded the four of us as blood brothers and that was no bad thing.

I was as patient as possible when we reach the mighty fortress. We found our quarters and while the other three went to explore the city I waited, kicking my heels, outside the chamber in which Earl Tostig, Earl Harold and my uncle were in conference. I knew that it was petty of me to expect to be seen swiftly but I felt that the news I had was of such import that the great men would need to hear of it. When they eventually left the hall Earl Harold and my uncle were still in deep discussion. I was acknowledged with a flick of the head but then ignored and I trailed in their wake like a child trying to attract the attention of a parent. The two men walked out of the hall and headed for the Roman walls. I dutifully followed. It seemed an age before they deigned to turn and speak with me but eventually they did. "Well nephew, having dogged our tracks for an unseemly length of time what do you have to tell us that is so important?"

"When I went home I found that my father has visited Scotland although he pretended not to and he travelled south with two strangers."

I felt sure that my information was of such importance that they would immediately act but their faces gave nothing away. "Your father went to Scotland and..."

"Well my lord he, well he was evasive when he told me and he didn't have a good reason. He travelled alone..." I could feel myself reddening and feel the flimsiness of my tale as I told it. I was making something out of nothing.

Earl Harold smiled and patted my shoulder. "Thank you for the information Aelfraed. It is good that you keep your eyes and ears open. Do not look so disappointed for your knowledge may be important. We, your uncle and me, have to think of the bigger picture."

Aethelward took my arm, "You did right to tell us and it may well be important but we need to think more on this."

I felt a little better, as though they were taking me seriously and we completed a circuit of the walls before returning to the hall as dusk settled. I had not been in the warrior's hall before and it was enormous. More importantly, it was filled with warriors, Thegns and lords. My comrades and I had been afforded great honour being allowed into the hall. I saw my friends and made my way towards them.

"Jorvik is a fine city," blurted Wolf. "I have never seen such stone. I wonder why the king does not abide here?"

"I think it is a little far north and besides the King favours the Normans, not the Northumbrians."

Osgar nodded, "And yet this city could withstand a siege far more easily than wooden Winchester. I agree with Wolf. If I were I king then I would live here. Far safer."

I felt proud that my two friends felt that way about my city. I had not been there often but I was proud of my heritage. We were the bulwark against the Scots and the defence against the Northmen. My good feelings were shattered when the hall doors burst open and Earl Tostig's Housecarls boisterously entered. Unlike us, they were armed and armoured and extremely loud. I suppose I should have expected that for it was their hall and we were guests but it seemed somehow false and over loud. The four of us drew back into the shadows so as to be inconspicuous. I suddenly saw my three brothers who appeared to be louder and noisier than the rest. I suspected they were drunk for they appeared to be unsteady upon their feet. I thought briefly about leaving, for I felt sure that if they spotted me then they would cause a quarrel. I was not afraid of a fight but I was afraid of letting down the Earl for I was his Housecarl. Ulf followed them in and I could see from his expression that he was not impressed. He saw us and wandered over.

"They are arrogant pups." We said nothing but watched them as they behaved like young boys rather than Housecarls. "It seems they chased the Scots over the border and they are celebrating their victory."

"Did they kill many?"

Ulf laughed and said scornfully. "They killed none! The Scots were already leaving and they followed them like a pack of dogs slink after the bear, afraid to beard it. They had yet to draw blood but they believe they are heroes all."

He went to the ale barrel and poured himself a beaker of the frothy beer. As he returned to us, Edward, my brother spotted me and, with Egbert and Edgar in tow, lurched towards us, "Why it is the runt! What brought you back from Harold's court, failed at something did you? Wet the bed because Nanna wasn't there?" He and my brothers thought that this was hilarious and fell about laughing.

I was unarmed but I moved forwards ready to smack Edward in the face. Ridley and Osgar held my arms.

"Ooh does my little brother think he can take on one of Earl Tostig's Housecarls?"

Ulf stepped forwards his hands like enormous pans. He grabbed hold of Edward's mail. "You have an ill-mannered tongue Northumbrian. It is Earl Harold to you and the warrior you abuse is a Housecarl himself." He dropped Edward, who had been dangling in the air, to the ground, "and you would be wise to watch your words around him."

I could hear from his slurred words that Edward was drunk and trying to impress both his brothers and the other Housecarls. "Earl Harold! Who is he? He has not defeated the Scots and sent them back over the border, that was the work of Earl Tostig a worthy warrior."

The hall fell silent as the other Housecarls saw Earl Harold, Earl Tostig and my uncle walk towards us. Edward and my brothers were so full of themselves that they failed to realise the perilous position in which they found themselves. We all smiled at them as the trio appeared behind them.

"Oh, my brother and his pathetic friends find it funny. You are jesters, now are you? Or have you fallen even further and now service warriors with your pretty little arses."

I felt Wolf stir beside me and I turned to him. "Forgive my brother, firstly he is drunk and secondly he was always a dick head."

Edward's hand went to his sword but it was grabbed by my uncle. "I apologise Earl Harold for the foul mouth of this toad who, I am afraid, is my nephew. He was deprived of my sister's wise words and dragged up by an apology of a man."

Egbert and Edgar dropped their hands to their scabbards but Ulf grinned evilly at them. "Please take out your swords and your bodies will be carrion bait by nightfall."

Earl Tostig's voice boomed out. "The three of you apologise to my brother and these warriors now."

Suddenly sobering, the three of them mumbled an apology to Earl Harold and looked to the ground in embarrassment. I could see that Harold was amused more than angered and may, even, have been enjoying himself. He turned to his brother, "Brother I forgot to introduce these four Housecarls. They were valiant warriors in the battle against Gruffyd in which they defeated his Housecarls and against the Earl of Mercia where they defeated his mounted horse." Tostig's Housecarls looked at us with new eyes for they had heard of the two battles. "This warrior," Harold put his arm on my shoulder, "also defeated the Welsh champion Gryffydd of Rhuddlan who had singled him out for combat."

Earl Tostig came and clasped my arm. "Let me shake your arm for I knew Gryffydd and he was a fierce warrior." He turned to my brothers. "Now aren't you glad that you did not try to spill blood here for if you had I am in no doubt that it would have been yours?" They all looked as though they wished the ground would swallow them. "You have disgraced my Housecarls and embarrassed me in front of my guests. Leave now and return to your home. I may send for you to rejoin my ranks," he glowered at them darkly, "or I may not! Now leave."

The three of them had the shocked faces of men who have seen their world disappear before them. They glanced pleadingly at the Earl who looked away and, as they left, gave me looks of absolute hatred. This was not forgotten.

Ulf leaned over and said, quietly, "I think you had best move around with your friends for a while. I don't think your brothers are happy men."

Chapter 7

When we eventually headed south again I was pleased to be leaving Jorvik. After my brothers' departure, it was a happy time and the Housecarls of Earl Tostig could not get enough stories about our battles against the Welsh and the Mercians. It seems that their forays against the Scots had either been badly timed or betrayed for they had yet to bring them to battle. Aethelward had been dismissive of this. "They need to keep men close to the border. Gods the Romans built a wall there. Could they not base them there?"

Earl Harold always seemed amused by my uncle's outbursts. "Not all leaders have advisers such as you who have such a keen insight into strategy. You and your nephew are both exceptions Aethelward."

I felt as though I were a giant when I was compared with my uncle for I had seen that he was one of the few men whom every warrior, even Earl Tostig respected. Ulf had snuggled into his bearskin as the north wind whistled around our ears high on the northern moors. "I hope the strategy you devised will work old friend."

Earl Harold nodded. "Do not worry Ulf it will. My brother and his Housecarls are itching to emulate us. When they invade the north of Wales we will take ship and attack him from the west. Between us, we will crack him like a nut at Yuletide."

Ridley and I looked at each other. We were going to war again. Perhaps our youth made us feel invincible but, along with Wolf, we felt that we could take on any enemy and defeat them, even the mighty, puissant Normans.

When we reached Legacaestir, Ulf left to fetch the Housecarls. The rest of the army would remain for Earl Tostig to command. I wondered about that for Harold was giving his brother the chance for glory and honour while he would play the part of a gatekeeper preventing Gruffyd from escaping. I answered myself with the same thought; Harold was not like other men. He was thinking of England and what was good for England. It did not matter to him who had the glory, merely that the result was the same; the Welsh eliminated as a threat and our borders safe. I have no doubt that if he had been in the northern lands then the Scots would not have raided with such impunity. The rest of us headed for Winchester where he would have to find the money for ships. King Edward had disbanded the fleet years earlier but the Earl and my uncle did not think that this would pose too much of a problem. It was drawing close to the end of the year and Harold hoped that the king would be in the mood to pay for the fleet; if not then I had no doubt that Harold would dip into his own coffers and come up with the required finance.

Winchester felt more like home than Medelai had as we arrived in the city. The warrior hall was almost deserted but it afforded us the opportunity to claim the best position for our beds. The Housecarls who had remained, to train new warriors and to rest injuries, told us of the problems there had been. The Norman knights had caused more trouble; Guy of Evreux, the reckless rider, had killed one of the king's bodyguards and had been sent home in disgrace. The others had left the king's presence and returned to London and the Norman Bishop who, to all intents and purposes, ruled that city. In some ways, I was pleased for it meant the Norman influence was no longer felt so keenly but I had been itching to try my blade against the arrogant Norman. I was sure that one day I would see which of us was the stronger but that day would be some time off.

It was the best Yuletide I had ever spent. We had the whole hall to ourselves and the absence of the Normans meant that King Edward and Earl Harold got on far better than they had previously. Even Aethelward seemed happy and reported to us that the king had sanctioned the purchase of the ships we would need. It seems that he had been warned of Mercian and Welsh intentions through his Norman allies and Harold's actions had neutralised that threat. It was at about this time that Edward named Harold as his heir. Of course, that meant little unless the Witenagemot proposed the Earl as a candidate for the crown in the event of Edward's death but it meant much for Edward was considered a noble king. At the moment that seemed likely as the only possible opposition would come from his half brother Tostig but from what I had seen he would give his support to Harold.

The world was a happy place and about to become happier. Ralph the Timid had been the Earl of Hereford defeated by Gruffyd and had eked out his last days in Winchester ruing the battle which had cost him his earldom. His children, Harold and Gytha were raised by Earl Harold's wife Edith. I had never met them before but, at a feast held to celebrate Yuletide, they were introduced to us, for they wished to meet the men who had killed their father's conquerors. Harold was slightly older than his sister Gytha who was a mere fifteen. As soon as I saw her I was struck by her beauty. Poets and singers speak of love at first sight. I do not know about that but I know that the moment I saw her I never wanted another woman. When the other Housecarls had been to whorehouses I had abstained and now, as I beheld the love of my life for the first time, I was glad. I was delighted when Earl Harold singled me out as the warrior who had killed Gryffydd of Rhuddlan for their father had spoken of the mighty warrior who had broken his charge. Gytha looked up at me with hero worship in her eyes and I am ashamed to say that I loved every glance and I found my head raised just that little bit higher. Harold and his sister plied me with questions about the combat and I repeated answers I had given earlier. My comrades became bored and wandered off, the others, too drifted off although I saw the Earl's wife, Edith giving us her full attention.

As we were alone, although in a crowded hall, I led her to a small trunk that served as a bench and we sat down. "You are young to be a Housecarl Aelfraed."

"I am older than you."

She giggled, "But I am a girl and I am not a Housecarl." Then she became serious. "I meant no disrespect. I merely thought that one so young had done well to achieve such fame."

"Fame? I think you exaggerate."

She became earnest again, her red hair framing her perfect face. "Oh no. You were the talk of Winchester even before the battle; the Housecarl who stood up to the Normans and protected the woman and her child; the young warrior who defeated a mighty bandit in the forests of Wales. You have renown Aelfraed, your name precedes you and it is said that you are a confidante of the Earl and his advisers."

I had to force myself to stay calm. I knew what my comrades thought of warriors who thought too highly of themselves and I did not want to lose the trust of my comrades. "I was lucky. I fight in a shield wall with many brave men. I could not have fought the Welsh champion had I not been protected by my friends."

She looked at me curiously. "What is it like to fight, to know you could die in an instant?"

"You do not have time to think. You fight to survive and you do what you must to live. I am glad that you will never have to fight."

I reached over to take her hand. She did not take it away but smiled up at me. "I am honoured that a warrior takes the time to talk to a young girl such as I. Promise me that when you are in Winchester you will visit with me and tell me of your deeds."

My heart was about to burst and I croaked, "Indeed I will I…"

Edith Swanneck, the Earl's wife, took Gytha's hand from mine, "Well I think Gytha, that it is time for you to retire." She gave me a knowing look. "I am sure the young warrior Aelfraed will need to tell his tale to others tonight."

The message was quite clear and I had no wish to annoy and alienate the wife of the Earl. "No, my lady and I apologise if I have commandeered too much of Gytha's time."

Gytha's eyes bored into mine. "Oh no Aelfraed. I can never have too much time with you."

In answer Edith, Harold's consort, swept the girl away to her quarters leaving me to be the butt of my friends' banter and cruel humour. "Making eyes at the Earl's ward!"

"Ah love at first bite!"

"He spears his first boar and fancies himself with the prettiest girl in the hall."

"Enough! Are we finished? Then lead me to the ale butt." I did not mind their laughter for I would have done the same in their position and I cared not for I now had something other than the life of a warrior to occupy my mind.

I did not see Gytha again for some as King Edward returned to London with Edith and their charges. We prepared for war and the second part of the assault on Wales. There were now many more recruits to the Housecarls of Earl Harold Godwinson. His victories had brought him greater riches and I knew, from my uncle, that we needed to have a solid force of Housecarls; I had seen the fyrd in action and although keen they were hopelessly undisciplined and unpredictable. We spent the next few months training new recruits and watched them suffer the same mistakes and indignities as we. The success we had enjoyed meant that the four of us had been promoted to the third rank of the wedge. Sweyn recognised that we worked well as a team and that was more important than the fact that the three of us were relatively young. We had served in two battles and been successful. To be fair our comrades did not disagree for our victory over Gryffydd of Rhuddlan had been the stuff of legend and they all basked in the reflected glory.

As well as training Wolf and Ridley improved their arms and armour. Ridley had a fine new helmet made with the nasal so favoured by the Normans. He had seen many older warriors who had no nose and, as he told us, as the best looking Housecarl he would keep his good looks. Wolf bought a magnificent axe. His own had been functional but its blade was not as long as ours and his new one was a thing of beauty. Ridley and I had given our two friends our spare horses and we were able to go hunting in the nearby forests as we waited for the orders which would take us to Wales.

We were privy to the information that we would be going by sea but we had to keep that knowledge to ourselves. It was amusing to watch our comrades watching the weather and commenting upon the state of the roads. We knew that when we went we would be sailing. That in itself was quite exciting for none of us, Osgar included, had ever been to sea before. The superstitious pair, Ridley and Wolf, was quite worried by the prospect whilst I was excited and Osgar viewed it as a chance to see his land from a different perspective.

"What if we sailed off the edge of the world?"

"Wolf, we know that Ireland lies to the west and the Danes have sailed further west to a land made of ice and of snow."

"How do you know that Osgar?"

"Because my young friend, unlike you I listen more than I talk and I have lived longer. I was told so."

Wolf was still not convinced and I could see the worry in his face. I liked my earnest young friend and sought to reassure him. "We will not be sailing out of sight of land and we will not travel far."

"Are you sure?"

"Aye I have looked at a map and we will sail from the Severn around the coast. It will not be a long journey."

"A map?" Anything which involved reading seemed like magic to Ridley and I resolved to teach him how to read when we had the opportunity.

"A piece of parchment which shows what the land and the sea look like from above."

Osgar laughed at the confused look on Ridley's face. "It was not drawn by a bird. The seamen who sail draw the lines to help them to navigate. I can see that the voyage will be an interesting one."

Just then the steely voice of Aethelward interrupted us. "You are like four old gammers who jabber about nothing except that you are gossiping about the Earl's plans which should remain secret."

I felt ashamed that we had been talking so loudly. "Sorry, uncle but we are excited. None of us has sailed before."

He relaxed a little. "It is not necessarily a pleasant experience but we will not be on the ships for long, however, we will not be able to take horses which means that you will all have to travel as lightly as possible. What you cannot carry you cannot take."

We were now a much larger band of warriors and the warrior hall was overcrowded. We looked forward to the time when we would board the ships. Aethelward gave us warning the night before we left allowing us to be slightly better prepared than the others and we set off across the western part of Wessex. This time we just had the Housecarls and were a mighty horde of armed and armoured men. When we reached the southern bank of the Severn estuary we saw, to our relief the fat-bellied ships waiting to transport us. They looked far too small to accommodate such a large number of men but Osgar was philosophical. "I am assuming that your uncle and the Earl have actually counted the men they need to take and I am certain that Sweyn will have done so."

He was right and, even though we were overcrowded, we managed to fit aboard. Unfortunately, we were shepherded below decks and it was only the Earl, Sweyn and my uncle who were allowed to stay above decks. We had no idea where we were for there were no apertures through which we could see. We knew when we were out in the rougher waters for the boat wallowed, dipped and rolled in the breakers. We had eaten sparingly but some of our comrades had had a hearty night and consumed much ale; soon the deck was slippery with vomit and the smell made many others bring back the contents of their stomachs. We found out later that the winds were favourable and gave us a speedy journey; even so, it took the better part of a day to reach our destination. As we tumbled from the boats we were all grateful that there were no enemies to greet us for we were in no condition to walk, let alone fight. Once ashore those of us who were able to, were formed into a skirmish line and we formed a wall of steel as the equipment was offloaded onto the beach. Despite my experience on the ship, I was pleased that they remained at anchor for we had a way out; the beach was surrounded by high and threatening peaks. As soon as I could, I spoke with Aethelward and found that we had landed in an unpronounceable place in the middle of Wales. We were as far from England as it was possible to be and were three hundred men who were alone. The ships were, literally, our lifeline.

The first night was the hardest for those of us who were fit as we had to shoulder the sentry duties. I had never had to perform such a duty and I found it challenging to stare out into the dark seeking unseen enemies; it was like the forest and the bandits all over again. I could see neither Ridley nor Wolf and I just hoped that they were close by. Every noise I heard made me start and jump. When Sweyn came around on his patrol I was relieved. His white teeth gleamed in the dark. "How is your first duty young boar killer?"

"I would prefer to face a boar or stand in the shield wall. I like it not lord."

I heard his laugh. "You will get used to it for this campaign will be more arduous than the one last year." He leaned in and I could finally see his features. "You have done well, Aelfraed, and we all think well of you but learn to walk before you try to run. Remember when you ran in the wedge for the first time. I thought then that it was a valuable lesson not just for combat but for life."

Enigmatically he left and I wondered to what did he refer? It was only later, for I had a long watch to keep, that I came to the conclusion that my intentions as regards the Earl's ward, Gytha, had been noted. Perhaps my confused parentage had created an issue. I had deduced that I was not the son of Edwin of Medelai. That in itself was not a problem. I did not have any filial allegiance to him and his sons but I wondered about my mother. In addition, it made me illegitimate. That was not necessarily a bad thing, for Earl Harold and Edith were not married and had children but Gytha was related to King Edward and that meant that any suitor would have to be vetted. I laughed to myself. I had had one conversation with her and already I wanted her for a bride. I had met one girl and she was the one. My friends were right to mock me, I was a fool.

The next day, despite my red eyes and tired head we shouldered our weapons and headed inland towards the heart of Gruffyd's lands. Aethelward and the Earl had had information that he was in the centre of his country where the mountains were high. We knew that the Earl of Northumbria was leading the bulk of the army south and we hoped to catch him between us; like a piece of metal between the hammer and the anvil. We saw ourselves as the hammer for we knew that we were the finest three hundred warriors in England. We had never been defeated and that bred confidence.

Within a day of leaving the estuary, we found our first stronghold. It was a small hill fort called Maen Llwyd. There was a small garrison but they appeared to us to be poorly armed. Sweyn lined us up in three lines rather than two. As usual, we were to the right of the second line. There was a small ditch and a palisade that ran around the mound. It was not steep and I suspect they had chosen the site as it was close to the river and could watch rather than protect. Sweyn walked up to the gate and called upon them to surrender. I am not sure that they understood him for his reply was a volley of arrows. It was a warning to us for they all struck his shield. Holding it above his head he retreated.

"Well my lord it looks like we will have to take this little pimple."

We knew that he was right. We could not leave it as it could stop us from leaving at some future time. We prepared to attack. If they only had arrows, then we would make short work of them. Aethelward and the Earl held a conference and my uncle came over to us. "I want you thirty warriors to attack the right side of the fort." The warriors he identified were the thirty of us on the right. I saw him go to the left flank and do the same there. It meant that the front of the fort would be assaulted by over two hundred warriors and they would face the main attack but our presence on the flanks would mean that the Welsh could not place all of their men on one wall. Once again, I saw the strategos that was my uncle.

As we edged around the side, making sure that we were well out of arrow range I wondered who would lead us. Sweyn stood before the main band while my uncle and the Earl waited behind. Soon it became obvious that we would lead ourselves. That was the first time I realised the status of a Housecarl. He was more than a mindless warrior obeying orders; he was part of a machine and each part was capable of acting independently. At that moment, I felt as proud and as honoured as I had ever felt.

Sweyn roared, "Forward!" and, holding our shields before us so that only our eyes peered over the top, we marched towards the stronghold. As we marched we banged our spears on the backs of our shields. It helped us keep time and it made a terrifying sound. The arrows began to thud onto our shields as soon as we were in range. Some stuck in the wood but many others pinged off the metal. When the arrows struck a helmet, it was alarming for the warrior as it made a sound like a small bell although none of the arrows penetrated, we all wore the best helmets we could afford. When the front rank reached the ditch we, in the second rank, halted to allow them to cross safely. The Welsh had sown the bottom with wooden, sharpened stakes and I saw three warriors fall backwards, their feet damaged by the pointed sticks. The other seven climbed to the top and then hurried to the wall where they stood with their shields above their heads to protect them from the missiles and stones thrown upon them. We were quicker across the ditch having seen the obstacles and we avoided the traps. Once we had attained the wall half of us protected the seven warriors with our shields while the other half jabbed upwards with our spears. The Welsh had not built the wall high enough and we were all tall warriors. Our spears pushed them back from the edge and the flurry of stones ceased. The seven warriors hacked at the walls with their axes their sharp blades making short work of the wooden structure. With the third rank behind us, we were able to prepare to assault. While the third rank watched and cleared the ramparts, we fell into a small wedge formation. Gurt was in the front and Ridley and I were second; with Wolf and Osgar on the left and right flanks, we felt secure. As soon as Gurt saw daylight through the wooden walls he shouted, "Push!" and we rushed the gap. His shield struck the hole and then the force of nine more warriors cracked it open like an egg. We were through!

To our left, we could see men still on the walls holding off Sweyn and our comrades. Gurt turned us and we ran at the warriors who were attempting to barricade the gate. Even had we not been reinforced by our comrades from the breach I am sure that the ten of us could have seen off the pathetically poorly armed men who turned in horror to see our spears and shields bearing down upon them. It was child's play. I stabbed forwards and saw Boar Splitter rip into the throat of the startled and surprised Welsh warrior before me. I did not penetrate far and, turning the blade, retrieved it to stab into the unprotected side of a man who had been too slow to turn and face us. By now men were coming from the walls to fight off this threat to the gate. Gurt shouted. "Wolf, Osgar get the gate open!" Ridley and I turned to protect the backs of our friends as they began to lift off the bars which held the gates in place. Four warriors, armed with shields and swords angrily raced towards us. I was to Ridley's right and exposed but I had Boar Splitter and the joy of battle was upon me. I stabbed forwards over the shield of the man in the middle and felt my spear slice into flesh. He fell back and I was able to deflect the sword of his companion on my shield and then I used the edge of Boar Splitter to slice across his unprotected head. Its sharpened blade sliced across his eyes and he fell screaming to the floor. Ignoring him I faced the man I had cut first and I saw fear in his face. He was terrified facing a mailed warrior a head taller than he with a spear that outranged his short sword. Bravely he came at me but without enthusiasm and with a flick of my shield I knocked his sword aside and as he raised his shield to protect his head I slid Boar Splitter hard into his midriff. He was not a big warrior and the blade emerged from the back. I dropped the spear for it would have been difficult to remove it and unslung Death Bringer whilst sliding my shield to my back. Someone must have been watching over me for as I did so I felt the thud of a spear thrown from the walls which thudded into my shield and banged sharply against my back.

I shouted, "Ridley" and, his opponents having been killed, he took out the spear and, in one easy motion threw it back at the man who had thrown it at me. His shocked eyes stared at us both as he tumbled from the walls. Osgar and Wolf had the gates open and our men poured through. The garrison immediately surrendered. We had won again.

As we consolidated our gains I looked around and could see few warriors who had fallen. Unusually Earl Harold had not had the prisoners killed as was our normal practice; instead, the ten survivors were being herded by a group of Housecarls led by my uncle. One of the newer Housecarls was punching the air in joy although I noticed his spear was clean, he had not drawn blood. "This is easy. If the rest of the Welsh are like this, we will be home in a week."

Ulf loomed up behind him. "Boy! These were not warriors, they were the men of the land, the fyrd, here to defend their country. When you meet real Welsh warriors then you can judge. Until then clean up the bodies."

I smiled at Wolf. "Were we ever like that?"

Osgar sniffed as he cleaned his axe. "What do you mean were?"

Osgar always had a way of bringing you down to earth. I retrieved Boar Splitter and cleaned my weapons. I searched the fort and found the well. Drawing a bucket, I drank heavily. Battle always made my mouth dry. Ridley and the others joined us. "Those stakes were nasty. The lads who were wounded have to go back to the ships; they cannot walk."

"Let us hope that we do not have too many forts to assault then."

I was intrigued by the prisoners and wandered over. My uncle was using one of the Housecarls who spoke and understood a little Welsh. To my ears it sounded like someone clearing their throat and spitting but, apparently, it made sense to the warrior. "Hobble them and tie their hands. They will be sent back to the ships with the wounded."

I felt sorry then for the captives. Their lives had been saved but not their freedom, they would become thralls, slaves probably working in the tin mines of Cornwall. Better to die fighting than live as a slave. I was close enough to my uncle and the Earl to hear their conversation.

"I believe that the king is close to Rhuddlan, on the border. There is a valley which runs north-eastwards and emerges close to Rhuddlan."

"That is close to St Asaph and the dragon mountain is it not?"

"Aye. If he retreats from your brother he could go three ways, west to his court but we have men there, south and that would bring him to us or towards the mountain stronghold."

The Earl looked northwards although there were many mountains between the dragon mountain and us. "Then I hope he comes towards us for it would take a year to winkle him out of that mountain." My uncle nodded his agreement and I prayed that Gruffyd would retreat from Tostig and come towards us. In those days, I believed I was invincible and the thought of fighting the whole of the Welsh army with but three hundred men did not worry me.

Now that the Welsh king had fewer options Harold sent two ships back with the wounded and the thralls and the rest to meet us off the northern coast of Wales. It seemed likely that we would have to fight him close to the heart of his dragon kingdom but we were in good spirits. Victory gives men that confidence and a confident army can defy any odds, well as we were to find out a couple of years later, almost any odds. In deference to his leg, Aethelward rode a horse as did Harold. We did not mind for we were Housecarls and marched proudly with an axe o'er one shoulder and a spear on the other. We marched in mail now for we were in enemy territory. As we marched I told my companions of the Spartans who had numbered three hundred, as we had and they had defied and held up the largest and greatest army the world had ever seen, the Persians and they had done so for ten days.

Ridley believed everything I said but Wolf was sceptical. "Three hundred held off tens of thousands for ten days? I cannot believe it."

"Ah but you see their king Leonidas was clever. He placed his three hundred in a narrow valley such as this." I waved my arm around the steep sides of the valley. They were so high that you thought they would fall in upon you, "he had his back protected by a thousand others."

"Ah, a thousand now this is more than the three hundred."

I shook my head. "The one thousand were like the fyrd and they did not fight; when the Spartans were surrounded they were sent away and the three hundred died to a man."

Osgar asked me quietly. "How do you know this?"

"Uncle told me. He heard the story when he was in Constantinople and it is famous in the Greek world."

My uncle's involvement in the story increased its credibility. "Did they have bows?"

"No, they had spears, large round shields and short swords."

"So they were Housecarls?"

I thought about it. "I suppose they were for they were the bodyguard to the king but they only had helmets, leather body armour and greaves."

Even Osgar was impressed. "Brave men then. And they all died?"

"To a man but, through their sacrifice, they won the war for the Greeks and defeated the Persians who had the largest army in the world at that time." We could all empathise with this for we would also sacrifice our lives for our leader and our country.

When we reached the long lake, we were at the narrowest part of the valley and Earl Harold made us camp at the northern end where we filled the entrance to the valley like a cork in a jug. Behind us, the land rose to the col which led to the lake. We could see a long way to the north-west but as it was coming on to dark we could not make out many details. We were all excited about the prospect of action. Ulf came to fetch myself and Ridley and took us to the Earl. Wolf and Osgar looked curiously on.

Earl Harold led us to one side, "You two are accomplished horsemen Aethelward tells me."

I suppressed a smile at the memory of Ridley's first attempts. But he had improved. "Thank you, my lord."

"Get out of those mail shirts and just take your spears and swords. I want the two of you to take these horses and scout out the land ahead. Find the Welsh but do not let them find you."

I felt honoured that we had been chosen and noticed that we were given no choice in this matter. "We will not let you down my lord."

Harold look surprised and then said, "I never thought for one moment that you would."

He left us with my uncle who helped us to disrobe. "Now be cautious Aelfraed. You are not going to fight you are going to look. Better return with a negative report than become embroiled in a fight." He looked at Ridley. "I asked for you because you are the sensible one. Look after this headstrong nephew of mine."

I did not know whether to be insulted or angry or pleased but Ridley beamed like the cat which has found an upturned jug of cream. Notwithstanding my reaction to the words, I was pleased with the mission and we headed down the other side of the pass. As we rode down I noticed that it was only wide enough for ten men at most. Any army ascending would have difficulty maintaining cohesion but then again, any force fighting them would struggle to maintain their ranks. The valley sides were still steep and covered in woods. Any Welsh army would have to keep to the flat land at the bottom. The stream to our right bubbled and burbled noisily but I knew that it would be no obstacle to warriors for although rocky it was shallow. This part of the valley would suit the Welsh. Darkness fell further and it was difficult to see as the last rays of the sun dipped below the mountains to the west. The horses were sure-footed and we relied on that to keep us safe. Suddenly my mount snorted and stopped. Up ahead I heard a whinny. I quickly dismounted and held my hand over my horse's nose. I did not want him to answer for the noise we had heard meant there were riders ahead.

Ridley skipped from his horse and we tied them to a tree. We moved quickly and silently towards the origin of the whinny. We moved away from the stream for its noise meant that we could not hear as well and our hearing was now more useful than our sight. The sharp-nosed Ridley held up his hand and I stopped. We peered into the dark. Ridley had either heard or smelled something, he later told me it was a smell, and after a few moments our eyes adjusted to the dark and we saw the white faces of the sentries. They too had tethered their horses to a tree. We could see two but suddenly a Welsh voice shouted from our left and we knew there were more. I gestured to the right and we returned to the stream. I stepped into it, its icy shock almost making me start, and began to walk slowly along the valley. I assumed that guards would not be looking in the stream for potential enemies and I remembered my first watch. Once we had moved a few dozen paces I calculated that we were within their picket lines and we headed for dry land. As soon as we left the water I felt the blood rush to my feet and the warmth was almost painful.

Ahead of us, through the trees, we could see the camp of the Welsh. It was difficult to estimate numbers but I counted forty campfires. It was a sizeable army. We suddenly froze as two men approached. We cowered in the bushes hardly daring to breathe. I cursed their arrival and feared that we would be discovered. They dropped their breeks and then turning their backs on the water they squatted. The foul smell which arose told me their purpose. When they had finished, they used some grass and then returned whence they had come. I led Ridley back to the stream, avoiding the place the warriors had used and then walked back up the valley. When we neared where I judged the picket line to be I glanced to the right but, seeing no one continued up a little further. It seemed an age until we found our horses. I was dreading returning to the Earl to tell him we had lost his horses but we eventually found them and trotted back up the valley. It was late when we reached the camp but Ulf and my uncle were waiting for us. They took us immediately to the Earl.

"Well?"

"The Welsh army is three miles away beyond the woods. There were at least forty fires and they have horses."

Harold seemed almost relieved. "Good! And you escaped attention?"

"No one saw us."

"Good. I am in your debt. I thank God for the day I came to Medelai and found you men and Aethelward." He turned to my uncle. "Once again you have chosen the field well. We fight them here, tomorrow."

Chapter 8

Wales 1063

I stood in the second rank. Boar Splitter rested behind my shoulder and I wielded Death Bringer. With my shield on my back, I stood awaiting the assault which we knew was coming. Those in the third rank waited with their shields ready to protect those of us in the front two ranks. So far it had been archers who had cost us the largest casualties and it was those in the rear rank who would stop the missiles. Earl Harold was counting on the fact they would use their archers first and then charge with their warriors. We knew that he had few Housecarls remaining for we had killed many of them in our first campaign and those that he did have would not face up to the whirling blades of one hundred fierce warriors. Some of us may have doubted that but not the strategy of Earl Harold and Aethelward of Medelai. No matter how many men we lost we could survive and more than that we would win.

The dismay of the approaching Welsh army was obvious as they trudged along the valley. When they saw us, perched atop the col spread out across their escape route we could almost hear their collective cry of despair. Gruffyd was no coward, despite his flight the first time we had fought, and he sent forwards his spearman supported by his archers. It was his archers we feared and as they drew back we all braced. It was hard to stand there without a shield and rely on the men behind for protection. Luckily the shields we bore were large and few men were hit by the missiles as they rained down. The shields and the armour meant that the wounds we suffered were light. The spearmen, who greatly outnumbered us advanced but we were confident. Standing above them our axes flayed a path at head height. The axes first sheared the spearheads and then the warriors' heads. Those in the front rank did not even see the enemies they killed; they were in the killing zone and brave warrior after brave warrior died without coming close to the shield wall.

The exhausted Welsh drew back and I could see Gruffyd conferring with his lords. It was a heated debate and we could see the gesticulating arms of his advisers pointing to the northeast, down the valley. It was infuriating to stand there knowing that the enemy had faltered but we could not attack as the terrain did not suit us. Had we had the fyrd with us then they could have been loosed to chase down the demoralised enemy. It was stalemate; they could not advance against our superior weapons nor could we end it.

Finally, Gruffyd took the decision for us and as flight after flight of arrows rained down upon us he and his spearmen left the battlefield. For a second time, he had evaded us. As soon as the arrows stopped the Earl gave the order, "Forward!" and we trotted forwards our shields held before us and our spears in our hands. Form his horse Aethelward could see that the Welsh were not heading down the valley but up a smaller valley which led west. He was heading for the mountain of the dragon and we would struggle to dislodge him from that lofty perch. The Earl sensed that this might be the last chance he had to capture the elusive king and he urged us on but a band of his bodyguards were there to prevent that. Just as we had blocked his escape route so the sixty or so bodyguards halted our pursuit. We would have to kill them before we could follow. They were brave men and all resigned to their fate. They began to keen a lament in their own language. As we advanced I felt its beauty wash over me; to the warriors who were about to die, it must have had a calming effect.

Sweyn shouted, "Wedge!" and we forgot about their song as we clashed our spears against our shields. There was a kind of symmetry to it all; our slow advance marked by our own rhythm and their steadfast song, almost a barrier in the valley. We could not employ our normal tactic of a run and a rush as the ground was too uneven and the last thing we needed was for someone to fall and disrupt the wedge. When Sweyn struck the enemy line, it was a crash of metal on wood and then, as we pushed on the ranks before us so the ranks behind pushed on us. We had the disadvantage that we were pushing uphill but we had the weight of almost three hundred men concentrated upon the tip of the arrow. Inevitably we split their line but they still fought, every moment they held us was more time for their comrades and their king to escape.

We were on the right in the fourth rank and the warriors who were on our side were slightly below us. Our spears outranged their swords and they frantically held their shields before them to protect themselves. The sheer weight of numbers began to tell and while the warrior before me could protect himself against Boar Splitter, Wolf's spear stabbed him in the side and he fell backwards. Their line was thin and we filled the gap so that the warriors were fighting before and behind. It could not last but they bravely fought on even after having suffered mortal wounds and we had to cut their throats just to make sure they were dead. We all remembered the story of how my uncle had been hamstrung by a warrior feigning death and we took no chances.

Ulf stood exhausted before me his arm bleeding from a sword thrust. "They were brave men and deserved a better leader than Gruffyd. "

I too was disappointed with the Welsh king and when Aethelward rode over to see how we had fared I told him so. He shook his head. "It is not easy being a king. The choices we have they do not for they are like the guardians of their land. Sometimes they have to live to regroup and defend the land rather than dying and allowing someone else to take it."

As I thought about that I thought of the wisdom of the words. He was right; we defended our lord, that was the extent of our decision making. We only had to think of the shield wall and naught else. We all turned, weapons at the ready as we heard horses clattering up the trail. To our relief, they were our warriors, Earl Tostig's scouts.

Sweyn led us along the path to allow the scouts to continue the pursuit of the enemy for there was no way we could close on the swiftly moving archers and horsemen. We began to help the wounded but as there were few of them we searched the bodies for any booty. The warriors were not laden with treasure but we found enough to make the exercise worthwhile. By the time we had finished, Earl Tostig and Edwin, Earl of Mercia had arrived. Sweyn led us down the trail to make camp while the leaders conferred. The mountain pass was cold but we were able to light a fire, unlike the previous night when we had had to remain hidden. We managed to catch some sheep and we roasted the meat. It was a little chewy but the hot food was just what we needed.

"All we need now is some ale to wash it down and we will sleep easy tonight."

"And tell me, Ridley, where do you think we would get ale here on this godforsaken mountain?"

"I didn't. I just said it would have finished the meal off."

Osgar shook his head, as he picked some meat from his teeth with the tip of his dagger. "Instead you have just made us pine for ale and thereby spoiled the meal. Well done Ridley."

My friend's face fell. He meant well and said little but when he did speak he frequently said the wrong thing. "Sorry, Osgar. I meant nothing by it."

I saw Osgar relent. Baiting Ridley was like shooting fish in a barrel and he patted the gentle giant on the back. "Never mind Ridley we now have enough coin to buy a barrel the next time we visit a town."

Our discussions were ended with the arrival of my uncle. He dismounted and joined us by the fire. We had saved him some of the meat and he gratefully gnawed on a bone. I noticed the pained expression on his face and I knew what caused it. His leg had been worsening of late and the cold, high mountains made it ache even more. I threw my wolfskin cloak over his leg and he nodded his gratitude. "Well, we will be out of these mountains soon. And for that I am glad."

I looked up in surprise. "We do not follow Gruffyd?"

Aethelward shook his head. "He is clever and slippery, nephew. He has chosen a route that only lightly armed men can follow. The Earl is sending the horse and the archers to pursue him and we go to Rhuddlan."

We were partly disappointed for we had wanted to finish what we had started but Rhuddlan meant comfort, food and ale.

The guards we had left at the fort looked disappointed as the army hove into view. The scouts and horsemen had returned to the main body to tell the Earl that the Welsh were ensconced in their rocky crags and an assault was a waste of time. The empty saddles testified to the fact that they had tried. Earl Harold was annoyed with his failure to destroy the Welsh wasp. He was also annoyed with his brother for not following the fleeing king closer after he had fled although he did not say that to Earl Tostig. Tostig took his portion of the army back to Jorvik leaving us with the same force we had had the first time we had fought Gruffyd.

I was invited to join the Earl, Sweyn and Aethelward as we celebrated high summer. There was little joy at the meal. "We will stay here this time for I want Gruffyd to suffer in the mountains. We will make him come to us!"

Aethelward leaned back to stretch his lame leg. "The problem we have is that the Housecarls are too ponderous to strike at such a mobile force as the Welsh." I could see Sweyn bridle at the implied criticism. "I mean no disrespect Sweyn you know that. I was a Housecarl and I know the value of that rock but sometimes the rock moves too slowly or the enemy evaporates before it, like fog on a spring morning. You need to have some lighter armed warriors who can force the issue or," he looked at Harold, "knights on horses such as the Normans use."

"That is something I think we can aspire to but we would need to train the men to do that. It would not happen overnight." He suddenly looked at me. "Aelfraed how long did you train to be a Housecarl?"

"Uncle began my training when I was seven."

Aethelward shook his head, "That was training to be a warrior you began your training as a Housecarl when you were twelve."

"So more than seven years to become an accomplished Housecarl." I felt myself redden at the compliment. "We would need seven years to be able to have a knight ready for war and I do not think that the Welsh and the Scots will wait seven years."

"You could go to Duke William and see how they do it? Perhaps ask for some advice."

Harold shook his head. "No, I think the Duke has his eyes on England's throne. I have heard it said that the Norman churchmen brought over by King Edward are here to prepare the ground for the Duke's arrival."

I leaned forwards eagerly. "We would fight the Normans?"

Harold smiled indulgently, "I don't think it would come to that, the Witenagemot would have to invite him to be king and if they did that then a war would be pointless."

"He might invade."

"Aelfraed he has horses, how would he transport an army that was big enough to defeat us? No, he would either be invited or he would not be a king."

My uncle had been playing with the pieces of the chess set which was on the table. "I would not be too sure my lord. Duke William's ancestors came from the north in ships. I am no expert in ships but, it seems to me that if they could get enough ships then they could invade."

The words of Aethelward made Earl Harold think. "Perhaps I need to discover if he could invade using ships. I know the Danes still use ships for war but they do not have horses."

Sweyn slurped the last of his ale and then put it on the table. "That still does not solve the problem of Gruffyd though. How do we get to him?"

Suddenly my uncle sat bolt upright holding a chess piece in his fingers. "If this was a chess game and we wanted to get the king, which piece would we attack if his knights and the bishop were protecting him and his rook?"

Harold and Sweyn looked befuddled. Perhaps because I knew my uncle better than they did and perhaps because I had played chess against him so many times, the answer was obvious to me.

"The Queen!"

"Precisely nephew."

The Welsh Queen was Ealdgyth and was the sister of Edwin of Mercia. She and her daughter, Nest, were obviously not with the king and I wondered where they were. Harold suddenly became interested. "So, if we use her to bait a trap…"

"That and offer a reward for the head of Gruffyd."

"Would his men betray him?"

"I do not know but he has deserted them twice before and failed to stand up to you. Perhaps he might but if we hold his wife and child then that just may stir him into action."

Sweyn belched, "But where in the Almighty's name is she? She isn't with him and she isn't here. She could be anywhere."

The thought suddenly came to me and I blurted it out. "Saint Asaph, with the monks."

When I said it, I felt foolish for the three men just stared at me but I discovered that they were staring because the answer was so obvious and yet they had failed to make the connection. "Well done Aelfraed. Of course, that is where she would be, close to the court and yet safe. We will ride there on the morrow."

I felt so proud when Aethelward came over to me and put his arm around my shoulders, "That was well done Aelfraed. I think today I saw the boy become a man."

As the one with the idea, I was included in the party which headed for the monastery the next morning. There were twenty of us mounted on all the horses that were not being used by the scouts. Although we did not wear our mail we had our weapons with us and there could be no doubt that we were belligerent.

Brother Aidan came to greet us. He looked from the Earl to Aethelward to me and gave a slight smile as he bowed. "I am afraid you will find no one here to fight my lord."

"You know who I am then friar?"

"We all know Earl Harold. How can we be of service?" Here he looked directly at my uncle. "As you no doubt know the monastery is poor, save for cheese and honey."

I think he meant to insult Aethelward and myself as he had known me when I was still a child but I was now older and had killed men. The friar's insults meant nothing to me.

"We seek Queen Ealdgyth."

A look of annoyance flashed across the monk's face and I could see the dilemma he faced. Should he lie to us or brazen it out and defy us. I knew that there were almost a thousand monks in the complex and they would fight if they had to. Harold could also be devious and he smiled disarmingly before the friar could lie. "I know that she is within your walls and I come to offer her my protection for her brother has now been made Earl of Mercia." He leaned forward to emphasise his next words. "And I appointed him. He would wish for me to look after his sister."

"And if she were within these walls would she not be safe here?"

Harold inclined his head, "I think the lady herself should make that judgement not you friar for, after all, you are a man of the cloth and not a man of the world."

I saw the monk become angry and he opened his mouth as though to argue but then thought better of it and returned the Earl's smile. "I will ask the lady but if she prefers to stay here…?"

"Then I would have to persuade her." The threat was subtle. It was in his tone and his words for his hand was upon his sword. When the monk re-entered the monastery, Harold turned to Aethelward. "This is more than a mere monk; this man dabbles in politics."

"I think you are right my lord." We cooled our heels for over an hour until eventually, the door opened once more and Brother Aidan stood there with Queen Ealdgyth. She was not as beautiful as the Earl's lady, Edith, but she had an attraction about her that stirred the loins. Her dark eyes were framed by her dark hair which gave her a sultry look. She enhanced the look by lowering her eyelids as she looked up at Earl Harold. I knew he was smitten when he leapt from his horse and dropped to one knee. "My lady I am here on behalf of your brother to offer you protection."

She smiled demurely and took his proffered hand. "And why would I need protection, my lord?"

"These are parlous times. Your husband has lost another battle." I saw the pained look on Brother Aidan's face at the word, 'another.' "And who knows when he will be able to return here. No doubts the monks here mean well but I am sure that my Housecarls can afford you better protection and I promise you, my lady, that when your husband sues for peace I shall return you to him unharmed. I swear it here in these holy grounds where the Saint himself lies interred."

It was a clever move from Harold to make such an oath. Any oath would be binding but his wording had been the key to his trick, Gruffyd would have to sue for peace and I could not see that happening. Ealdgyth was torn but I could see that she too was attracted to the Earl. The small child with her, her daughter Nest, clung to her mother's skirts and the Queen looked down at the child and then at the Earl. "Under those conditions, I submit myself to your protection." She turned to Brother Aidan. "Thank you for the sanctuary you offered. I will go with the Earl."

"Are you certain, majesty? You will be safe here I can assure you of that. No matter how many men are sent to get you, you would be protected."

I saw Harold's face harden and his hand slip to his sword. "Be careful what you promise priest."

He turned to face the Earl. "I am a man of God and I do not fear the sword."

The Queen came between them. "No father, I go of my own volition and I would not wish harm to come to you."

The Earl pre-empted any further discussion by mounting the Queen on one of the spare horses we had brought. Nest was placed behind her mother. I watched Brother Aidan as we left and I could see the anger. I hoped that the oath Harold had sworn would not be broken.

That evening I saw a different side to Earl Harold for he became the gallant, the would-be suitor to the Queen. It felt unseemly to me for he had a wife, Edith; I knew that they had not married in the church but they had children and the Queen herself had a husband. I did not know what was going on in his mind. Years later I discovered the truth that the Queen was distantly related to King Edward and Earl Harold was strengthening his claim to the throne. I also believe that he did find her attractive and the feeling appeared to be mutual. The feast that Earl Harold gave was as magnificent as could be expected this close to a war but it was aimed to show him off at his best. I have to admit that he was a fine-looking man. I was never a Catamite but had I been one then the Earl would have been someone who would have attracted me and women found him even more attractive. That evening he was as amusing and funny as I have ever heard. It is said that the way to a man's heart is through his stomach but the way to a woman's heart is through her laugh. The feast proved to me that, for a woman, at least, that was true. I was sat across from them next to Ulf and Sweyn and I saw the accidental touching of the hands and the simpering looks they exchanged. When the Queen's servant took Nest to bed I saw Harold flash a knowing look at Sweyn who immediately stood. "Thank you my lord for such a magnificent feast and now I think it is time for us to retire."

The older men knew what the statement meant but the younger ones like Wolf looked disappointed that the feast was ending. Of course, it was not for we retired to the warrior hall to continue drinking whilst the Earl and the Queen slipped away. I believe that was the night that Harold fathered his first child with the Welsh Queen.

The next few days were the courtship of the Queen. Earl Harold took her hunting, he composed songs and poems for her and he played with Nest. I found it distasteful. I was wandering around the grounds of the palace and I thought I was alone until I happened to overhear a conversation between the Earl and my uncle who were on the other side of Yew hedge. Once again I conveniently forgot the words of Nanna advising me not to eavesdrop.

"But my lord the Queen is married and there is the Lady Edith."

"Do not lecture me Aethelward of Medelai! What I do, I do for the kingdom. Never forget that or forget who you are."

"I speak to you as a friend for I know what it is that drives you. It is not just England it is the fact that she is a beautiful woman and you yearn for such women. I remember…"

"And that is why I forgive such familiarity but do not press or I may forget old alliances. Advise me on military matters and not on matters of the heart or of politics."

When he stormed out I waited, still hidden and watched as my uncle limped out, his face suffused with anger. It was the first time I heard him have cross words with anyone and the first time that I saw rage upon his face. It would be some years before I found the reason. In the end, it was a moot point for the next day a rider came in from Gruffydd Ap Cynan. He had a small escort of riders and held in his hands a bag. He waited patiently outside the gates of Rhuddlan and Earl Harold, my uncle, Sweyn and Ulf rode out to meet them. They were all armoured and armed but the meeting was peaceful. After a long discussion, the bag was handed over and the two parties split up. Sweyn carried the bag into the fort and called over one of the Housecarls. "Fetch me a spear!"

The man went to the armoury and found a Welsh spear. When he returned Sweyn took from the bag the head of Gruffyd Ap Llewellyn, the first and the only, King of Wales. He stuck it on the spearhead and then climbed the ramparts to place it there for all to see. My uncle exchanged a look with Earl Harold and then he dismounted and led his horse to the stables. I was desperate to know what had happened and I raced after him.

He removed his saddle and, turning, saw me behind him. "You think that you know a man when you have fought with him but you do not. I grow weary."

"What happened to the king?"

"The Earl's decision meant that his men decided that he was too dangerous to be allowed to live and they killed him. The new King of Powys is Gruffydd Ap Cynan, the uncle of Cynan Ap Iago. I think we will be travelling back to Winchester."

We did indeed return to Winchester but not before Earl Harold married Ealdgyth and strengthened his claim to the English throne. The Housecarls did not know what to make of it for we were all fond of Lady Edith but Earl Harold was our liege lord and we obeyed him in all things. We all liked Ealdgyth and could understand his lust but this had an unseemly feel to it.

When we did leave, it was without Earl Harold. The army left Rhuddlan after first destroying its defences. We might have agreed on peace but we were not leaving the Welsh anything which might harm us in the future. The Earl and Sweyn and a number of lords left with the fleet. Aethelward told me later that the Earl intended to scout out the French coast and ascertain for himself the feasibility of a Norman invasion. I think he would have wanted my uncle to go with him but since their argument relations between them had been cold. It is interesting however that he chose my uncle to be his wife's protector.

For my own part, I quite enjoyed the journey south. The towns and villages we passed through feted us as heroes for removing the threat of the Welsh. My uncle also assigned the four of us to guard the wagon containing the Earl's new wife and I found her a pleasant woman to talk with. She was lonely and Nest was a silent child so she enjoyed talking to us and I must admit flirting with me. I do not think that she found me attractive but of the four of us, I was the one with whom she liked to converse. I actually found myself feeling sorry for her. It was obvious that her father had married her to the Welsh king for political reasons and she did appear to be genuinely in love with Harold but she was also a woman who seemed to like the company of men. My main concern was quite selfish, Lady Edith looked after Gytha and I did not want my chances with her being jeopardised.

When we reached Winchester, we expected a storm but Lady Edith was still in London. The whole of England knew that they were married but not in the eyes of the Church, it was called in the Danish manner which meant they had chosen to be a couple. His desertion of her was no crime although many of us felt unhappy about it for we liked Edith Swanneck. The storm we did get was not one we expected for we discovered a few days after our return that Earl Harold had been shipwrecked in Normandy and was now a prisoner of Duke William. To the country, it was bad news but to the Housecarls, it was devastating as we had not been there to protect our lord and, at the back of our minds, all of us wondered at the oath he had taken at the monastery. Perhaps God was punishing him for his actions with the Queen. The breaking of an oath was the most serious offence a warrior could commit and Harold had violated that by lying with the Queen and making his heirs.

We all turned to the two leaders who remained amongst us, Aethelward and Ulf. "What do we do? Take a ship and rescue our lord?"

Aethelward shook his head. "No, for he will not be harmed. It will cost the Earl something, some land, gold, I know not what and then he will be returned to us, until that day we protect his lady and his land."

As we dispersed to the warrior hall we discussed my uncle's words. We had not thought that Ealdgyth was in danger but Aethelward was wise and the Lady Edith was known not to be pleased. Killers were cheap and there were many potions and poisons to be had from strange women who lived in the forests. There were many enemies of Earl Harold who would use his absence to their advantage. It was not the work to which we aspired but if protecting the lady was our only task then we would perform it to the best of our ability.

When King Edward arrived, we all breathed a collective sigh of relief that Lady Edith was not with them. For myself, I was disappointed as Gytha remained in London with the Lady. The King brought with him the Norman Archbishop of Canterbury Robert of Jumièges. The Archbishop was the most martial looking churchman I had ever seen. Were it not for the fact that he was introduced as such I would have taken him for a knight. Instead of a sword, he carried a mace. He was a cruel-looking man and his arrogant face showed the low esteem in which he held us. King Edward was looking frail for he was not a well man and I wondered then at the capture of Harold. Had he been betrayed to keep him from England? None of us could work out how he had come to be shipwrecked in Normandy. I was in no doubt that if the King died whilst Harold was in Normandy then this Archbishop would do all in his power to secure the throne for his sponsor, Duke William.

King Edward had obviously come to find out about the Welsh campaign and Harold's marriage. Ridley and I were chosen to be the guards as Aethelward, Ulf, the King and the Archbishop held conference. It meant that we could overhear most of what was said. I took it to be an honour for us to be chosen, it meant that my uncle trusted us to keep the confidences we shared.

"Firstly, Lord Aethelward is Wales secure? That is the most pressing matter."

"It is your majesty. With the death of Gruffyd, the kingdom has split into smaller factions. The Earl of Mercia is a good leader and he can keep them in check."

We could not see the faces of the men inside and heard only the words. When Robert of Jumièges spoke, we could recognise his voice because of his accent. "It is a pity that the Earl's brother Tostig has not had the same success with the Scots for we hear that Northumbria is an unhappy place."

I knew that to be true and wondered if my brothers had yet been reconciled with the Earl. I still wondered about the visit my father had made to Scotland but that puzzle was too difficult to solve.

"The Scots we will deal with later. Now Lord Aethelward what of the marriage the Earl made. Was it well done?"

There was a silence and I could almost picture my uncle trying to speak the truth without harming his friend's reputation. "They were married sire, at the monastery of Saint Asaph and the marriage was consummated before the Earl left on his ill-fated voyage."

The heavily accented voice of the churchman broke in, "Not ill-fated, my lord, for Duke William is protecting your Earl and he will return to England, eventually."

The word 'eventually' had a chilling ring to it and I wondered how much Robert of Jumièges knew about the whole incident.

"We will remain in Winchester for a while I intend to give a feast in honour of the victory over the Welsh."

The feast was a double-edged sword for whilst it would honour us it was my uncle and Ulf who would have to do the work and prepare for the feast. Once again Ridley and I found ourselves at the forefront of the work and we did not see much of Osgar and Wolf over the next few days. Many lords began to arrive at the city for the feast which was becoming grander by the day. Every house and hall was occupied by armed and armoured men. On the day of the feast, I had been sent to

Lady Ealdgyth to escort her to the hall. I took Ridley, Osgar and Wolf with me. I had learned in the battles we had fought that life is easier with men around you whom you trust. The walk was not far but the streets were thronged with people. Many chancers, charlatans and ne'er do wells had descended upon the town to make money from the visit of the king. The four of us formed a solid phalanx around Ealdgyth who clung on to my arm. I felt my body swell with pride that my Earl's lady trusted me so. As we crossed the main road my eye was suddenly drawn to two men, on horses, who were just entering the gate. They were the men who I had last seen with my father. I said quietly to Osgar, "Aren't those the men we met the day we returned from hunting?"

Osgar glanced across quickly and nodded, "Aye it looks like them."

I could not leave the lady but I determined to seek out my uncle as soon as I could and give him the information. By the time we had reached the hall and safely delivered the lady some time had elapsed. It took me some time to find Aethelward but when I did he took my words seriously.

"You are sure that the men were the same ones who were with your father?"

"Yes, uncle and Osgar and the others confirmed it for they saw them too."

"It may be harmless but I believe you when you say that they acted furtively. It is too much of a coincidence that the king is here and the Earl is not and these men choose this moment to visit. Where are the others?"

"They guard the lady still."

"I will see them relieved then you take them and scour the town for these men. When you find them bring them to me for questioning."

"And if they will not come?"

"Then that will confirm that they are here for nefarious purposes. Be on your guard!"

We searched every part of the town of Winchester from the lowliest and flea-ridden alehouse to the houses of the rich and well to do. The only clue we had to their whereabouts was their two horses which we found tied to a rail outside a notorious whorehouse. Osgar went in as a potential customer but when he returned half an hour later he returned empty handed. "There are four whores in there and they were all occupied but not with the two men we saw." He grinned, "They were Housecarls so I left them to it."

Aethelward and Ulf were disturbed by our news. Ulf scratched his beard thoughtfully. "You lads are the only ones who know them so we need you to walk the hall this night. I will warn our men that there may be two Scots in our midst and to keep watch."

When he left to pass on his instructions Aethelward had a troubled look upon his face. "I had hoped, Aelfraed, that you were wrong and these men were innocent visitors but all you have told me leads me to believe that they are here on a mission. Describe them to me." He looked at the others, "And if he omits anything then speak up and add it."

"They were both redheaded and had beards." That in itself was not unique amongst the Scots. "They are both big men."

Aethelward leaned forward, "How big? Ridley or you?"

"As big as Ridley."

"Well one of them was but the other was a little shorter and thinner."

"When you saw them today did they have weapons with them?"

I thought about it and then looked at Osgar for help. He looked into the distance and then said. "I saw swords on their horses when they rode in the streets but there were none on the mounts when we found them."

"No shields?"

We shook our heads. "Not that we saw."

"This could be for a meeting with someone who wishes ill to England or it could be someone who intends to harm someone."

I looked up in alarm. "The King?"

"It could be. He no longer has bodyguards and relies upon his hosts and his Norman friends. Or it could be that Ealdgyth is the target." I looked at my uncle with a shocked expression and he shrugged. "Just because we treat women well does not mean that others do so. She is the Earl's lady and to strike at her here in the heart of his land would be a blow." He peered at each of us in turn. "Arm yourselves well tonight. If they are killers, then it will be knife work. Use swords and daggers. You will need to work out how you will watch over the King and Lady Ealdgyth. Fortunately, they are now in the same building and our task will be easier."

I suddenly had a thought, "And what of you uncle? Everyone knows that you are the Earl's adviser, perhaps you are the target."

I could see that the thought had occurred to him too. He shrugged. "That may be the case but I can protect myself and besides I am expecting it. The King and the Lady are not. Their protection is in your hands. God be with you. You will need all your wits about you tonight and tomorrow we will scour the town thoroughly for these two visitors."

Chapter 9

The watches we had kept on campaign felt like child's play compared with the stress and the tension of watching for the two strangers. We worked as pairs with Osgar and Wolf walking the outside of the hall whilst Ridley and I watched the inside. The kitchens were a nightmare with cauldrons of boiling steaming liquids and servants taking in platters of food. We began to see shadows where none existed and sudden movements acquired sinister overtones. By the time the food had all been served and the guests were all drinking we were exhausted. I watched my uncle and saw that he barely touched his ale but his eyes flicked constantly around the room, diligently scrutinising the guests for signs of the red-haired warriors.

As the evening came to an end and the guests left I felt as tired as though I had fought in the shield wall for a day. The main guests were staying in the hall which meant that we did not have to follow them. Aethelward joined us. "Osgar and Wolf can come indoors now for the guards outside have been told to stop anyone from entering."

Wolf and Osgar had had the same experience we had and I could see from their eyes that they too were tired. It seemed that we had made a mistake and there would be no threat to anyone's life. Aethelward was not certain. "This would be the best time to strike in the small hours when the birds of the night rule and the owl is king."

All of us shuddered involuntarily for the owl was a frightening bird and was a symbol of ill omen. I hoped that I was wrong but part of me wanted to see the warriors again so that I could ask them about my father. Aethelward retired to his room for we thought he might still be a target. The four of us prowled the dark hall without a light for we did not want to give anything away.

Ridley and I stood in an alcove close to the King's chambers whilst the other two guarded Ealdgyth. "They say that the spirits of the dead walk at night." Ridley looked up to the rafters in fear, "and they say that the dead men who died unnaturally here come back at night to haunt the living. What do you think master?"

In truth, I believed that the dead walked at night but not in a sinister way. "Do you remember Nanna?" In the darkness, I felt him nod. "I believe that her spirit is here and watches over me. I believe that she protects me in death as she did in life."

"And will she protect me, master?"

"Aye, for she loved you as my friend. I fear not the spirits of the night, but I do fear the blade of an unknown killer."

I found my eyes droop in with the tiredness and the tension. I kept jerking my head up and staring around in panic. I felt that if I just closed my eyes for a moment then I would be fresher. Suddenly I snapped awake again and this time my nose could smell something that had not been there before. I nudged Ridley and he too was awake swiftly and instantly alert. He said nothing but we both stood in the shadows and let our eyes seek out that which was unnatural. We could see the drapes which covered the door to the King's quarters, in the antechamber was Robert of Jumièges. I saw the faintest movement from the shadows but it was enough for me and I drew my sword and slipped silently down the side of the rough lath wall which was in deep shadows and would hide me. Ridley, faithful and loyal Ridley, emulated me and I caught the faintest shining glimmer from his sword. Ahead of me, I detected an arm and I moved forward quickly. The floorboards were old and one squeaked beneath my feet. I saw the killer's eyes as he turned to face me. He was fast and his blade leapt towards my throat, I barely had time to fend off the blow with my gauntlet but I grabbed his arm as the blade sliced along my cheek, spraying me with my own blood. It was then that I smelled him and knew what had awakened me for he smelled not of men but of perfume. He grabbed my sword hand and we wrestled around. He was strong, of that, there was no doubt, but I was younger and I pushed back with my right hand. If the edge could get close to his throat its sharp blade would slice through his skin and end his life. He shifted his body so that I lost my balance and I felt myself going backwards. Once he had me on the floor then I would die. I saw his face close to mine and I threw my head back and butted him on the nose. I heard the cartilage crack as his nose broke and he could not help but fall backwards. We both lost our grip and, as I fell to the floor, I slashed out with my sword and felt it slice through the hamstring of his right leg. He crumpled in a heap. I stepped on his sword hand and held my blade to his throat. I glanced behind me and saw Ridley withdrawing his sword from his dead opponent's neck. Wolf, Osgar and Aethelward had heard the commotion and joined us.

Robert of Jumièges came out of his room sword in hand. His eyes flashed around and, seeing my opponent on the ground he stabbed him in the throat crying, "Assassin!"

I turned in horror to my uncle who grabbed the churchman's hand. "Why did you do that? We could have questioned him and found out whom he served."

The archbishop looked flustered. "I thought he might try to kill the King. I was protecting his royal person."

"He was disarmed. I had my foot on his hand."

"I could not see that. Who can think in a moment, besides it is obvious they were sent by Malcolm Canmore, they are Scots."

My eyes narrowed and I looked at my uncle. How could he have known that? Before we could speculate the King emerged. Robert reacted quicker than I could. "Majesty these two Housecarls have just saved your life and foiled a plot to kill you."

The King's grateful, eyes widened and he embraced first me and then Ridley. "Tomorrow we shall reward you."

Other guards arrived, having been summoned by Ulf who looked darkly at Aethelward. My uncle shook his head and turned to the four of us. "You have done well and saved the King, now you need to get your rest and we will talk in the morning." The message was obvious, talk in private where the Archbishop could not hear us.

I found it hard to sleep as I ran the events through my head. My father was involved with the two Scotsmen and so was the Norman churchman, that was obvious, but what linked them and what was their purpose? My head was too fuzzy with the action and tiredness. This was all I could know I would need daylight and my friends to unravel the knotty problem.

Before we had a chance to discuss the events we were summoned into the presence of the King. The Archbishop stood behind him his darting, dark eyes never leaving our faces. The King looked a little calmer than he had the previous night. "We would like to thank these two brave Housecarls for their bravery in saving the life of ourselves. As a reward, I am giving each of them a piece of land and title in their native Northumbria. To you Aelfraed of Medelai I give the parish of Maiden Bower close to Topcliffe and to you, Ridley son of Oswin, I give the parish of Coxold and title therewith." One of the priests with him gave us both a document with the royal seal appended. We both knelt and kissed the proffered hand. "Today we will return to London knowing that our city of Winchester will be well protected by Earl Harold's brave Housecarls."

When the King's retinue had left, I noticed the look I was given by
Robert of Jumièges; it was a look of pure hate. I had, in some way,
unwittingly earned the enmity of a mighty Norman. We were still
exhausted the next day but I sat with Ulf and my uncle to run through the
events. Aethelward agreed with me that the Norman bishop had shown
his hand by acknowledging that they had been Scottish assassins. The
only way he could have known that was if they were involved. The fact
that he disposed of the loose end merely confirmed that he had known
something. "But it is your father and his involvement which is more
worrying. We know that the Normans want Edward dead and Duke
William on the throne. With Earl Harold, a prisoner of the Duke it would
be a perfect time to remove the King of England and then the Council, of
which the Archbishop is a member, would have the Norman Duke as
king."

Ulf looked at Aethelward, "The sooner the Earl returns the better."

When I left the hall, I was thronged by my comrades who were
delighted that I was now a lord. I had not thought of that but I did feel for
Ridley. He was now superior to his father. His parish was smaller than
mine but would provide an income. The two were adjacent and I knew
that our lives had changed forever at that moment. I was now Aelfraed of
Topcliffe and Ridley was the Lord of Coxold. Neither of us knew that we
would hold those titles for a mere three years but once given they could
never be taken away. We were lords. We both wished to travel north to
see our lands but we knew that to do so whilst the Earl was a captive
would have been dishonourable so we stayed. I used the time to question
Ulf and Aethelward about my responsibilities. I learned that both men
had lands of their own but used a steward to manage them. Neither of us
wished to be absent landlords besides the thought of riding to battle at the
head of my own men appealed to me.

Surprisingly quickly Earl Harold was returned to us. There were
rumours that he had sworn an oath to support the Duke's claim to the
throne should Edward die but he assured us that it was a lie. We believed
him because he was our liege lord, but I for one was not convinced. He
seemed inordinately proud of the fact that I had acquired lands and
immediately acquiesced to our request to visit them and have some time
away from his Housecarls. The one regret I had was that I did not get to
see Gytha but I did impress upon both the Earl and my uncle that I
desired to make her my bride and, now that I was a lord, I could so. They

patronisingly smiled and nodded; they did not know me. I meant it and one day I would achieve my aim.

We parted from our friends Wolf and Osgar. They both nodded to us and said, "Farewell my lord."

"I will never be my lord to you two. You are our friends and remain so. I will be insulted if you refer to me as my lord again. I am Aelfraed and this is Ridley and we will always be Housecarls."

Their smiles at my words showed me that they were happy and the two of us headed north up the great Roman road. We had not travelled far when Ridley spoke, "Master. Could I visit with you at your demesne?"

"Firstly, I am not Master and secondly, why?"

He hung his head. "I am pleased that I am a lord but I do not know how to act. If I watch you then when I go to mine own lands, then I will not look quite so foolish."

How I loved the simple uncomplicated Ridley. He never let me down through our whole lives and I never had a better friend. At that moment, I knew that I could not let him down and I agreed. I knew that I would protect Ridley with my life and he would become a great lord, as I hoped to be.

When we crossed into Northumbria we detected a change. There were more beggars and the people appeared to be less well off than those in Mercia. We stayed in a small inn close to Doncaster and when they discovered that we were Earl Harold's Housecarls and that we had fought the Welsh they relaxed. We found out that Earl Tostig was taxing the life out of his land and the people were suffering. He was using the threat of the Scots as the excuse but, as the innkeeper told us, the Scots still ravaged the land despite the high taxes.

We bypassed Jorvik for I had no wish to swear fealty to such a man. I would claim my lands first and then visit Jorvik. I know that sounds cowardly but I did not like Earl Tostig and never had. Another part of me worried that I might see my brothers. I was not afraid of my brothers but I had no wish to spill their blood and if we met again then I knew it would come to that. So, we eventually came to Maiden Bower at Topcliffe and I fell in love with it immediately. To the northeast lay the hills of the white horse which seemed apposite bearing in mind that that was the sign of Earl Harold. The parish itself was at the junction of two rivers and was close to the great Roman road. I could see now that King Edward had given me a strategically important post. If someone could build a fort here, then they could deny any invader passage south. I wondered where the previous owner was.

When we reached the small village, the Steward came to greet us. "Greetings my lord, how can I be of service?"

I glanced over at Ridley who was watching my every move. "I am your new lord," I flourished the document given to me by the King. "I am here to claim my demesne. This is Ridley lord of Coxold."

He and his wife fell to the ground. "I am sorry my lord no one warned us."

"Rise err ..."

"Thomas sir, Thomas of Topcliffe and this is my wife Sarah."

"Well, Thomas I would like to inspect my lands. Do you have a horse?"

He looked panicky. "Er yes sir. But it is not ..."

I knew he looked at our fine mounts and that his would be a nag at best. "It can be an ass for all I care, Thomas, just so long as we can see my lands this day." I smiled as I said it and to my relief, he smiled too. This would work.

I was pleased when we visited the farms for it looked to be a prosperous place but I was concerned with the finances. "Thomas, tell me, the farms are producing much?"

He beamed at me, "Oh they are doing very well. God has been kind to us and we have not had floods."

"And the last lord, before me; when did he die?"

"He went north ten years ago to fight the Scots and did not return. He had no heirs."

"So, the profit from the estate. Where does that go to?" I kept my voice even for it seemed to me that there should be a horde of silver and I could see no evidence of that. Thomas looked like an honest man and his words had sounded truthful but there was a gap between what I had seen and what I could touch.

Thomas was a bright man and he understood the implications of what I had said. "All of the money is given to the church for the priest to care for. He was the friend of the lord."

I smiled, I could see the picture clearly now. My run in with other men of the church, latterly the Archbishop, had given me a different perspective to the men of the soil who saw them as Christ's protectors on earth. I saw them as greedy, voracious and political beasts who feathered their own nests. "Then let us visit with the priest and find the lost money for we shall need men at arms and money for building."

The Steward looked up at me. "Building? Men at arms?"

"Tell me, Thomas, what do you do when the Scots come through rampaging or the Danes?"

"The Danes have not done so for years but when the Scots come we go to Ripon or Jorvik."

"And that can be done swiftly?"

"Oh no, my lord. We leave the farms and get there as quickly as possible. The Scots never take everything, they always leave a little and we start again."

I sighed and looked at Ridley who understood me far better than this man of the soil. "If we had our own castle and men at arms then all the valuables could be gathered and protected and the Scots would leave empty handed. We would not need to start again and we would have more money."

I could see that he was dubious but it mattered not for I was lord and I would make that decision. Thomas was there to carry out my orders. The church was a fine stone church with a small bell tower. I could see that it did well. The priest who greeted us was a round, well fed man called Osbert. When I introduced myself, a cloud appeared to pass across his face and he glanced at Thomas. "Welcome my lord I am pleased that the King has sent another master for the land."

"Could we go in the church father for it is cold?"

In truth, it was not but I wanted to see the interior before he had the opportunity to hide what I knew we would find in there. "Please, it is your parish church now."

"It is, isn't it priest?" The harshness of my tone made him flinch. Inside I was immediately struck by the gold which glittered on various objects, the crosses, the communion plate all had the tinge of gold. I wondered what we would find in his dwelling? "My Steward tells me that he has been leaving the profits from the estate in your care." I smiled disarmingly at him, "I would like to thank you for that. Of course, now that I am here I will, of course, require my gold."

I have seen men pale in battle but never in a church. He paled. The blood drained from his face. "But my lord, the church needs upkeep and…"

I picked up the golden crucifix. "This does not look like the roof or the walls." I gestured at Thomas who was behind me as though he feared the priest. "I am sure that Thomas here, being a good Steward will have kept a good accounting of my money." Thomas eagerly nodded. I pointed a mailed finger at the shaking priest. "That amount is what I expect from you so let us go to your dwelling and begin to count out the first amount that I will take with me today."

"But my lord I must protest. The bishop in Jorvik loves my church and he would not wish it to be as it was."

My voice lost its sweetness. "Listen, priest, this is my church and the Bishop can go and kiss his own arse for all that I care. My people have suffered at the hands of the Scots whilst you, no doubt, were safely behind Jorvik's walls. I am here now and things will change. Do you understand me?"

I could see from his frightened piggy eyes that he did and he led me to this home which was a fine stone dwelling and, as I had expected, well furnished. He went to a trunk and took out a wooden box. He took a key from around his neck and opened it. There was a quantity of silver in there but not what I expected.

"This is it?"

"The rest went into the church, my lord."

I grabbed a handful of his cassock. "Then get it from the church or Ridley and I will rip it from the walls ourselves." His face was filled with fear. I heard Thomas have a sharp intake of breath. I saw, on his table two silver candle holders and I grabbed them and dropped them into the box. "Ridley, Thomas, find anything else which looks valuable and you, my pudgy little friend, have one week to find the rest of my gold."

Whilst my companions cleared out the house I returned to the church and took all the silver and gold ornaments I could find. My absence had emboldened the priest. "My lord I must protest. When the Bishop..."

"Never mind the Bishop what about the Earl?"

He looked nonplussed. "The Earl?"

"I assume you have been paying his taxes?" I knew that he had not and his skin whitened once more. He had gambled on the Bishop protecting him but Earl Tostig valued gold above the church.

His shoulders sagged. "A week my lord."

As we rode back to the Steward's house I wondered where he had secreted the rest. Probably in Jorvik with some of the Jews who lived there. It mattered not to me and if he ran, then good riddance, I already had enough to make the start I want to on the improvements to my estate.

When we returned to Thomas' house he said, "My wife and my family will move into the barn, my lord."

It took me a moment or two to understand that the house he occupied was the lord's house. It was a rough building and not worthy of a lord. I assumed that the previous occupant had not stayed there much. "No Thomas. Lord Ridley and myself are used to privations and we will sleep in the barn but on the morrow, we will purchase the men and materials we need to begin on my home." He tried to protest but I waved them away. "Is the inn still on the Roman road at Catherick?"

"The Angel? It is my lord."

"Do not prepare any food for us we will visit there and we will see you on the morrow."

As we rode the few miles north to the inn Ridley asked me all the questions that had been simmering in his mind. "How did you know that the priest had been stealing from you?"

"The things he had in the church and his look. Brother Aidan was a real churchman and he had a lean look about him. The priest was too well fed."

"I would not know what to look for."

"I will visit with you when you go to your parish."

"And why do we visit the inn?"

"We both need men at arms and our parishes will not have them. We can spread the word and the inn is the best place for that. There will be many men without lords and if they travel south they will have to call at the inn."

The rest of the questions were easily answered and Ridley appeared satisfied with the answers. His problem was that his father had ignored him and he lacked confidence. The Housecarls had given him confidence in war but not with people. I hoped that he would survive but I knew that I could not be watching over him all the time. He would have to make his own mistakes and live with them just as I would make my mistakes.

The Angel, so called because of the small crudely carved wooden statue of a winged angel which adorned the door lintel was a popular inn. I would have stayed there but I knew that, until the priest made good with his promise to repay the money, I would have to cut my cloth accordingly. Everyone stared at us as we walked in. To me the sight of heavily armed men was normal but here, on the road, it was unusual for the lords normally stayed in each other's homes when they travelled the land. The landlord took one look at our weapons and decided to defer to us. "Welcome to my inn. How may I serve you?"

"Two ales for a start and food if you have it."

"Aye, sir we have a hunter's stew on the pot and freshly made bread."

"That will do." I turned to face the patrons but continued to talk to the landlord. "I am the new lord of Topcliffe, Lord Aelfraed, and this is the master of Coxold, Lord Ridley." I felt Ridley squirm for he was still unused to the title. "I am seeking men at arms to serve with us landlord, if you hear of any men seeking employment then please direct them to my demesne."

"Certainly, my lord." I could see from his face that he was adjusting his prices to accommodate the new landowner. He pushed two old men away from the table by the fire and pulled out the crudely carved chairs for us. We sat there supping the frothy ale from the two goblets fashioned from some animal horn. The food when it came was tasty and filling. We were both used to hard rations and any food would have been welcome. When we had finished two men came over, their heads bowed. I say men but they were only just in their twenties. The taller one spoke first, his accent had the hint of the coast further north; it was recognisable for strangers thought it sounded Scots but we, in the north, could differentiate.

"My lord I am Osbert and this is Branton my brother; we are from Persebrig." I knew of it. There were Roman ruins there and it guarded the river which divided Northumbria. "We served a lord who died fighting the Scots and we seek employment."

"What weapons did you use?"

"My brother is a skilled archer and can use a sword. I can use a sword and a spear and I can ride."

"Where do you stay this night?"

He jerked his head to the left. "In the barn."

"If you will come to my home and sleep in the barn as we do I will try you out tomorrow. If you are not suitable I will pay you to help build my castle and if you are then you help me to begin my retinue."

He grinned. "Then we will come with you my lord and we will be suitable."

"We will see. When we leave then join us."

They both repeated their thanks and returned to their table. "Do you see Ridley? We are here but a moment and I have two men. When the word spreads, we will have many men for there are always swords looking for new masters."

As we left, having paid the landlord, I repeated my request. "Remember landlord I am not far from this inn and I like it. You will have good custom from me and my friends if you serve me well."

I could see the greed in his eyes as he effusively thanked us and we headed back south. Branton and Osbert had celebrated with much ale and were quite noisy as they rode along the Roman road. We had to go at a slower pace as they were afoot but I did not mind. I listened to their words to gauge the kind of men they were. Osbert was definitely the leader and I picked up that he had been the leader of the warriors of the lord he had served. That suited me for I needed someone who could be decisive and take command. They fell into the hay and fell asleep before Ridley and I had taken the saddles from our horses.

"We could have made them do this?" grumbled Ridley.

"We could, but I intend to work them both hard tomorrow and an early night will mean I will have greater work from them."

I was up before dawn for I was excited. When we had ridden around the land the day before I had seen, just north of the church, the perfect site for a defensive home. The river made a curve and a small stream joined it. With a little judicious engineering, the smaller stream could be a formidable barrier. I rode out to it. Dismounting I reached down to grab a handful of bare soil. It was malleable. I led my mount to the river to drink and examined the river bed. There were many stones there which we could incorporate into the building. As I mounted my eyes were drawn north-west to Medelai but fifteen miles distant. I wondered if my father and brothers knew yet that they had a new neighbour and he was a member of their family. I had been tempted to ask Ridley's father for help with the building but I decided against it. I wanted to be slightly more secure for I knew that my brothers still harboured dire thoughts.

By the time, I had returned Ridley and the brothers were awake and eating the bread and cheese provided by Thomas' wife. I talked as I ate; Nanna would have disapproved of such bad manners but time was of the essence. "Thomas, I need men of the parish to come and start the building of the citadel. We will need them for two days, no more. Then I want you to go to Ripon and buy tools. Take the silver box. If there are any carpenters or masons on the land let me know otherwise you can hire a couple for a few days. While you get the men Ridley and I will give these men at arms a try."

The words had come out in a torrent and I think they overwhelmed Thomas who, none the less mounted his nag and rode off. I would need to think about buying horses for breeding. There were some horse farms to the east and that would be another task. I was suddenly aware that there were not enough hours in the day. The one commodity we had plenty of was weapons for Ridley and I had collected them from the men we had slain. I chose two of the short swords and gave them to the brothers. Ridley and I used our own.

Branton looked worried, "My brother told you my lord that I am an archer."

"Do not worry, Branton, you need not be a champion but in my experience, archers sometimes run out of arrows and I wouldn't have you sitting on your arse while we do your fighting eh?"

Osbert laughed. "Come on brother you are not as bad as you think." He took a good stance with his feet well balanced and I watched Branton copy him.

Ridley and I advanced and swung our blades. The metal clashed and clattered as we exchanged blows. I did not expect either of them to give us a good match for we were Housecarls, I just wanted to see if they were afraid and they were not. After we had disarmed them a couple of times I was satisfied. "Branton get your bow and show me what you can do."

Grinning he went into the barn to get his bow and his quiver. I saw that he had but three arrows, a sure sign that things had been hard for them. He carefully took out his bowstring and strung his bow. He selected the best arrow he had and smoothed the goose feathers with wetted fingers. When he was happy he turned to me, "Target my lord?"

I shrugged. "You know your own skill better than I. Impress me!"

I could see that he relished the challenge. His eyes scanned the land and then he smiled. A crow was perched atop a tree. I estimated that it was at least two hundred paces. It would be a difficult shot. He drew back and then the arrow flew. With a half squawk, it fell to the ground.

I nodded, "You are both hired and it looks like we have supper. Now come along with me for the four of us will work as labourers this day, not warriors."

By the time, Thomas' wife had brought us refreshments, just after noon, I could see the difference that we had made. The twenty labourers were a mixture of men, boys and old men; I suspected that some of my people had not come, and remained to tend their own land. I would deal with that later but I did not really mind for it afforded me the chance to get to know my men. These would be the men I would lead when called by the Earl to supply the fyrd; the digging of the ditch showed how they could work together. Branton and his brother were a revelation for they took to decision making quite early and I was pleased that I had hired them. I sent Osbert off with six men to cut down some saplings for the palisade and by nightfall we had a mound surrounded by a wooden wall as high as Ridley. "You have done well men and when you return tomorrow I will reward you."

I could see from their faces that they had not expected that and they left cheerfully. As we trudged wearily back to the barn I turned to Ridley. "Two more days my friend and then we will go to Coxold to claim your land. Osbert, we will need horses for you and your brother. We will need to look like warriors of note."

Later that night, after we had eaten and Thomas had returned my depleted funds, Ridley and I equipped the two men at arms. We had our old leather helmets which we gave to them. We had spare swords and daggers but neither shield nor spear. Osbert solved that problem. "When we have finished the walls, I will make our shields and I will find a spear staff. Branton can make his own arrows; he is a skilled fletcher."

I had noticed a flock of geese but so far, no smithy. While the brothers began to try out their new weapons I sought out Thomas. "Do we have a smithy on the land?"

Thomas shook his head. "No, we go to Ripon when we need iron work."

"I shook my head. That is no good. We waste time and we need one here. When we have built my house, we will build a smithy close to the palisade and we will find a smith." Thomas looked at me as though I was a magician. His expression told me that he thought they would be hard to find. I knew that I would find one.

The next two days were hard work but we were rewarded by the house appearing at the top of the mound. We used stones from the river to give a sound base and to build a tower at one corner. The doorway was built halfway up the tower with a ladder next to it. Thomas looked at the structure doubtfully. "It will not be easy to get in and out my lord."

"I know but that is its function. If we are attacked by the Scots I intend to make it as hard for them to get in as possible."

I rewarded the workers with a halfpenny each and they went away happy. We left Thomas to finish off the roof and the lath whilst we rode down the road to Coxold. I could see that Ridley was eager to emulate me and, having managed to acquire two sorry looking horses the four of us rode east. Osbert had performed well and the shields of the two brothers were painted with my red horse. We were hardly Housecarls but, armoured as we were, we looked martial enough. The two parishes were remarkably close to each other and we were but a couple of hours apart. It was smaller than Topcliffe but it had a fine old church, St Michaels and, as we later found out, a less avaricious priest.

All of Ridley's fears were allayed when he met Garth, the Steward. He was an old white-haired man but he was delighted to see a new lord. "Jove himself has sent you, master, for we have been praying that the King would send a saviour to us and here you are."

We discovered that the previous lord, Ragnar, had been part of a plot to invite Harald Hadrada to come to Jorvik. He had been executed and his land taken by the crown. All the monies from the estate had gone directly to the crown for the priest, who was a holy man, refused to flatter and fawn on the Bishop. Now that Ridley had arrived things could only get better. He also had a fine house partly built of stone and I think he felt guilty that I had so little by comparison. When he offered to house me I shook my head, "I am pleased, my oldest friend, for it means I can take my men back to my demesne and build that up without worrying about you!" I took him to one side. "I feel a storm coming Ridley. The attempt on the King's life was a sign and since we have returned I sense that people around here are unhappy with the Earl. War will come sooner, rather than later and we should be prepared."

Chapter 10

Jorvik 1065

War did come but not as swiftly as I had expected. We had the autumn and the winter to consolidate our holdings. My citadel was finished and I was proud of my tower. Thomas had managed to acquire a blacksmith, Ralph of Thirsk, and we had not only produced fine weapons and mail but also improved the tools we used on the farm. The money the priest had returned was not the full amount but I knew that I had had all that he could lay his hands on and my threat of exposure meant that he worked for me and not against me. My people were religious and the last thing I needed was to alienate my church. My retinue was now larger. We had four men at arms and two archers not counting the brothers. During the winter, I had seen that Osbert was a good warrior and he now fought in my old armour with sword and spear. It felt good to be riding the hills with my men. Ridley too had four men at arms and his property was doing as well as mine.

When Earl Tostig raised the taxes so much that I knew people would starve, we refused to pay. We were not the only ones and were not singled out but when we heard that the Earl had led his Housecarls from Jorvik to collect the taxes we knew that trouble was coming and prepared accordingly. I ensured that there were plenty of supplies of food in my tower. If we were attacked, then my people could be safe behind my wooden walls and we could laugh a siege to scorn. I invited Ridley to join me but he had become quite attached to his land and determined to defend it. He did take up my offer of weapons for his fyrd however for my smithy, a huge man called Ralph, made fine short swords and axe heads. With Osbert training my fyrd after church on Sundays I was confident that they would fight well.

One morning one of Ridley's men galloped in on Ridley's horse. "My Lord, Thegn Ridley says that there are armed men heading up the road from Jorvik intent upon taking taxes."

"Up the Roman road?"

"Yes sir. My master is waiting there now for you with his fyrd and his men."

"We will be there shortly."

"Thomas, ring the bell for the fyrd and get the people in the citadel. Osbert, prepare the men."

We had been planning this for some time and the fyrd and their families flocked to the citadel. Taking their tearful goodbyes, I led my forty men down the road. I took just one horse for I knew that, whatever occurred, it would be axe work. Ridley had remounted his horse and was at the head of his thirty men. He grinned at me as I arrived and I was astounded by the change the winter had wrought. He was a far more confident man than he had been and the looks on the faces of his men showed that they had loyalty to this young lord who had thrown himself into his work with energy and humour.

"How many are there?"

Ridley shrugged, "The man who told me was not good at counting." He shouted over to a young eager looking man with a billhook. "Robert, come here."

"Yes, my lord?"

"How many men did you see?" He looked at me in panic. "I swept my arm around our gathering. "More or less than this number?"

He seemed relieved. "Less but they were all armoured." He pointed at Osbert. "They looked like him."

"Any riders?"

"Just one at the front."

"So, they are men at arms and not Housecarls. If it is a small number, then it will not be the Earl."

Before I could ask Ridley leaned over to me and said, for all to hear, "You command my lord. My men are yours."

I was grateful. "How many archers do you have?"

"Five."

"Branton take the archers and Lord Ridley's over to that stand of trees on the right. When I shout, 'Branton', then keep loosing arrows until you have none left." Grinning he gathered his band and left. "Osbert gather all the men at arms and line them up before the fyrd." I dismounted and led my horse to a tree behind our force. Tying him there I returned to the front line. We had ten men with some sort of armour. Only three of us, Ridley, Osbert and myself had mail shirts but the other seven all had helmets and shields. They each had a spear and then either a short axe or a sword. The fyrd were armed with everything from hayforks and billhooks, to hatchets and daggers.

"Some of the Earl's men are coming up the road. They want to tax us so that we starve and they want to take the food from your bairns' mouths. They think they will walk in here and take it. I think we will stop them." They all gave a ragged cheer that gratified me. "We at the front have the armour and we will do any fighting, although I hope that they will return from whence they came peacefully. Your job is to stop them from attacking our sides. When they charge us, push against our backs as though we are a bull you are trying to shift." They all laughed at the image. "No one charges until I give the orders. Is that clear?" I had hardened my voice at the end so that they knew I meant it. I turned to the front rank. "I will be in the middle, Ridley to my right and Osbert to my left. The rest of you split yourselves evenly."

The waiting was the hardest part. I was never a patient man. Osbert sensed my frustration and he began to talk to the man next to him just to break the silence. Osbert was, in his own way a very clever man; he had the ability to get anyone to do what he wanted through persuasion, not force. "Is this your first battle then?

"Aye, it is."

"Well remember that if we keep shoulder to shoulder we have more chance of winning. Isn't that right Lord Aelfraed?"

"It is Osbert."

"And our two Thegns fought against the Welsh King. Thegn Aelfraed killed their champion and made them run so you need not fear, we have two heroes with us this day."

I felt uncomfortable at such praise but when I glanced around I could see that everyone looked prouder and more confident, including Ridley. My ears were spared any more unwelcome praise by the sound of a horse's hooves on the cobbles of the old Roman road. There was a hollow before us and I saw the mailed rider appear over the top. I could not see his face for he had a helmet with a nasal and a mail coif. He also had a kite shield and I wondered if he were a Norman or merely someone who aspired to be one. Our sudden appearance was unexpected which relieved me for it meant they had no scouts out. The line of mailed warriors suddenly spread out behind the rider and I saw that there were but twenty men and only ten had mail shirts. I was confident that if we held our nerve we could defeat them.

The rider rode forwards and halted twenty paces from us. He pushed the helmet back as he said, "Well, well this is my lucky day for not only do I get to take prisoners back to the Earl but I get to kill the Runt!"

It was Edward! "Well brother, a little premature. You can return to the Earl and tell him that his taxes are too high and we will not pay them. When the King hears…"

"Forget the King, it is Earl Tostig who rules this land, not the weak man of the cloth who spends his days in prayers." He saw Ridley for the first time. "Another throwback to be killed." His face became puzzled for the first time. "Where is your lord, the man you serve?"

I laughed. He did not know who we were. "I am sorry, brother, I thought you knew. The King gave me Topcliffe and I am the Thegn of that land."

Ridley's voice came out overloud but was effective for all that. "And I am Thegn of Coxold!"

My brother's face was partly hidden by his mail coif but I could the anger in his face and his eyes. "All that this proves is what a dotard the King has become for appointing two runts to be Thegns. You have made my work today an easy task brother! Charge!"

I had been expecting such treachery and I shouted, "Branton!" I knew that he would do his job and I almost laughed at the ragged, uneven line which lumbered towards us. This was no wedge, not even a shield wall this was a line of ten warriors having a foot race to see who could reach us first. That suited us and I lifted my shield to cover my face and prepared Boar Splitter to spill blood. I noticed that Edward had not charged but sat watching his men as they closed with us. His face suddenly fell as the arrows rained down on his force. Four arrows pitched some of those in the rear rank to the ground. The rest of the rank slowed up, looking for the hidden archers, and it was then that I knew we would win for the front rank now had no support.

The first warrior was so desperate to reach me that he had outrun his fellows. Boar Splitter pierced his skull and spitted his brain. I allowed the blade to fall away and drew my axe. Next to me, Osbert had killed his man, as had Ridley. There was just the second rank before me and I swung my axe above my head and roared forwards. The poor warrior before me stood no chance and his head was taken cleanly off by Death Bringer. The blood showered the man next to him and the head rolled along the ground to lie looking at the sky with a surprised look. Edward's horrified face suddenly saw the dead warriors and the rest looked over to their leader for help and for leadership. In answer, Edward dug his spurs into his horse's flanks and galloped down the road, back to safety. The six survivors turned and fled leaving just the dead, the dying and the wounded on the battlefield.

Behind us, a huge cheer erupted and I heard one cheeky voice say, "Now can we charge?"

Laughing I turned. "No, good fellow, for that is our first battle over and we won!" I quickly checked the front rank of my men. Two of them had suffered slight wounds but I could see that they were minor enough to become marks of glory in the future which would be revealed in years to come when the battle became far bigger than it had been and far more heroic. Apart from the three killed in the middle two more of the mailed warriors had died and three of those in the rear. There were seven wounded men who lay in terror on the ground. I knew what they feared, that they would be slaughtered where they lay. As Branton and his archers appeared and began to collect the spent arrows I turned to Osbert. "Take the men at arms, Branton and his archers. Make sure they have gone." I looked at the wounded. "You have a choice. You can surrender now and live or we can kill you where you lay."

It did not take them long to discard their weapons. I turned to the fyrd, "Those who have animal husbandry skills see to these wounded men and do not harm them," I paused, "unless they show signs of flight."

Ridley and I took a couple of the fyrd to strip the bodies of armour and to search for any wealth. We piled the arms and armour at one side. "Get wood and kindling. We will send these souls to their heaven." We had just piled the bodies when Osbert and his men returned. He wandered off to the side and when he appeared again I saw that he had the head of the man I had slain. "Wouldn't want him to meet his God with half of him missing."

The men were in good spirits and laughed at the dark humour. The wounds having been dressed I spoke to the prisoners. "You seven have a choice. You can join us, either as one of Thegn Ridley's men or one of mine. Or you can leave and follow your master back to Jorvik."

One of them stood. "That is it? You will allow us to leave? You will not have your archers shoot us in the back?"

"You can leave and you will not be harmed. You will leave all weapons and armour here but you can follow my brother if you wish."

Suddenly the man's look changed. "That was your brother? Then you must be Aelfraed who fought Gryffydd of Rhuddlan."

I was too modest to reply but Ridley beamed from ear to ear. "That he is! And I was there to witness that combat!"

"Then we are lucky to be alive and I for one will gladly serve such a warrior."

By the time we headed back to our homes all seven had joined us. The spokesman was a fine warrior called Aedgart and I came to rely on him almost as much as Osbert. When we reached the citadel, the relieved folk of my estate all went home and we celebrated with ale and a deer

Branton had shot on the way back. I looked around at my army. From small beginnings, we had grown and I now had ten armed and armoured men at arms and five competent archers. I felt like a lord but I wondered what Earl Tostig would do to the two lords who had dared to question his authority. At the time, I did not know that others had joined in the putative rebellion against the unfair taxation as far as I knew he would come north with a larger army and vengeance on his mind. I turned to Osbert, "I think tomorrow we build a tower and improve the gates for the next time we may well have to defend our demesne."

Osbert nodded. "I would not worry for when the word gets out about today we will have others choosing to fight for you."

"But could I afford them?"

In answer, he held up a purse. "It seems your brother ran rather swiftly from the field and dropped this. I suspect it is someone else's taxes but we can use them eh?"

I opened the purse and saw that it was not just silver and copper, there were gold pieces. I wondered when he would miss it.

In the end, he did not come but Earl Harold did. We heard that Earl Tostig had been driven from his capital by the inhabitants of that city and he had fled to Scotland. Ridley and I took our men to Jorvik to meet with Harold and the new Earl of Northumbria. When we reached Jorvik it was as though a feast was being thrown for the whole country. There were many armed men but every street had people laughing, joking and drinking to celebrate the defeat of Earl Tostig. We found Ulf and the Housecarls at the warrior hall. Leaving Osbert to find a field for our men, we entered. It was more than flattering to be greeted so warmly. Wolf and Osgar were effusive but they had seen our men behind us as we had arrived.

"Truly you are lords with your own retinue! I can remember the days when you could not keep your feet in a shield wall."

We all laughed heartily at that. When we told them of Edward and our battle they nodded sagely. "Aye well your brothers and your father have joined with the Earl in Scotland and I can now understand why they did not fight if your brothers are a measure of his men. No offence Aelfraed."

"And none taken Ulf, I agree with you." My uncle, the normal fount of all knowledge was with Harold and I was desperate for news. "Who is the new Earl of Northumbria then?"

Ulf had the good grace to be shamefaced as he stammered his reply, "Er Morcar."

I was stunned. Ridley looked at me with a confused expression on his face. "Who is Morcar?"

"The brother of the man he appointed as Earl of Mercia, Edwin and the brother of Ealdgyth his wife."

Even Ridley could see nepotism at work and he gave a quiet, "Oh!"

"Your uncle is here," ventured Wolf and then he added cheekily, "and one of the ladies of the court, Gytha."

I ignored his attempt to make me feel foolish. "Gytha is here? Is she married yet?"

The four of them fell about laughing. When Osgar had dried his eyes, he said, "You are one of the brightest minds I have ever met Aelfraed and yet where this girl is concerned you are like a moon calf, all doughy eyed and tongue-tied."

"Wait until it happens to you Osgar."

Wolf laughed. "He is married to his axe; have you not seen the small hole at the end of the handle? Just the right size for him!"

It was good to banter again and be with comrades who had shared the line of death. I liked Osbert and the others but I could not let my guard down as I could, here amongst my fellow Housecarls.

We were summoned to the church for the swearing of the oath. The Bishop looked less than happy about the situation but he had to suffer in silence. I knew, from my tame priest, that he was as corrupt a churchman as it was possible to be, perhaps Morcar would be able to control him but he was younger even than Ridley and I hoped that his brother Edwin, Earl of Mercia, would be around to give him the support he needed.

When we emerged, Harold sought out the two of us. "I hear you two have been routing the lords of the north."

I smiled. "It was a skirmish, nothing more."

"No Aelfraed, I am proud of you because that was the stone which started the mountain to fall. Others took heart from your stand and your victory. I am indebted to you once more."

"In that case my lord may I ask a boon of you?" I saw the irritated look flash across my uncle's face but I ignored it.

"And what boon would that be?"

"I would like to court the Lady Gytha."

"I thought you had grown out of that fancy but as she is not promised to anyone I will give you permission to speak with her but, young

Aelfraed who has less land than most unless she is of the same mind then I will seek a more powerful suitor for her."

Ealdgyth arrived at that moment. "Who are you marrying off now husband?"

She was still as beautiful as ever. I had heard that she had lost her baby but I could see that she was with child once more. Earl Harold disappointed me. He saw Gytha as an object, a pawn in a game of chess for him to play or to lose at a whim.

"Aelfraed here would woo Gytha."

In answer, Ealdgyth threw her arms about me and kissed me. She had always been fond of me. "But of course, he shall woo her and they shall marry. Oh, this is wonderful." I was delighted to see the look of disappointment on Earl Harold's face. He was rarely thwarted and I was glad that his wife had his measure. "I will arrange the meeting myself. Come in the morning to our residence and she will be there awaiting you." She kissed first me and then the Earl and left.

The Housecarls looked bemused. It was as though a tornado had crashed through the town and then left.

Aethelward put his arm around my shoulder and Ridley's. "Come you two for we have much to talk of."

When we were some distance from the Earl he suddenly became serious. "It does not do to upset the Earl."

"But he said he had no plans for her."

"Not at the moment but he is always planning for the future. And now, how are your lands? I heard about your brother, well done."

"Our lands are better now."

"We have men at arms," blurted out Ridley.

"I know and it is good for we will need them soon."

I saw an alehouse and we went in. "Why uncle what do you know?"

Ridley went to get ale while my uncle explained. "The King is not well and I do not think he will last more than a year or two. Duke William is spreading the story that the Earl swore fealty to him."

"Is it true?"

Aethelward shrugged. "I am not sure. Oaths do not seem important to the Earl unless someone swears one to him."

"I hear my father and brothers are fled with Tostig?"

"Aye and I should apologise to you. When we were last in Jorvik you warned me of your father but I could not believe that my sister's husband was a traitor."

I shrugged. "I could have been wrong. I was younger then."

"No Aelfraed I should have trusted your instincts. It seems he was in a plot with the Normans and the Scots to rid the country of Edward. It would have allowed Malcolm to claim Northumbria and the Duke the rest of the country. War is coming. I am pleased that you are here for Morcar is young and will need wiser heads to aid him."

I looked shocked. "I am not wise. I am of an age with Morcar."

"Yes nephew, but you have seen and done more than he has and more importantly you have the brain of a strategos. I am getting old and I have no son but if I had one I would he was like you. You make me proud as you would have made my sister proud had she lived."

I never cried as a grown man, I had not cried since Nanna died but that day in the alehouse with Ridley and my uncle I was close to tears. "I will not let you down uncle."

He then gave me the smile that Nanna always gave to me and which my father never had. "You will never let me down."

We three sat in a comfortable silence and then I made the whole scene embarrassing. These two were the two closest people to me in the world and I felt I could say anything. "Who is my father? It is not Edwin."

Ridley stared intently at his ale as though trying to read the runes of the froth. "No, it is not Edwin."

"Then who is it?"

"That I cannot tell you for, unlike some men, I have an oath which I took."

"Did my mother love my, my real father?"

Aethelward smiled, "Oh that she did Aelfraed. It was wyrd."

"And Edwin, did he know that…"

"That his wife had been unfaithful? Aye, and it cost her, her life."

Once, when we were campaigning in Wales I stood atop a high crag and the world below me seemed to spin. Had Ridley not pulled me back I think I would have plunged over to my death. As I sat in the alehouse I had that same feeling of falling into a deep dark hole. Even Ridley had finished studying his ale and he sat open-mouthed looking at me. My uncle put his hand on my arm. "Now that he is declared traitor I can tell you so that you feel not the shame of his name."

"He killed her?"

There was a silence as Aethelward sipped his ale. "Aye, he killed her. I did not find out until I returned at Nanna's request and I would have killed him then but your grandmother forbade it for your sake."

Suddenly many events surrounding my uncle's return made sense as did many of the stories Nanna had told me which I had not understood but now did. She had been preparing me for the news which she knew would shatter me. I said no more on that momentous night for my men at arms found us and we spent the rest of the night carousing and listening to Aethelward's stories of the Varangian guard. But in my mind, I swore an oath that Edwin of Medelai would die at my hand and my mother would be avenged. I think my heart became a little harder that night. I still did not know who my real father was but that could wait until my blade sank into that evil man's heart.

Ridley was worried about me and, the next day, as we walked to the Earl's house he spoke quietly to me. "Are you all right Aelfraed? I have never seen the black anger upon you as I did last night."

"Thank you, my most faithful and oldest friend. Yes, I am not losing my mind as I thought I was last night but I am resolved to kill that black-hearted murderer."

He nodded his agreement as though that was inevitable. "Of course, you know that you will also have to kill your brothers."

Ridley did not think of himself as clever but where people were concerned he was a genius. Of course, I would have to kill my brothers for they would avenge their father. "I know."

"And I will be there beside you as your friend." Wise men say that you are stuck with your family but you choose your friends. I was glad that, all those years ago, when Aethelward had first arrived, that I had chosen Ridley for I could not have chosen better.

By the time, we reached the Earl's home my mind was, once again, calm. The Earl had taken over the old Roman headquarters building, which was a fine stone structure built in the Roman rather than the Danish style. It was one of the Housecarls who opened the door and he grinned at the two of us. Somehow it made me feel much better; I now had friends, friends who would give their lives for me; what did I care for Edwin and his brood?

The whirlwind that was Ealdgyth rushed up to me. "I have prepared Gytha to greet you."

I looked at her in panic. "You have not told her?"

"You goose! I am not Earl Harold! I am a woman and know what it is to be in love. Go and woo her."

"But Earl Harold said…"

"Earl Harold knows the correct way to hold a spear and that is all. Now go!"

When I entered the chamber set aside for our visit, I saw that the Earl's wife had made sure that we were alone but the inside was all functionality. There were two high backed chairs and a table. The Lady Gytha sat at one of the chairs. When I approached, she leapt to her feet. My first view of her since that day so long ago in Winchester confirmed that she made my heart sing and my head light. She was a little thinner and gaunter but that had merely accentuated her beauty. Her smile, however, made the dour room spring to life as though someone had brought in a vase of flowers.

"My lady…"

I had waited so long to see her, I had badgered so much to meet her and I had dreamt so long of the moment that I was suddenly tongue tied and I just stood there with my arms open.

She took my hands in hers and inclined her head to the side. The magic of her touch made my skin tingle. I felt just as I did before the shield wall advanced full of joy and fear all at the same time. I tried again. "My lady I have thought about you every day since we first met. I know that I am a lowly lord of a small parish and you are a high-born lady from a powerful family but I would if you would have me, woo you." When the words tumbled out I felt foolish. I had meant to say 'marry' but the word woo had erupted from my mouth and sounded pathetic. I looked to the ground shamefaced. "I am sorry my lady for I am a tongue-tied warrior who knows not how to speak to someone as beautiful as you. Please say that you are willing to see me again I beg of you."

In answer, she leaned up and, standing on tiptoe for she was much shorter than I, she kissed me gently and chastely on the lips. "My lord, I too, have dreamt of you. When I heard of your bravery in saving our King it only confirmed my feelings for you. Your lowly parish does not worry me for I would be with you even in a cow byre. You do not need to woo me for I am yours already."

"Then marry me."

"Yes, my love, I will."

Ealdgyth must have been standing outside the room for she suddenly burst in, her face filled with tears. "You goose, I thought you had lost her! Woo her indeed!" She kissed Gytha and then me. "We must see the

Bishop and have you married as soon as possible before the Edith Duck-legs hears of this and tries to stop it."

I looked confused as Gytha giggled. "I think my lady is making fun, for it is Edith Swanneck."

"I knew she had the name like some ugly part of a bird. No matter. Now you must be apart until you marry that is proper." I flashed a surprised look for I remembered how she and the Earl had thrown themselves at each other. She knew the look and shrugged. "Aelfraed, Gytha has never been married before. Now go and buy some decent clothes and I will send for you when the Bishop is ready."

The Earl's lady was like a force of nature but she got things done and was as good as her word. Almost before I had time to turn around and change into my new clothes the grinning Housecarl came to the inn with the message that all was ready.

Ridley came with me as did Aethelward, Ulf and my men at arms. They were a little awed to be in such a magnificent church with the Bishop conducting the service. When the Earls and the other lords entered, I could see from their faces that they thought they had been transported to some fantasy land. I knew that it was a fantasy and the service flew by in a blur. Ealdgyth had made a bedroom in their quarters available to us and when we found ourselves alone, as the others feasted and celebrated I suddenly felt frightened for I had never been with a woman before. I had heard the stories men told but, as with all stories that men tell, I knew that most of it was an exaggeration. I wished I had spoken with Aethelward before we left but then this was out of his area of expertise as well.

The room, thankfully, was lit by just two candles and the half glow allowed us to move towards each other half-hidden. I enfolded her in my arms and noticed again, how small she was. I leaned down and kissed her on the lips as she had kissed me. This time we pressed in hard to each other and I felt her lips part slightly and a tiny tongue darted to touch mine. I felt as though I had grabbed a burning brand and a shock of excitement raced through my body. I felt something I had never felt before. Suddenly we were both taking our clothes off and climbing onto the bed. The sheets seemed icy against our hot bodies but neither of us cared. I knew not what Gytha was feeling but if it was only half of what I felt then she would be ecstatic. Despite the fact that neither of us knew exactly what we were doing our bodies did and as I entered her for the first time she gave a small moan of pleasure and then just as suddenly as it had started she gave a squeal of delight and I was spent. We lay back on the bed and she nestled her head in the crook of my arm. I kissed her gently on the eyes and said, "Gytha, I love you."

She leaned up and kissed me on my lips, "And Aelfraed, I have loved you since the day I first saw you."

Thus, I was married and the next year was the happiest of my life.

Chapter 11

Maiden Bower 1065

When we returned to Topcliffe, accompanied by my uncle, Thomas and his good wife were delighted to have a lady of the manor. I was, of course, given looks of disapproval for not having warned them so that they could prepare the house. I have to admit that it showed it had been created by a man and was both martial and functional in nature. There was no natural light save for an arrow slit in each of the walls. Fortunately, that was easily remedied as the upper walls were wooden and we had more light. Gytha, for her part, was delighted. For the past few years, she had moved around the country, first with Edith and latterly with Ealdgyth and to have such rough clay with which to work made her clap her hands in glee. When I mumbled my apologies for the Spartan nature of the room she hugged me. "No husband! I would not have it any other way for the home is my domain and I can do with it as I like."

As a high-born lady and a relative of the Earl, we had been given a substantial dowry and the first thing we did was to send Thomas' wife, Sarah, with Gytha and an escort of men at arms to purchase all that she needed to make the house a home. Aethelward and I toured my lands and he made many comments about possible improvements. As we neared my boundary which ran along the Roman road he looked into the distance.

"Let us visit Medelai."

I had often thought, myself, that I might like to visit it now that my family was no longer there. "If you want to uncle."

He looked into the distance and spoke without turning as we rode. "It is the Earl's wish for now that the family has fled and been declared traitors, it becomes the property of the crown. It has been given to me."

I was delighted for Medelai was a neighbour, not as close as Coxold but to have Aethelward as close as that... "Will you live there?"

He shook his head. "I am no farmer. I am a strategos and I would have refused it but for the memory of your mother. It will, in some way, repay the pain she suffered at your... at Edwin's hands. No, I go to see Ridley's father and arrange the business side of the estate." He glanced at me. "If you remain in the area then I would appreciate your keeping an eye on it for me."

"Of course." There was an underlying message in his words. "You say if I remain in the area. Why should I not?"

Even though we were out in the open he lowered his voice. "I told you that war is coming and that may well be in the south if Duke William comes to claim that which he believes he was promised by the King." King Edward's sojourn in Normandy had made him lean towards all things Norman and now it was coming back to haunt him. "You are too valuable a warrior to waste your time kicking your heels in the north. If war comes you and your men will be needed at the Earl's side, at my side."

We rode in silence. I had not thought of myself as a valuable warrior. I was not yet ready to hang up my axe for I had not even reached my prime but having taken a wife I was ready to play the dutiful husband. When war did come, I had assumed it would be the Scots from the north and I would be defending my land. I would have to rethink my position and discuss it with Gytha.

The estate had a forlorn feel to it. My father had rarely been there before but at least Oswin had kept it looking well. There were few workers in the fields as we rode up to the gates of the hall. Oswin bowed to Aethelward who came straight to the point, "The King has decided that for his rebellion against him your master and his family have forfeited this estate which now belongs to me." He flourished the legal document before Oswin but did not allow him to read it. He looked around at the yard. "Things do not look good Oswin. Do I need a new Steward?"

Oswin paled. He had a comfortable home and lifestyle. If he were to be thrown off the land he would have nowhere to go. "No, my lord but when the master left many of the men went with him and..."

"And you could not be bothered to hire new ones." He leaned down from his horse to put his face close to the Steward's. "I am going back to Winchester but I am leaving the Thegn of Topcliffe to watch out for my affairs. It is not far and you will visit him once a week with a report on the estate and any profits which have accrued."

He looked puzzled. "I do not know the Thegn of Topcliffe my lord, how..."

I had been waiting for this moment, "Oh but you do Oswin for I am he and should I be absent when you call then travel down to Coxold and report to the Thegn of Coxold for you know him also." I paused dramatically, enjoying the tension and the cruelty of my next statement, "for he is Ridley, your son."

I thought I had gone too far and the Steward's heart would stop and he would drop down dead at our feet but he recovered himself. "Congratulations my lord." He turned to Aethelward. "It shall be as you command my lord."

"I will take the estate accounts with me to read at my nephew's demesne. They will be returned to you when I have scrutinised them."

Whilst Oswin was not happy about losing the documents he had no recourse. I suspected he would have preferred to have some time to adjust them but this way Aethelward would see them, warts and all. This was confirmed as we rode back to Maiden Bower. "I am not a man for figures and roods and the like. Is your man sound?"

"Thomas? He is everything Oswin should be but is not."

"Good, then I will let him look at them and give me a report. I am not a man to read columns of figures," He grinned. "I was just trying to put the wind up the old bastard anyway. I never liked the way he treated Ridley and you."

I laughed. "Will you be advising the Earl then?"

"Yes, but I think he will soon be king for Edward is not well and speaks to his priest more than his advisers."

As we rode east towards my land I could see that the summer was over and the first signs of autumn were upon the land. If Edward was ill now, then the winter would surely finish him off as it did with many old folk during the harsh winters of Britain. "When the King dies, I want you to bring your men down to London. The Earl will need your support."

"And Gytha?"

"She too, nephew, for the Earl's lady is fond of her and she will be safe there."

"What of my lands?"

"Remember Aelfraed that the lands were given to you by the crown, besides, Ridley could watch them for you could he not?"

It had never occurred to me that I might be fighting without Ridley by my side. How different from a couple of years ago, when we tramped around Wales and only thought about surviving the next combat and now we had estates and people to worry about. I began to envy Osgar and Wolf who still enjoyed their lives as Housecarls. "Of course, I trust Ridley with my life."

Aethelward stayed for a week before a messenger arrived to say that the Earl was returning south. Gytha had made a great fuss of my uncle; she had had more contact with him at court and she knew him to be a true and honourable warrior. As she said to me one night as we cuddled beneath the linen she had bought, "I have seen many deceivers and flatterers but you and your uncle are not among them. In these troubled times, it is good to have a rock on which to rely."

She threw her first feast on my uncle's last night at Maiden Bower. She invited Ridley and Osbert. I think Branton was a little put out but the room we used was not large. Already my lady was making plans to have a bigger hall built. It felt strange to be sat at the head of the table facing my wife with my three guests arrayed down the side. Sadly, it was one of the few times we were able to do that at Maiden Bower. My three friends made a great fuss over Gytha who loved every minute of it. At court she had been ignored as the more powerful ladies, Edith and Ealdgyth were the nectar for the butterflies. Ridley seemed as much in love with my wife as I was and he watched her every move.

Towards the end of the evening, when the toasts and thanks had been made, my uncle rose unsteadily to his feet. He had drunk more than I had ever seen him drink and I take that as a compliment that with us, his family, he did not need to be guarded. "I would like to thank my nephew Aelfraed and his lovely wife Gytha. This," he waved an unsteady arm around the hall, "feels like home. And Aelfraed, if I have not told you before I am as proud of you as any man could be."

Osbert and Ridley gave a, "Hear! Hear!" and banged the table with their hands. Gytha looked on proudly.

"I know that I will be seeing you soon, both of you when you come to London." Gytha looked at me in surprise and I shook my head as much as to say *'we will talk later'*. "When you do then I will show you my hospitality." His speech over he slumped into his seat.

Later after Ridley and I had put him to bed and Gytha and I were alone she pouted and asked, "When were you going to tell me that we were going to London? Am I not your wife? Do you not consider my feelings?"

Osgar had warned me that women were not like men. They expected to be talked to. It was not that way with men and certainly not warriors. "My love it is not certain. Aethelward said that the King is not well and if he died then we should go to London to help the Earl be crowned. That is all. The King still lives. My uncle was talking about some time in the future."

She immediately regretted her words, I could see that in her crestfallen face. "I am sorry. I thought he meant sooner rather than later." She began to cry and I held her in my arm.

"What is the matter? I am not upset."

"No, but I was cross with you, and I should have trusted you." She paused and dabbed her eyes. "There is something I should say," she took a deep breath, "I am with child. You are to be a father."

Suddenly her tears were explained and I hugged her tightly. "That is wonderful news. When?"

"In the spring."

"That is the perfect end to a perfect day."

And so, my life changed again. Gone was the carefree Housecarl; now I was a landowner, a husband and about to be a father. I wondered if I would ever have those days of freedom again. I didn't regret the marriage but I now looked back on my time as a Housecarl and thought it short. Now, as I look back on my life I can see that it was those happy days which were short for just after St Andrews day I received a message from Aethelward. We were to go to London. I had two frenetic and hectic days as I arranged everything. Ridley happily took over the management of my estate and promised that his men at arms would protect mine in the event of any Scots' raids. He now had a sizeable retinue for the steward had husbanded my resources well and without Tostig's taxes, we were all more profitable. Thomas and his wife were sad to see Gytha go for she had brought a breath of fresh feminine air into our masculine world.

I now had twelve men at arms and eight archers. Not a huge army but one of which I was proud. The men at arms all had a shield with my red horse painted upon it. Six of them had mail shirts while the rest had leather armour. Everyone had helmets with nasals, a spear and a sword. As soon as I could I determined to get an axe for Osbert, my sergeant at arms for he was a handy man with the weapon. Branton and his archers had leather armour, a short sword and a buckler. They also sported leather helmets; I remembered when that was all that I had had and how it had helped to protect me. I now had a magnificent helmet made by Ralph. It was simply constructed with a steel crown and a nasal but he had worked brass and copper around the rim to give added strength and to make it look even finer. My men were well trained and I was loath to lose them so I have given them the best that I could.

Gytha was a good rider. I offered her a wagon but she laughed it away. "When I am bigger then I will travel like an old lady." She was more than competent on a horse and it meant that we travelled quite quickly. With our own mounts and some I borrowed from Ridley, we were able to ride down the Roman road south. The inns and taverns were well protected and we now had enough money to pay for us all to be comfortable. We reached London within a week. We could have travelled quicker but I was aware that my wife was with child and I wanted to do nought to jeopardise that.

Ealdgyth insisted that we stay with them in their magnificent home and my men at arms were accommodated with Harold's Housecarls in the warrior hall. After the quiet of Maiden Bower London seemed to be filled with noise and bustle; more importantly, it was filled with intrigue and politics. I could see why the Earl was in London and not in his homeland of Winchester. The dying King was surrounded by Norman churchmen all trying to get him to nominate Duke William as his heir. His last announcement before he slipped into an uneasy sleep was that Earl Harold was to be the next king. For many, that would have been enough but the Archbishop of Canterbury had not given up on persuading Edward to change his mind. Earl Harold always kept one of his trusted men close to the King's chamber so that when he woke and needed to take sustenance they could ensure that the Normans did not influence the sick man. There was something macabre about those of us who waited outside the door for, when I was assigned that duty, I felt like a carrion bird ready to pick over the corpse.

I was grateful for the sanctuary which was Earl Harold's home. Ealdgyth was with child and she and Gytha were like two broody hens, not that I would have dreamt of saying that to either of them. Marriage had taught me that silence from a man was always preferable to the witty comment his fellows would enjoy. Fortunately, I was able to spend a good deal of my time with the Housecarls and I trained with them. My men at arms were used as a rank behind the rear rank. As Sweyn said, now much greyer since his time as a prisoner, "We need men who can stand and fight whether they be Housecarls or warriors for the working day." Osbert loved his time with my comrades. He confided in me that he had always aspired to be a Housecarl but events had got in his way. I wondered if I would ever have enough money to be able to afford Housecarls of my own.

It was when we were training that news came in of Tostig and my brothers. Malcolm Canmore had declined to support an invasion of Northumbria. He was, as they say up there, 'a canny Scot'. He had enough spies in the English and Norman courts to know that those two behemoths would fight to the death for the rich land of England and at the end of that fight, he might just be able to walk in and take it painlessly. Why risk his men in an attack against the two Earls, Edwin and Morcar, both of whom were worthy opponents? More worrying was that Tostig and his Thegns had taken ship for Norway where it was said, they were trying to persuade Harald Hadrada to claim the English throne for himself.

As we rested and ate bread and cheese my uncle told us of Hadrada. "I fought under him in Constantinople. He was a good warrior and very brave. He is no longer young but he was a strategos and understood how to win at war." He looked at each of us in turn. "If you face him do not underestimate him. He is like a good chess player or even a magician, he has you looking one way and then strikes where you least expect it. The only saving grace is that he would be fighting alongside Tostig."

Osbert was new to this level of discussion. "Why is that an advantage, my lord. I thought he was Earl Harold's brother?"

Ulf grunted, "Half brother. The half they normally throw away!"

"We have fought with him and he is not reliable. He is always looking for the easy victory and the gold at the end of the rainbow. We could have saved many men's lives in Wales had he pursued Gryffydd more closely."

"When he sent my brother Edward to fight us I knew then that he was not a good leader. Do you remember Osbert?"

"Aye, he was not a good leader but how does that reflect upon the Earl."

"The Earl knew that neither Edward nor his brothers could be relied upon. They showed that when we met them in Jorvik and yet he still appointed him and gave him men. Aedgart, you fought under him that day what is your opinion of him?"

"Who Edward or the Earl?"

I liked Aedgart for he was a plain speaker and always spoke the truth no matter how unpleasant to the listener. "Both."

"The Earl talked a good talk but he was always behind the front rank. Edward just copied him. A real leader would have got off his horse and led us in a wedge, or at least fought alongside us."

Osbert smiled, he enjoyed banter with his friend. "But you would still have lost."

Aedgart smiled and shrugged. This point had been debated and argued amongst our men often but the feeling was that the right side won because of leadership. "So Osbert, it is not Tostig we fear but Hadrada."

"Well he is getting old, perhaps he will stay in his hall and at least we know he will not try the icy Norwegian waters before late spring."

Ulf threw an indigestible crust into the river which flowed nearby. "Which just leaves us with Duke William. Lord Sweyn, you were at the Norman court and saw their army. What do you say?"

Sweyn had had a hard time in Normandy and had not enjoyed the experience. He and the Earl had fought for William and earned his praise but Sweyn was still bitter for he had been the butt of many unpleasant comments. "Well he won't come until late spring but when he does then watch out. If he can get his horses across the channel, then we will be in trouble and he has crossbowmen. The bolts can go through mail."

None of us liked that thought. Most arrows rained down from the sky and you could use your shield but the bolt had a flatter trajectory and was harder to see. "We just use our shields then."

"Aye Ulf but he has archers as well. It means that you need two shields. When the enemy horse come at you they have a bloody great spear, tipped with metal. If you are lucky your axe can break it but if you don't then it will pierce your mail like a ripe plum."

There was an uncomfortable silence as we digested that information. When Aethelward spoke, his voice seemed unnaturally loud. "There are two answers to that problem. One is mounted archers who can ride at the flanks of the charge and pick off the horses and the second is to have ditches and pits with spikes."

"That sounds too defensive. You mean you don't attack?"

Aethelward smiled at me. "When you defeated your brother did you attack?"

"Why, no."

"You outnumbered him and yet you just stood, why?"

"His men were better armed and better quality than my farmers."

"Precisely. Your men at arms absorbed the attack and allowed you to win. I do not think that we will be using the wedge against the Norman horse. Perhaps if the Earl of Mercia brings his mounted men then we might be able to attack."

Ulf asked, "Why is he not here, along with his brother?"

"Tostig. If he attacks Jorvik then the earls must be there to defend it. Do not worry we have more than enough men on the south coast to repel an attack. He has to get his horses off his ships and that is when he is vulnerable. I have advised the Earl to keep us as close to the south coast as we can and as soon as the fleet is sighted then send the army there to fight them on the beaches and drive them into the sea."

Aethelward's comforting words reassured us and gave us hope through the long winter ahead.

King Edward died in the dead of winter. He slipped into a deep sleep and did not awake. We wasted no time in having the Witenagemot confirm the Earl as king. The only voices which might have dissented were the Norman clergy but the Housecarls who stood behind the council persuaded them to be silent. Harold was crowned King and it was the proudest moment in my life for I had helped an Earl become a king. I was in no doubt that it would make me more important for, after the Earls, I, along with Ulf and Aethelward was seen as the next order of commanders. When we fought, I would lead not only my men at arms but those of other lords who would flock to the banner of the White Horse. There was also a good omen in that Ealdgyth gave birth to twins Harold and Ulf. His namesake was inordinately proud of the fact that the Queen had chosen his name. It also helped me for I felt less guilty about leaving Gytha alone. She was now waiting on the Queen and the two were inseparable. It meant that I was able to train with the men at arms ready for the war to come.

We saw little of my uncle and the Earl for they were busy looking at maps and listening to the reports of the ships which brought news from foreign ports. One spring morning we were busily working with the Housecarls when the Earl and my uncle rode up. Their faces were serious and they summoned me to a conference with Sweyn.

"Bad news Aelfraed, my brother has persuaded Harald Hadrada to invade Northumbria."

"When your majesty?"

"Soon I fear. I want you to return to Jorvik with your men and apprise the Earl of the danger. We need to raise the fyrd."

"And what of the Normans?"

Aethelward became a little impatient. "You are not the only warrior we have nephew. We might just be able to defeat them without you, it will be hard but…"

The King put his hand on my uncle's arm, "Aelfraed is thinking of not only us two but his wife, are you not?"

I nodded. I could not take Gytha into a war zone and yet, if I left her in London she might be in a battle and I would not be there to protect her. I knew that Aethelward was worried about me and had not meant what he had said. "Will Gytha be safe here?"

Aethelward clasped my arm. "I give you my word."

All things considered, Gytha took the news well. I think that the Queen had warned her of my impending departure. Her affection for me remained unabated. Gytha told me that the Queen loved my honesty as well as my courage. "It is a sign, my husband, of the esteem in which the Earl holds you and the trust he places in you. I would be at your side but I am afraid that I am a little ungainly at the moment." She glanced down at the bump which seemed to grow bigger each day.

"My uncle has promised to look after you should…"

Tears sprang into her eyes and, throwing her arms around me, she hugged me tightly. "You will return and I will still be here when that day comes."

Our parting was tearful but sweet and my men impatiently waited for me to mount. As I headed north, with the Thames at my back I wondered when I would see my wife again. My men were full of cheer for the Earl had paid for mail shirts for all of my men and arms and Osgar had given Osbert an axe as the two had become friends. With the pack horses laden, and no pregnant woman to worry me we covered the two hundred odd miles in less than five days. We rode hard for we knew that the Danes could land at any time. I sent the men at arms on ahead to prepare Maiden Bower for defence and I retained Branton and his archers as I went directly to Jorvik and the court of Earl Morcar.

The Earl must have had word before my arrival for there was a great deal of movement around the city and I was pleased to see the defences being strengthened. The Danes were not known to have siege weapons and if we failed to defeat them then we would, at least, have the security of its Roman walls to protect us. I was admitted as soon as I reached his headquarters. The warriors all knew me, I was the Hero of Rhuddlan and bards wrote songs about me. As I stepped across the ancient portal I just felt dirty and tired, as un-heroic as it was possible to feel.

I always liked Morcar. He was not as flamboyant as his elder brother, the Earl of Mercia but he was earnest and brave. He was a man on whom you could rely. Later, in more peaceful times he showed himself to be resilient and resourceful too but that was in the future.

He greeted me like an old friend, "Welcome Aelfraed. Are you the vanguard? Does the King follow?"

I shook my head. "No, my lord. The King waits for the Normans who threaten our south coast."

He looked sad and downcast for a brief moment. "I see intrigue here. Earl Tostig chooses his moment well."

I wondered about that. The mysterious assassins were linked to the Normans and Earl Tostig by my father. I thought about the damage the traitor could have done. He had been privy to all the debates and councils. I was just grateful that my uncle had not trusted him and kept valuable information to himself. "The traitor knows the city perhaps we ought to look at changing the way it is defended."

He looked at me curiously. He knew from the talks around the fires that I had been part of the discussions with Aethelward and Harold before the battles in Wales and I knew that he respected my opinion. "How so?"

"Everyone knows of our Roman walls and the river so if we add defences which were not there before then we may surprise an attacker. He will see what he expects to see."

"Come we will walk the city and you can advise me." As we headed towards the river he added, "My brother is bringing his Mercians to aid us."

"And that too is worrying."

"Worrying? That my brother comes to aid me?"

"No, my lord but your brother has the only cavalry who can stand up to the Normans and they will be here in the north if the Duke attacks."

He laughed. "Aelfraed your mind works in a different way to mine. You are correct it would be better if he was with the King but I fear that without him we would have little chance."

"How many men can we field?"

"With my brothers and the fyrd ... probably a little over five thousand."

Not as large as most armies and smaller than the King's. I wondered if it would be enough. We had reached the southern gate and the river. "If they come by sea they will have to head north from Riccall. This is the first place they would strike. If we damage the river defences, then the river will flood this land and make attack impossible. We could use the other gates and protect them in different ways." When we had walked the whole area, we decided to deepen the ditches on the other sides of the city walls and sow the bottom with wooden stakes. I remembered how a few had been effective in Wales. The Danes had destroyed all the towers but one and I suggested that the Earl build wooden ones to allow us to defend it better.

That night as we supped in his quarters he asked me how I would fight if I was the general. It was the first time I had thought about commanding more than a handful of men and so I visualised the chessboard and imagined that Tostig was my opponent. "Hadrada will have the advantage for he knows where he will land and we do not. We cannot keep the fyrd waiting all summer for him or the people will starve. We need to use the demesnes on the river to watch with riders and warn us when they approach. Our problem will be gathering our forces together. The Danes have the advantage that they will all be landing at the same place and be an army already. We should have some means of slowing them down. Your brother's horse would be perfect for that. I know, having faced them that a charging horse is terrifying."

"And yet you defeated them."

"My uncle chose his defence well. If we can find out where they are and slow them down, then we can gather the men at arms and the fyrd can be raised. We know that they will have to land in the south so perhaps gathering the men at arms now in the city might save time but it will impose upon the supplies for this city. How are you fixed for a siege?"

"Enough water but we lack food and it is just spring now."

"Then we must get more. Tell your lords to bring their own supplies when they are summoned." I shrugged, "My Steward will have to provide for my men." The Earl looked downcast. "Fear not my lord for these warriors fight like us. Man to man with shield wall and axe. We can beat them. If it were the Normans…"

He shook his head sadly, "I fear that day is not long off Aelfraed."

And he was right.

I left the next day to begin gathering the men. I had given Osbert instructions for the smith to produce better weapons for our fyrd. They might not be armoured but they could at least have a functional weapon that might actually hurt someone. I had already asked him to begin making helmets before we left but that was a long and hard process and it was swords and spears that we needed. As we neared Coxold I called

Branton, "Ride to Lord Ridley and ask him to join me at Maiden Bower and request him to get his Steward to cut a hundred ash staves." Branton knew me well enough not to waste time with questions and he rode off while we headed to my home.

It was reassuring when I saw the tower rising above the gate and the men at arms on the walls. Thomas and Osbert ran to me as I trotted through the gate. "Welcome my lord I have done everything which Osbert asked of me."

"You are a good man Thomas and now you must begin to preserve meat."

"Meat my lord?"

"Aye for I will be taking my men down to Jorvik and we needs must provide for ourselves." I turned to Osbert, "When Branton returns send him with his archers and those of your men who are good hunters. We need as many wild pigs and deer as they can hunt."

"It is spring my lord."

I knew what he meant. We liked, whenever possible, to preserve stocks by only hunting the older beasts in spring. It made the rest of the herds and flocks stronger. "Tell him to try to take older ones but we must have food. How are the weapons coming?"

"Ralph has produced fifteen spearheads and now is working on the swords."

"Good when Ridley comes we should have the spear staffs. We will need arrows too but Branton needs to get the food first."

"Aidan can fletch; I will set him to work." Osbert gestured at the floor of the farm. "We have enough goose feathers."

"Thomas, warn the fyrd that they will be needed sooner rather than later. We will not take the old ones, they can work still and we will leave those younger than ten. The others will be needed as slingers."

Thomas looked troubled. "It has been a harsh winter, my lord."

"It will be a harder summer." I smiled, he meant well, "do your best old friend and go to Medelai and bring any surplus."

Thomas snorted, "It is easier getting blood from a stone than ought from that man. I know he is Lord Ridley's father but…"

"Don't worry, Lord Ridley feels the same. Osbert, send Aedgart, I think he will get the necessary blood from this stone." Osbert grinned Aedgart was his friend but was one of the toughest warriors either of us had ever met.

Thomas ventured, "And the Lady Gytha, my lord, how is she?"

"Thank you for asking Thomas. She blooms. Being with child suits and she is with the Queen in London so she will be safe. Lord Aethelward protects her."

I could see the relief on his face. This was why we were fighting, for decent men like Thomas against tyrants like Tostig and my brothers. It was why we would never be defeated because we fought, like Housecarls, for each other.

Chapter 12

Summer arrived and there was still no sign of Tostig and his Danish allies. Morcar arranged for beacons to be built and lit when the fleet was sighted. It all meant that we were slightly better prepared. The news that the Normans were still in Normandy also helped us to sleep easier in our beds. The delay increased the size of my retinue as my name and reputation drew volunteers who wished to join my men. Osbert, Branton and Aedgart were more than up to the task of finding the best and getting rid of the rest. Ridley took some of our cast offs, but not many. By early summer I had forty warriors, fifteen archers and twenty-five men at arms, fifteen of whom were mailed. The fyrd were all armed with spears. Most had a shield and many had a sword. Even the boys were armed with daggers. Ridley had a similar number with less mail as his estates were not as rich as mine and I have to say that Gytha's dowry helped. Needless to say, we were both proud of our men. We had spent the long early summer days in mock battles using sticks and shields. We had many bruises and occasionally it became heated but we knew that we had better warriors for all that.

The rider from the Earl of Mercia arrived at the gates one day in August. We had wondered when the message would come. "My Lord Topcliffe, the Earl says that the Danes have sailed and are heading west."

"Ride to Lord Ridley and tell him the same. Where do we gather?"

"Easingwold my lord."

Morcar had taken my advice and was gathering his men away from the river. I did not know how long it would take them to reach our shores, that would depend upon the wind. I idly wondered whose side God was on; ours or the pagans? I went to Thomas and Sarah. "While I am away old friend the estate is yours. I know that you will look after it and manage it well. If I should fall," I saw Sarah's hand go to her mouth in horror, "It might happen. Then look after the land for the Lady Gytha and my son. If we lose then Tostig and the Danes will return but you have lived through that and will do so again. I have not taken all the fyrd; when you are able bring our people inside the walls. Ralph can make more weapons and you can, at least, defend yourselves." I was touched by the tears in both their eyes. Sarah kissed my hand and I embraced her and I clasped Thomas' arm. "Farewell, my friends."

"Take care, my lord."

As I mounted my horse I thought that we all looked like seasoned warriors. With twenty mounted men at arms and ten mounted archers, we were more mobile than most and I wondered if we would be needed to travel south after we had defeated the Danes to fight the Normans. I was confident that my men could make a difference. The fyrd looked like warriors too and not the ill-armed rabble I had seen in Wales. They all had weapons of war rather than weapons to hand and the fifty men and ten boys followed the men at arms proudly out of the estate.

We headed down the Roman road. I had sent word to Ridley and I felt a lump in my throat as his warriors joined us. He had fewer weapons for his fyrd and fewer mail shirts but it was an impressive host and he rode next to me, his retinue joining mine to fill the road. We encountered other lords who were also heading south. They all looked enviously at our men and armour and, indeed, our numbers. It pleased me that so many had heeded the call for I had worried that there may be others like my father who were on Tostig's side but the numbers on the road made me think that my brothers were an exception.

Easingwold was a huge armed camp. The Mercians were a large contingent and you could smell where they were camped from the horses and their distinctive aroma. The two Earls had tents side by side and leaving Osbert and Aedgart to sort our men out Ridley and I went to the two Earls to gather intelligence. Morcar was delighted to see me and greeted me effusively. Edwin was more reserved but I think he was trying to maintain the position of general. In Aethelward and the King's absence, he was the senior warrior. "When did the fleet sail then?"

"One of the traders in wood who use the port of Whitby said he saw them gathered at the Danish port and they were boarding."

"So, they may not have sailed or they may have." I could see that they had had the debate themselves. "But if your horsemen are watching the river…"

Edwin dismissed my words with an imperious wave of his hand. "My brother told me of your idea but you are not a horseman Aelfraed. You cannot keep horses on patrol and then use them in war." I could see that Morcar had put my ideas forward and I was horrified that the leader of our army had ignored my advice. I bit down a retort. I was just another Thegn and my association with Harold and Aethelward meant nothing. I was a young lord but I knew that if the King had been with us he would have listened.

"So, they could have landed?"

"I did order beacons Aelfraed, as you suggested and they have not been lit yet."

"Well, at least we have time to prepare our strategy for the coming fight. I had hoped that the Norwegian King would fight the Danes rather than us."

The hint of a sneer appeared on Edwin's face. He had changed since he had been so grateful to us for defeating the Welsh. "Are you afraid, Lord Aelfraed? The hero of Rhuddlan?"

Again, I fought against the instinct which would have snapped a reply. "No, my lord, but I would prefer that King Harold did not have to face the Normans without your horses."

I was pleased with the look of embarrassment on the Earl's face. "When the Normans come then my horse will be ready."

I worried that even if we did defeat the Norwegians then the Earl would lose more horses than was safe for the army. I held my counsel. It was obvious to me that Edwin Earl of Mercia would do it his way and any advice would be for guidance only. Already on the first day, my heart began to sink. I felt Ridley's shoulders sag as he stood next to me. Ridley had heard of my ideas and thought that they were sound. "Well my lord I will go and see to my men." I had hoped we would have been invited in for a conference where we would feel part of the planning but I did not think that the Earl of Mercia took advice.

Later when I sat with Ridley and Osbert we all agreed that this lack of information could be disastrous. It was Osbert who had the idea. "My lord, do we need to stay here?"

I looked at him as though he had two heads. "We are with the army. Do you mean return to our home?"

"No, my lord but if we were south of the city then we would, at least, have advance warning of the enemy approach."

I slapped him on the back. "That is genius Osbert but more than that, we have horses, we could do what I urged the Earl to do and patrol the river. Ridley, how many horses do you have?"

"Fifteen."

"With my thirty that gives us a sizeable patrol. I will visit the Earl in the morrow and suggest this course of action." I was pleased that we had a course of action. Ridley still looked troubled.

"What is it, old friend? I can almost see your mind working and coming up with problems."

"Easingwold is some way north of Jorvik. I am no strategos," he grinned, "I am neither Aethelward nor Aelfraed, but it seems to this dull mind of mine that if we were closer to the city and the east then the host could close with the Norwegians quicker."

"Your mind is anything but dull my friend and I am glad that you reflect more than I for it helps you to see things which I miss. I will hazard with the Earl tomorrow."

I was not sure how the Earl would take my advice. Perhaps the fact that his sister had married the King made him feel superior to others who had fought more than he. I knew that Morcar, whose land this was, would heed it but his elder brother appeared to be using his prerogative as elder to take charge. I knew that I would have to be subtle and calm. My temper could have the opposite effect to the one I intended. The two Earls were outside their tent discussing matters with their sergeant at arms.

"Ah Lord Aelfraed did you sleep well?"

"I did my lord and it gave me some ideas which I would like to put to you."

Morcar's eager face was in direct contrast to the scowl which appeared on Edwin's. The Earl of Mercia was a cautious man as he had shown when he conspired with Harold to remove his father. "We are always keen to hear ideas."

I smiled my most engaging smile. "Well my lord, I fully understand that you do not wish to tire out your mounts by patrolling but my men will be fighting on foot. Have you any objection if I take my men and Lord Ridley's to watch the river with our horse? We would be able to warn you of the enemy's arrival and join you swiftly."

Morcar eagerly looked at his brother. I could see the Earl of Mercia working out if he would lose face in this. I had looked at the suggestion from every angle and felt sure that he could not. "That seems a good idea. Thank you Aelfraed, I am glad that your mind is still as sharp as ever."

It was now time to make him bring his army further south. "Of course, if the army were further south and east then we would have fewer miles to cover to bring the barbarians to brook. I will leave with my men. We will be close to the bend of the river between Fulford and Riccall."

"Wait, I think that if we were," he lifted the calfskin map he held in his hand, "at, say, Stamford Bridge we could respond to their advances swiftly."

"An excellent idea my lord. I think you have come up with a strategy of which the King would be proud." The preening smile told me the best way to deal with the Earl of Mercia, use flattery.

As we walked away Ridley grinned at me. "Well done, he does what you wish and believes it is his idea."

"Chess, Ridley, chess. I will teach you one day."

We found a dell by the river a mile or some from Escrick. We were close enough to the big bend in the river where a fleet could land its men and yet but a couple of miles from Jorvik. Aedgart set up a camp in the Roman style with stakes around a rough perimeter and he organised the men while I prepared the patrols. "We will keep five horses here as a reserve. Ridley, you take your ten, Osbert you take ten, have Branton take his archers and I will take the rest. No armour and no axes. We scout not fight. I had copied a map from the one Edwin had had. We need to scout from Riccall to Goole. We will stagger the patrol by an hour so that we do not tire out the horses. Remember that we are watching for ships or signs that the ships have already landed."

"Surely they will leave their ships where they land?"

"They will, Ridley, but if I was Hadrada I would land scouts ahead of the boats to make sure that scouts like us did not spot him."

Osbert nodded his head, "Then I hope that Hadrada is no Lord Aelfraed."

I led my small patrol first. I had given myself the least men; it was not vanity, it was eagerness. I wanted to be able to reach the mouth of the estuary quickly and satisfy myself that the preparations were in time and they had not landed already. As we rode along the river I cursed that King Edward had got rid of the fleet. Had we still had ships then one could have stood off the coast and warned us of the fleet's arrival. This way we could only react to the Viking moves, we could not initiate. He would always have the advantage.

The first week showed me that he had not arrived and my relief was tinged with doubt. Suppose the patrols were all a waste of time? The Earls had set up camp at Stamford Bridge and that part was satisfactory but all I was doing was working my men hard. When I confided in Osbert and Ridley they both laughed at me. "My lord if we were not patrolling we would be sat around the camp and the men would be bored. They would gamble and they would fight. This way every man has to ride two days out of three, the third day he trains. This is making us better warriors for we now fight as one band, not two. I for one would not change this strategy and the longer the Vikings take to come then so much the better."

"No Osbert, it is not, for the sooner that they arrive the better. We need to defeat them and then head south to aid the King for the battle for England will be fought in the south, not here in the north. This is a distraction."

It was towards the middle of September and the men of the fyrd were becoming anxious for it was harvest time. I wondered if they would arrive or not. Perhaps it was a feint and they were landing further south, suppose they were allied to Duke William? If that were the case, then the King would be caught between two armies and he would surely need us. Eventually, Branton galloped hard to meet me as I led my patrol east.

"My lord! The Norwegians, they have come."

We raced along the banks to the bluff close to Riccall, overlooking the river. There I beheld a mighty fleet of dragon ships. The river was filled with the dreaded longships which were spilling their men ashore. They were spreading like ants from a nest. Had the army been handy then this would have been the time to strike for they were neither armed nor armoured but the warriors were many miles to the north. Our task was to scout and we began to count the ships. After we counted two hundred it became difficult but that gave us an estimate. Sending Branton back to Ridley with orders to break camp and head north to Jorvik, I kicked my horse and led my warriors north to Stamford Bridge.

As I arrived it seemed that I had arrived none too soon for the men sat sullenly around with no sense of order. Morcar ran to meet me while Edwin came at a more sedate pace to preserve, I do not doubt, his dignity.

"News my Lord Topcliffe?"

"The Norse men have arrived at Riccall. We counted more than two hundred ships."

Edwin paled a little. "That would give them in excess of eight thousand men."

"More, my lord, for there were other ships further distant we could not count."

He looked around at the camp. "We have barely six thousand men. It will not be enough."

"It will my lord if we choose the right ground." He looked at me with a question in his mind if not on his lips. "Close to Fulford, we can block the road to Jorvik. The river and the marshes can protect us and make him fight on a narrow front where his numbers will not matter."

"That will not suit my horse."

"With respect, my lord, the bulk of the army are on foot; had we an abundance of archers then we could threaten them with your horse and massacre them with arrows but we must fight with what we have."

"Very well." He turned to his brother. "Have the army moved to Fulford." When Morcar ran off to give the orders Edwin turned to his sergeant at arms. "Send a rider to the King. Tell him that a mighty host has landed at Riccall and the Earls of Mercia and Northumbria, need his help."

The sergeant left quickly. I was appalled. "My lord, the Normans!"

"The Normans have not yet come. If the King comes north, then we can defeat these Norwegians and then march south to meet the Normans with a much larger army than he has."

"But if they land now then they will be unopposed."

"But we do not know that." He shrugged. "If they have landed then the King will not aid us and the land will be stained with our blood and bones."

He turned his back on me and headed for his tent. I was dismissed. I wished my uncle had been with us for the Earl might have listened to him. What was I but a Housecarl who had been given a parcel of land for one brave deed? And yet I could see that we could have held them at Fulford or even beaten them. I rode back to my men with dread in my heart.

I cheered up when I reached Fulford for my men were in good heart having warned the rest of their danger they felt they had already played a part. Ridley had spied the piece of high ground where the marsh protected one flank and the bank of the river the other. "Good position Ridley."

He beamed with pleasure, "I have been watching you and slow as I am, I do learn."

I ordered the men to make it a defensive position. To my dismay, Edwin did not like the position I had chosen and he placed his men with their flanks secured on the bank of the Ouse while his brother anchored his men close to the Fordland marsh. Leaving my men on the high ground I rode down to the two Earls. "My lord the high ground gives us an advantage."

"But this gives us more for we have a narrow front."

"We have nowhere to retreat!"

"We will hold them here. Our flanks are secure; place your men in the centre with the other warriors."

He strode off the decision, a disastrous one as it turned out, made. I rode angrily back to my men. Ridley could see my anger and he said calmly, "We fight by the river."

"Aye. If things go ill there will be no place to retreat." I turned to Osbert, "Get the men started down the hill but keep the horses here." He gave me a questioning look but followed my orders. I looked down the road to Riccall. It meandered its way from the southeast which meant the Norwegian would approach the same way. There was a leat near Naeburn which was hidden by a small wood. I did not want to be north of the city if the Norwegians were victorious; the King would come from the south and I needed an escape route that way. I did not tell this to Osbert and Ridley for I knew that they trusted me. "Osbert, take four men from the fyrd that you can trust, men who know horses and have them take the mounts down to Naeburn and hide them behind the trees. Tell them to guard them until we come."

Osbert was clever enough to see where I was going with it. "Suppose the Vikings come?"

"I do not think they will but if they do then they should take the horses south. At all cost, the beasts must not fall into their hands."

Nodding he left to select his men. I peered down the road and could see no movement. If the men left now they would be gone before Hadrada arrived. I turned to Ridley as we watched our men trudge north. "Whatever happens I do not wish to be incarcerated in Jorvik. Tostig knows it too well and it will fall quickly."

He looked at me in surprise. "You think we will lose?"

"Look at the way we are arrayed. The horses are trapped by the river. They cannot charge and the ground is boggy. On the other flank, the secure swamp is a prison; it keeps the Earl there. They outnumber us and I think that the Earl of Mercia is relying on Harold to come to his aid."

Ridley looked appalled. "But the King is a hundred and ninety miles away."

"Exactly. Even if the messenger rides his mounts into the ground he will take three days to reach London and then the King will need the best part of a week to reach us. I want to be free and not trapped behind the city walls. We can do mischief to their ships and we can cause trouble so long as we have horses."

"Which is why you have sent out horses away."

We marched down with the last of our men and placed ourselves in the centre of the line. I knew that it was the place of honour but also that it was the most exposed, if either flank fell then we would all die. I placed our men at arms in two lines and behind them Branton's archers. Behind that, in neat and ordered ranks, unlike the other fyrd I could see, I placed our fyrd. I felt proud that they looked so military whilst the others looked like farmers out for trouble. I called Branton over. "I want you to conserve arrows. When you are each down to your last ten then tell me. "We had spare arrows but I knew that mine were amongst the few that the army had. If we had to fight our way out, then the archers might just be the weapon that would save us.

I looked at the men around me. There was the Thegn of Scarborough to our left. His men were hardy farmers and fishermen and although he had few mail shirts many of his men wore helms. To our right was the Thegn of Skipton. He had mountain folk and some of them wore mail. Both men were older warriors, veterans of wars against the Scots. Our shield wall in the middle would be the rock on which the enemy broke, of that I had no doubt. I hoped that the Norwegians would attack us piecemeal for in that lay our only chance. I estimated that they outnumbered us by three thousand men and, in terms of trained warriors, by over two to one for the fyrd, although keen and brave, would not stand long against a Northman.

This time Edwin had placed a rider on top of the high ground we had vacated. I cursed the Earl again for the high ground now aided the enemy rather than us. He would be able to see our numbers while we had no idea about his. Suddenly the excited rider galloped down and yelled, "They are coming, and I have seen Hadrada!"

He said it as though it was Jesus himself who had appeared! "Well, it looks like we will get to fight today."

Ridley laughed, "Was there ever any doubt?"

I looked for Edwin to ride out and encourage us with brave words but he and his riders sat behind his spearmen and fyrd. That particular formation meant that the cavalry would not be able to charge. It would, however, have easy access north, back to the city. I looked to my left and Morcar waved. He would not speak if his brother did not. His men were arrayed like mine and his Housecarls formed two solid rows. Behind them were his spearmen and then his fyrd.

No one was going to speak. I would have spoken to the army but it would have seemed impertinent and a challenge to the Earls; right now, we needed cohesion and unity. I turned to face the men of Coxold and Topcliffe. I spoke loudly enough for the men of Scarborough and Skipton to hear me. "Men of Topcliffe and Coxold. You have marched far from your homes to fight this invader from beyond the seas and the tyrant who taxed you to starvation. These men from the north are renowned fighters but I tell you, I Aelfraed of Topcliffe who fought alongside Thegn Ridley against the Welsh King and killed their champion," There was a huge roar, not only from my men but from those on either side, "that you need have no doubt that you are all better warriors and remember this, they have never seen the men from the north fight. I have and believe me if you scare them half as much as you scare me they will run back to their dragon boats as soon as they can." The men laughed and then cheered. I did not feel ashamed for having brought up my one victory, men needed to believe that the man who led them was a hero. I saw Edwin's sour look- it mattered not for he had had his chance and spurned it. At least the men in the middle would stand. One effect of my speech, however, I could not anticipate. While I had my back to the hill Hadrada and Tostig had appeared. The cheers and shouts from the middle meant that they saw that as the stronger part of the line. It saved us from the first assault but helped us to lose the battle.

Hadrada was an impressive looking warrior. Aethelward had told me that he had made a fortune when serving the Emperor in Byzantium. He had virtually bought Norway and had almost captured Denmark. His armour was the finest that could be bought and gleamed as though gold. I knew it was not gold for steel was better but he looked imposing. Tostig lurked behind him looking as furtive as ever. I knew that he would not be in the first ranks who charged. I looked for my brothers and my father for I assumed they would be with their traitorous leader.

I saw the Norwegian King pointing ahead, even though I could not see them he was directing. Suddenly it seemed as though I would get my wish and they would fight piecemeal for the first band which rose over the hill headed steadfastly in a wedge formation and they were aimed directly at Morcar. I had thought that the King would have brought all his forces up first and attacked on the whole front. This suited us. As I watched the men approach I saw that they only had shields, helms and spears. They were not armoured! These were not his best warriors; these were the fastest. If this was his whole attack, then Morcar would easily defeat it.

The few archers and the slingers hurled their missiles thinning out the wedge. I could see that they were not the best warriors for it took time to fill the ranks of the dead. When they struck Morcar's line it took barely a step back before it began to move forwards. As soon as Morcar's men began to move forwards the warband crumbled and began to edge back towards the swamp. I could hear the roar of victory as Morcar and his men pushed the defeated and demoralised warriors into the swamp where they became easy prey for Morcar's men and they were soon despatched.

Hadrada had seen his first attack fail and he launched another with two larger warbands. They headed for the gap which had now opened up between Scarborough's men and Morcar's. Morcar and his men were too exultant pursuing the fleeing warriors to notice their predicament. As they closed I saw that these were better armed; these had axes and mail shirts. They marched purposefully and they banged their shields. These were hardened warriors; these were like the Housecarls. One band veered right to strike at Morcar's men on their flank and in their rear whilst the other headed towards the remnants of Morcar's right side and Scarborough's men. This was where my uncle would have been able to see the whole picture and move troops around. Our leaders were stuck on the flanks, fighting their own battles.

"Angle left!" My voice pierced the sounds of battle and the men of Topcliffe and Coxold, well trained as they were, performed the action instantly. The others were slower but they fell in line and we had a solid shield wall which was now at a slight angle to the rest of our line. "Rear rank brace!!

Their wedge could not keep a tight formation because of the muddy ground and some men slipped. They hit the Thegn of Scarborough's line but the line only went back two steps and then the other warriors pushed forwards. Ridley and his well-trained men at arms began to push against the side of the shield wall and slowly overcame it. I then saw, to my horror that our enemies had launched the rest of their men against Edwin, Earl of Mercia. Had I been on top of the hill I would have done the same for I would have seen the fyrd and lightly armoured spearmen to the fore. The warriors now trudged towards them, relentlessly banging their shields they were the elite; these were Hadrada's own men, paid for from his booty. "Topcliffe angle right!" My men and Lord Skipton's all turned to face this new threat. It meant that we had an arrow-shaped line and

Ridley and I were its point. Ironically no one was attacking us- for the moment. "Branton, get your archers and slingers to thin them out."

Branton's men rained flight after flight on the mailed and armoured axe men who thundered towards the spears and fyrd of Mercia. As well as the arrows the stones from the boys peppered them and soon they were edging even further left, towards the river. Had Edwin had his armoured men in the front rank we might have been able to push them in the river where they would have drowned in their heavy mail but we were unable to do anything until Morcar defeated his foes. So far neither Boar Splitter nor Death Bringer had drawn blood and it seemed that they never would when Morcar's men broke and ran into the swamp, much as they had driven the first warband there. The Norwegians pursued them to continue their slaughter. The second warband now turned all their attention to the fragment of Morcar's men and those of the middle.

"Skipton, watch those near the Earl. Branton, continue to thin them. Topcliffe, angle left." Our only hope was that we could break this warband and then turn to support Edwin if he survived.

Osbert and Aedgart were to my left and right. This was my first battle without Ridley and Wolf at my side but I was confident in my sergeants. I began banging my shield with my spear and my line took it up. I could see the rear ranks of Ridley's men moving back slightly as more warriors turned from the pursuit of Morcar to attack the centre. "Run!"

We hit the Norwegian line at an oblique angle. They had been so preoccupied with the left that they had ignored us. Their left side was unshielded and our spears found no obstacles. I had taught my spearmen to aim for the vulnerable part under the arm and they did so. The men before us died and fell to a man and we were on to the next line. I had withdrawn Boar Splitter from the first victim and he continued to slice into unguarded flesh. Eventually, I heard an order barked out in an unintelligible language and the Norwegians slowly turned to face us. The ease of our victory had given us confidence which meant that my men were not worried about the mailed warriors who faced us.

I yelled, "Fyrd! Push!" And I felt the reassuring pressure from the shields behind me. Because we had approached as one and the Norwegians had turned from their battle we had the advantage. I sought out the fiercest warrior who faced us. A mighty warrior wielding an axe. Most men feared advancing against the axe but I used one and knew its weakness. There were no others slicing in unison and, as the axe head slipped down I thrust Boar Splitter at his unguarded neck. With a surprised look, he dropped his axe and fell to the floor. I stepped into the breach and I was now the point of a small wedge. The next warrior had a sword and a shield. I could see from his face that he anticipated defeating me. His grinning face seemed to mock me. As I pulled back my spear I punched with my shield. He had covered his face with his own shield to protect himself and did not see the blow which struck his hand and knocked him to the ground. As I stamped down on his face I heard his scream as the warrior behind me speared him. It was then close-in work. The Norwegians were brave enough but we had had a cohesive shield wall at the start and we had maintained it. I know not how long we fought but I knew that I had never fought as long before.

And suddenly there was no one before me. As the wounded were despatched I quickly looked around. Morcar and his men were fleeing north to Jorvik pursued by exultant Norwegians. I spun around and saw, to my relief that the Thegn of Skipton was still there but of Edwin, there was no sign. Branton pointed North. "They have all fled my lord and are heading for Jorvik."

I looked and could see that the bulk of the Norwegian army, led by Hadrada and Tostig were racing after Edwin's horsemen. On the ground, close to the river lay the fyrd who had been sacrificed to allow the horse to escape. There were four lords left on the field, which was littered with bodies, the remains of their commands and the few men of Morcar who had sought protection from us. In all, we numbered less than two hundred. Thankfully I could see Scarborough, Skipton, Ridley, Osbert and Aedgart. We had survived.

"Branton, throw your archers out ahead and see if there are any men there. Make sure the road south is clear."

The Thegn of Scarborough looked at me as though I had lost my mind. "But Jorvik and the Earl are North!"

"And so are nearly ten thousand Norwegians. South there should be none and within a week King Harold or Aethelward of Medelai should be coming up that road." I raised my voice, "Any who wish to go north be my guest but I go south. I do not relish fighting my way through that horde and then be trapped behind stone walls." I saw Osbert grin as no one moved. "Aedgart, get the fyrd to take any weapons and armour they can but be quick. Osbert, get the wounded together."

He looked at me and I knew what he was asking, "And those too wounded?"

"A sword in the hand and I will send them to their god."

Osbert shook his head, "No my lord. I am the sergeant at arms, it is my job." Osbert left to perform the grisly but necessary task of dispatching those too wounded. Skipton and Scarborough came to my side with Ridley. "Where to my lord?"

"Down to Naeburn where we have some horses then we will find somewhere to hole up whilst we decide our next move." Out in the marches and by the river we could hear distant screams in the dying September sun as the Norwegians massacred the fyrd who had not made the walls of Jorvik. The army of the north was no more and if Duke William came now then England would be part of Normandy.

One of Branton's men ran up. "My lord, no one ahead of us. The trail to the leat is clear."

Right men let's move. Aedgart, bring up the rear. Archers pick up any arrows as we go." Had any Norwegians been lying in wait for us then we would have all died where we stood for we were exhausted, thirsty and hungry. God was smiling on us that day for we made it to the trees unharmed and unseen. We put the wounded on the horses after Branton and two of his archers had taken three horses to find us a camp for the night.

We headed down the road towards the river. We were of course on the wrong side of the river for safety as Ridley pointed out to me. "If we get to the river what then? There are no bridges south of the city."

"True but we can see what mischief we can cause the Norwegians. They think that we are defeated and holed up in the city. They do not know that we have escaped. We know this land and they do not."

The Thegn of Skipton asked, "And the wounded, the fyrd?"

"You are right. They cannot stay for it would not be fair. We will make a raft and ferry them across the river. They can make their own way home for they will be on the other side of the river. We will send two riders down to Harold to apprise him of the disaster and then we can gather our strength and then begin the fight back."

"Is it not over?"

I looked at the Thegn of Scarborough. "It will be over when our bleached bones lie on the soil and we become part of the land for which we fight. Norwegians do not take prisoners. Would you allow Earl Tostig to be a tyrant once more? Besides my friend, the Normans are coming. This is not the end, this is the start of a war and the lucky ones are the ones who are dead already."

Chapter 13

Stamford Bridge
September 1066

Although we found that we were fewer in number than the guards Hadrada had left, we were all warriors and most of us were mounted. Skipton had sent some of his men at arms back as escorts for the fyrd and wounded for he had the most casualties. Ridley and I had lost but three men each and we loaned their horses to the lords and their sergeants. Branton had found the fleet and, to our delight found that it was only guarded by a few warriors.

"He has most of his men with him. If we attack the guards, then he will have to send men down to protect the boats and there will be fewer left to besiege Jorvik." I knew that the fewer men around the walls, the less chance the Norwegians would have to capture it.

We left the horses on a bluff and crept down at dawn to the boats. Each boat had four men guarding it. We counted the ships and saw that there were three hundred. Although we would be outnumbered if they all attacked us by attacking boat by boat we could do much damage before they could gather their numbers.

Branton and his archers had collected arrows from the battlefield and were well stocked. We used their skills to kill the sentries on the first five boats before the alarm was raised. It was not combat, it was a massacre, as sleepy warriors without armour staggered ashore to fight us. We hacked holes in the planks of the ships, which had been dragged to the shore, with our axes. The damage we inflicted was repairable but it would take time and in many ways, it was petty; we might not be able to bring them to battle but we could annoy them and hurt them. When we saw a hundred armed warriors running down to fight us I led my men back to the horses and we rode away, their jeers and catcalls ringing in our ears. This was not an honourable war, this was a necessary war.

We saw the fruits of our labours the next day when Eystein Orri arrived with over five hundred warriors. Hadrada had sent a sizeable force to protect his ships and they looked to be hardened warriors whose presence would be missed when the King came north. Our foray was over. That night our messengers returned from King Harold with two of the King's retinue. "The King desires you to find out the whereabouts of the Norwegian army. We are here to act as messengers, lord."

It was to the point! "Right lads, we head north!"

We moved cautiously with Branton and his scouts ahead of us but the land was empty save for the carrion which feasted on the dead of Fulford. I had expected Norwegian patrols but there were none. As we approached the city walls Branton returned. "There is a thin line of warriors guarding the Mickelgate."

"Any sign of fighting?"

He looked puzzled. "No. The sentries looked like they were there to stop anyone getting in rather than attacking."

I held a conference with the other lords and Osbert. "I had not expected this. We know that the Norwegians have not left and they have not taken the city what is he up to."

Osbert scratched his chin, a sure sign that he was thinking. "We need a prisoner or two."

"Can you do that?"

He grinned evilly. "With Branton and Aedgart I could have the King's crown and be back in Topcliffe before he knew it was missing."

"Go then but, Osbert?"

"Yes, my lord?"

"Try to get one that speaks our language eh? It makes questioning a bit easier."

They took five men with them and, in the early hours of the morning they returned with three bleeding and bruised prisoners. Two of them were Norwegians but one I recognised. He had been a farmworker at Medelai. Ridley also recognised him. "Aidan!"

"So, my brothers are here?"

"Yes, and when they find that the Runt lives they will have you all for breakfast. "

Aedgart's blow was so hard that it made me wince. "Be polite! You don't need your balls to answer questions."

"What is happening in the city?"

He spat a gob of blood out and I am sure I saw a tooth amongst the mess. "The Earl of Mercia has surrendered the city and they are negotiating the terms."

Skipton could not contain himself. "The craven coward!" I could not blame him for many of his men had died ensuring that the Earl could escape to safety. We all valued our men and none of the four of us would have thrown lives away as needlessly as the Earl of Mercia did.

I put my hand on his arm. "This is not the time for judgements." Turning to Aidan I smiled. He had been one of the fellows of Edward and he had enjoyed taunting me but I knew his mind. I could see that he fancied that he had tied his horse to a wagon that promised success, money and power. He thought they had won. He did not know, as we did, that Harold was on his way north and the unruly, ill-disciplined Norwegians would lose. "And if I wish to surrender to Earl Tostig will he be in the city?"

More confident now he glared at Aedgart and snapped at me, "You can crawl to Stamford Bridge where the Earl and the King rest, preparing to slaughter your men, again." The last insult was spat at me.

I nodded, I had the information I required, and they were to the east of the city at Stamford Bridge. I smiled at him, "Thank you." Turning to Aedgart I said coldly, "Kill them!"

Aidan screamed his insults but they were in vain as the three of them had their throats slit and they fell dead at our feet. "You may return to the King and tell him Stamford Bridge. We will scout out a safe route to get there and meet you here."

We knew that the main army was at Stamford Bridge but were they on both sides? Branton reported a wood about a mile from the bridge and we went there to hide our horses. Leaving the bulk of the men to prepare a camp I went with the two brothers and Aedgart to spy out the bridge. Ridley wanted to come too. I took him to one side, "I need you here should aught happen to me. Skipton and Scarborough are good men but you are a leader. I trust you Ridley and I feel safer with you at my back."

Mollified he agreed and, after taking off our armour and helmets we took swords and daggers and set off towards the river. Night came earlier this late in September and soon made us difficult to see. As the chill set in I regretted not bringing my cloak but as we neared the bridge it was too late to do anything about that. Branton had sharp ears, he was the best scout we had and when he held his hand up we all stopped. As we waited in the dark we heard the voices which had been masked by our footfalls. Branton slid onto his belly and we all followed suit. I was the last man in the small line for I was the biggest and, if I am honest, the least effective amongst the four of us when it came to sneaking around. I might be the master of the shield wall but when it came to crawling around quietly, I was out of my depth. All that I could see was Aedgart's arse rising and falling and I had to stifle a giggle; I knew not why. I could have stayed at the camp but I knew that it was important for the eyes of a strategos to evaluate their defences and not an archer who might miss some crucial detail.

I saw Aedgart's grinning white face turn to me and his hand gestured me forwards. Branton had cleared a space and I saw that we were slightly above the bridge and looking beyond it. The fact that the bridge was but thirty paces away told me that the bulk of their army had not camped on this side. That gave King Harold an immediate advantage. There were six men lounging on the bridge with beakers of something in their hands, I assumed that it was ale. I focussed on looking beyond the bridge. What I observed made my hopes rise. There was no organised camp and, most importantly, no defences on the eastern side of the river. The few campfires told me that the men on this side would not halt Harold. They had no idea that the King was on his way and, as they had defeated the northern army, and the city had surrendered they had won and they could wait out those in the city. I saw the greedy fingers of Tostig all over this. He would have been happy for the city to surrender rather than have it assaulted and the booty taken by greedy Norwegians. This way it would be handed over formally, keys and all. Their defence was the river and that was all. From the campfires, I could see that they were spread out over a large area. Even allowing for the Norwegians who had returned to Riccall there had to be at least eight or nine thousand men in the camp, a sizeable force. I was worried that, after a forced march from London, Harold and the army would be exhausted, not the best conditions in which to fight.

Suddenly I realised that I could understand the guards on the bridge, they were Northumbrians. I looked down and began to listen to their conversation.

"What I want to know is how come it is us daft buggers who are stuck on this fucking bridge while the Viking bastards are getting pissed on the other side of the bridge?"

Another voice, less drunk mumbled, "Keep your voice down! Remember what Lord Egbert said, if we let them get drunk then we will have the first choice of the booty when we enter the city."

The first man, who looked vaguely familiar spat over the bridge into the river. "That is a fool's dream these hairy arsed bastards can hold their ale. They could be as pissed as a churchman and still be able to get to the booty first. Lord Egbert is talking out of his arse. Now if Lord Edward had said that…"

I then remembered where I had seen the man; he had been with my brothers when they had arrived, drunk, in the warrior's hall in Jorvik. I did not think we would learn anything else of use and I slipped back to return to Ridley and the others. I was awoken, in the hours before dawn by the arrival of King Harold, Sweyn and Aethelward.

They looked exhausted but greeted me warmly. "Well nephew, I am pleased that you survived the disaster at Fulford."

Before I could give him an account of the battle an impatient Harold shot an irritated glance at Aethelward and took my arm. "That is in the past Aethelward. Aelfraed, you scouted the bridge tell me now of their dispositions."

I smiled, "It is as though they wish us to be victorious your majesty." I relayed to him the information we had discovered and the fact that there were Northumbrians who were aiding Tostig.

"Well done Aelfraed. How many men are there west of the river?"

"No more than a thousand majesty."

"And your men can watch the bridge without being seen?"

"Yes, I will send them out again at dawn."

"Jorvik has surrendered?"

"Aye but as yet they have not handed it over. Hadrada seems happy enough to wait and save his men."

"Morcar and Edwin may have slightly redeemed themselves although I would have preferred them to fight for we would have attacked his forces whilst they were engaged."

Aethelward spoke in the dark. "And the fleet?"

"We damaged a few of their boats and they drew off a force to protect them. Perhaps one in ten of the army is now waiting some way south, close to Riccall."

"Excellent that was well done but it means, my lord, that we will need to leave a force here to repel them should they try to reinforce Hadrada."

"No, I want to defeat this Hadrada once and for all and then get back to the south coast. We will risk the boat guards attacking us. They are many miles to the south. At least we have time to bring the army here and attack when we choose."

"Where is the army, your majesty? "

"Close to Elvington." I could detect a tinge of sadness in his voice. "I would have camped closer to Fulford but I did not want the heart ripped out of my men seeing the scene of the battle." He turned to me. "Tell me now what went wrong?"

I wondered how to say that it was his appointments as Earls which had led to the disaster. I remembered my uncle's words about truth and I did not try to gloss over any of the errors. "Our intelligence was not as it should have been. Mercia did not wish to tire out his horses scouting and we only had a warning if but a few hours. Then the place of battle was badly chosen. The Earl declined to claim the high ground. Finally, your majesty, his dispositions were a little flawed. The Earl of Northumbria had a swamp on his flank and a stream behind. The Earl of Mercia anchored his horse by the river but placed spearmen before him."

"And the centre?" I suspect that Aethelward knew the answer to that question.

"Ridley, Scarborough, Skipton and myself were given that honour."

I saw the look exchanged between the two friends. "And the battle?"

"It started well enough. Earl Morcar pushed back the weaker troops before him but they lost cohesion and when Hadrada fed in his better troops they recoiled and had nowhere left to go but the swamp. They then attacked Scarborough and Ridley. At the same time, he attacked Earl Edwin and many of the fyrd were slaughtered or pushed into the river."

"And you nephew?"

"We were the point of the arrow fighting on two sides but we were helped by the fact that they pushed on either side. When the Earls fled the field and were pursued our small band of survivors were left with the dead. We headed south and that is when we attacked their fleet."

The silence which followed was eloquent. The flight of the two leaders before the battle was decided was criminal in the eyes of Harold and Aethelward; the choice of the battlefield was another. I had fought enough times with the two men to know that a well-chosen battlefield could save men's lives and win the battle. "You have done well Thegn Aelfraed. When we have time, we will reward you."

"Thank you, majesty, but I require no reward; just the opportunity to find my brothers on the field for they fight with Tostig."

"Edwin and his brood are here?"

"Aye, we captured one of Edward's men and heard others. They are here all right."

"Well, Aelfraed if you send your scouts out and Sweyn you bring the army here we can prepare to end this debacle. When they have arrived, we will choose the moment to attack."

By the time the army had arrived it was noon and the day, for late September was unseasonably hot. Branton had returned and told us that the Norwegians were lazing around the camp and engaged in horseplay in the river. The King and Aethelward held a brief conference. When they gave us their orders we were all eager to bring this horde to battle. Aethelward addressed the Thegns. "We attack those on the western bank first. Lord Aelfraed will lead the attack for his men have had time to rest and the King's Housecarls will be in reserve. When those on the western side have been disposed of then the Housecarls will attack the bridge and lead the assault on their main camp."

Ridley and Scarborough patted me on the back and I did feel honoured. My men also took the fact that we were to be the vanguard as a mark of honour and their prowess. As we gathered in the woods I ordered Branton and his archers to precede us with all the slingers. Placing Ridley to my right and Skipton and Scarborough to the left we began to advance. I was overjoyed to see that the Norwegians had no armour and their arms were stacked. It would not be a victory filled with honour but I had no doubt that our attack would be successful. The flights of arrows killed all they struck. I dressed my shield wall once we emerged into open ground and then roared the charge. It was not combat, it was a massacre. No one could stand against us and soon the bridge was filled with fleeing warriors eager to escape the deadly blades of my vanguard.

We should have been able to win quickly that day for our surprise was complete but three warriors thwarted us. Scarborough and Skipton were closer to the bridge than I and they led their men across the narrow bridge. The three men who faced them were naked save for their axes. I could see, from their wild appearance that they had worked themselves up into the state that the Norse called berserk. It meant they would fight to the death and would be impervious to wounds. Aethelward had told me of such men and even he feared them for it took many blows to kill them. It struck me that they must have come from the eastern side of the river or they would be already dead and would not have time to work themselves up.

As it transpired Scarborough raced across the bridge with his men at arms to attack the three naked men wielding double-handed axes. Scarborough was a brave and doughty warrior but he had no chance against those three warriors. His head flew from his body to land with a splash in the river below. His enraged men threw themselves at the berserkers but swiftly followed their lord to their deaths. Skipton was more cautious and he led his men towards the three with spears levelled. In part, it worked, for one of the berserkers was pierced by four spears. Even mortally wounded he still threw himself at Skipton with his axe.

The brave Thegn calmly decapitated him. Stepping over the body his small band advanced but Skipton fell to the leader of the remaining two. As I heard the tramp of feet as Sweyn and his Housecarls arrived to begin their assault I could not but help admire the remaining two brave men. The blood dripped from their bodies from their wounds. In a detached way, I thought that if I had not used Branton and his archers to kill the others they would have had arrows enough to kill these brave men. Skipton's men threw themselves at the last two berserkers to gain revenge for their dead lord. Although most died one of Skipton's brave Housecarls dived with his sword forwards to strike one berserker in the neck and throw him from the bridge. He was dead before the berserker hit the water as the last man killed him.

"Right lads we have pissed around enough. Let us show this big bastard what the King's Housecarls can do."

Sweyn's words were greeted by a roar. I stepped forwards. "Sweyn wait."

"What Aelfraed, you want more glory?"

"No old friend I want to save some lives. Branton." My archer appeared and I threw him Boar Splitter. I had spotted a half-barrel they had used as a boat tied to the bank. "Take the barrel and go beneath the bridge." Branton was a clever warrior and he grinned as he saw what I intended. He took two of his archers and pushed off. "Now you can attack Sweyn and I will get my glory later." I grinned to take the arrogance out of my words.

He patted my shoulder and shouted. "Wedge!"

I saw the formation take shape and smiled as Osgar stepped out. "You can always join us, my lord. We still have room."

"Now that you are here you will not need me."

The berserker prepared himself. The wedge could not be its normal shape for the bridge was only wide enough for four men but Sweyn stepped forwards and I saw Ulf at his right shoulder. Even without Branton, I thought that they would be victorious but there were almost forty dead men on the bridge who urged caution. The Norwegian was hurling insults at Sweyn but they were unintelligible gibberish to us. It mattered not as long as his focus remained on the wedge.

The bridge was not built in the Roman style, out of stone, but in the Danish manner, out of wood and the boards had split over the years. I saw Branton position the boat beneath the feet of the warrior who braced himself for the attack as he swung his huge axe around his head.

Suddenly a look of surprise erupted on his face as Boar Splitter slid up between his legs splitting first his manhood, ripping into his bowels and entrails and eviscerating him. Although I could not see I knew that Branton would push up and then twist the weapon to withdraw it. As I saw the bloody mass of gizzard and guts spill onto the bridge I knew that the berserker was dead. Sweyn stepped up and with one blow cut the man in two. The wedge poured over the bridge.

I felt my uncle's hand on my shoulder. "You did well Aelfraed but I am afraid that those brave men undid your good work." He pointed to the shield wall which was now being formed on the far side of the bridge. The men were not in armour but they were ready. This would not be a quick day's battle, this would be two similar armies standing toe to toe and it would be the last man standing. "Take your men across the river and stand to the right of the Housecarls."

He limped off to instruct the other leaders. A grinning Branton appeared with Boar Splitter in his hand. "We should rename this Dane Splitter!"

"You did well. Get your men to gather as many arrows as you can and then line up behind us."

We lined up some way short of the Norse line. We knew that they had no archers and that they could not and would not charge and we stood there with impunity, our warriors trading insults with the enemy. We all became silent when Harold rode up unaccompanied. He rode towards the twin standards of Tostig and the Norwegian King. No one tried to molest or attack him and he faced his half brother.

"Brother. It is not too late to rejoin your English brethren and to turn on this Norwegian usurper."

"I hear that Duke William calls you usurper."

"You would have a Norman as king of England?" Tostig had no answer and was silent. "I will give you my Earldom, Wessex and all its lands if you join with us and fight Hadrada."

Those Norse who could speak English began to mumble at this although the Norse King stood impassively, his great axe resting on the ground. I could see that the idea tempted Tostig for Wessex was the richest part of England. The greedy Tostig, no doubt thinking of the Danegeld in the past, slyly asked, "And what would you offer Hadrada?"

Harold looked contemptuously at the Norse King and said, "Six feet of ground or as much more as he needs, as he is taller than most men." We were all close enough to hear this and the whole of the English army burst out laughing. One of Hadrada's men, aroused by the insult hurled his spear at Harold who merely turned his head and it sailed over his head to land harmlessly at my feet.

I picked it up and turned around, "Here Branton. In case you get the chance to geld another Norseman." As the spear was passed back, my men laughed at the joke.

When Harold returned to our ranks we knew that the time for humour was gone and it was now the serious business of fighting and dying for his face was both sad and serious. He knew that this day would see many Englishmen die and more importantly there would be fewer Englishmen to face the Normans when they eventually arrived. Had his brother accepted his offer who knows how different the future might have been?

He nodded to Sweyn who shouted, "Wedge!" and my old comrades formed themselves into a wedge. We would not be following suit for Aethelward wanted us to bring the maximum blades into action while we faced unarmoured foes. Sweyn and his Housecarls would be facing the elite of the Norse army and they would be the hardest to defeat. The three berserkers had given us the measure of our enemies.

As we walked towards the waiting enemies I glanced down their line to see if I could see my brothers but their banners were not in evidence. Perhaps they had fled before the battle. That would not have surprised me but it would disappoint me for I wanted to end this and send my brother's souls to the next world. I hoped that their perfidy would cause them to burn in the Christian hell but I cared not so long as they were dead. That day we were not at the heart of the battle for that honour was reserved for Sweyn and my comrades. We could not see what went on there but we had more than enough to do with the enemies before us. "Branton, save your arrows; for they will strike only shields. Kill any who are on the ground and save your arrows for easier targets."

"Yes, my lord."

I heard Ridley's voice call from the right. "I have seen your brothers! They are to the right of me!"

I cursed. If I left my place to fight them then I would leave Osgar, whom I could see a few paces to my left, exposed. My personal fight would have to wait until later. "Keep an eye on him."

"It will be just the one as these Norse look to be big buggers!"

After that, there was no time to talk. "Men of Topcliffe let us avenge our friends. Charge" We were only ten paces from the Norse but we managed to gather impetus and clashed with them. Even as we struck,

Boar Splitter lanced towards the face of the warrior before me. My shield arm reacted before my eyes and deflected the axe which hacked at me. I stepped over his body and noticed that Osbert and Aedgart had killed their opponents. My next enemy had seen what I had done and he was prepared with his shield close to his face. I feinted with my blade and punched with my shield. He went backwards but did not fall for those behind were pushing hard against him; this was a shield wall. The two lines were now locked and I was too close to him to spear him but the man behind him was now close enough and Boar Splitter struck his eye and entered his brain, he fell back and the pressure before us lessened. We pushed forwards and while punching with the shield I head-butted the man facing me who had no nasal on his helmet. The crack of the bone-breaking and the spurting blood told me that I had hurt him. Dropping Boar Splitter, I drew my sword and stabbed him beneath his shield. He too fell. Glancing to my right I saw that Osbert still stood but he had taken a spear cut to the cheek. Aedgart's arm was bleeding. Our enemies were making life hard for us despite their lack of armour.

Although we were not in a wedge the three of us in the centre of our line were gradually edging ahead of our comrades. My men were well trained enough to take advantage of this. I was confident that Osgar to my left and Ridley to my right would protect my flanks and I pushed forwards. Had I been an eagle soaring high in the sky I would have seen the effect of this on the enemy line for we were forcing apart the centre of the Norse line from the Northumbrian traitors on their left. It was slow and it was inexorable but it was inevitable. Branton and his archers were spilling across the field along with the local fyrd to kill and despoil any Norse that they found; ahead were the enemy but behind us lay only the dead.

The Northumbrians and Norse who fought us could see the banners of their leaders edging away and they renewed their efforts against us. Rather than weakening us, it helped for when they swung their blades and axes they were exposing themselves to counter blows. Had they been armoured the blows would have done little damage but they sliced and slashed into unguarded flesh. Weakened, they continued to fight but were wounded as they were, doomed to die. Suddenly we found ourselves with allies and friends to our rear as we split the army into two. Unknown to me, Aethelward had seen what we were doing and it was being repeated on our left as he directed the battle from his horse. Within an hour, we had split Tostig and Hadrada from their men.

For my part, I had to concentrate upon those to the fore. We cursed and we swore and suddenly I was aware that those before us were English. We had fought through the Norse to the traitors. "Let's kill these treacherous traitors and send them to hell!"

It was when they began their chant that I knew I faced the warriors of my brothers, "Runt! Runt! Runt!"

Rather than enraging me, it calmed me. I glanced along the line to my right and saw Ridley at the head of his wedge but, like mine, it was barely formed. I shouted, "Topcliffe, Coxold halt! Wedges!" My brother's men were too surprised to react quickly for they were neither well trained nor led but our men were and we had two wedges in the blinking of an eye. I sheathed my sword, slipped my shield around my back and drew Death Bringer. Being at the front I did not have to worry about the rhythm of the swing and I started the deadly dance of death. I knew that the two friends Osbert and Aedgart would already be in time with both me and each other. My first victim started in horror at the blade which seemed to sing as it sank towards him hacking down his neck and into his chest. The second one was a lucky hit for I caught the next fellow on the upswing, the edge slicing upwards from his chin. Osbert and Aedgart were equally successful and those behind, using swords and spears, were also winning their combats. We were deep in their lines and the terror was everywhere. I saw Egbert two ranks ahead of me. Even as I swung my blade, I was able to detach my thoughts from what I was doing. Egbert should have been in the front rank as Ridley and me but instead, he had a wall of bodies before him. I wondered why I had grown up living in such fear of a bully, a cowardly bully at that.

The warrior before me was so intent upon my blade that he lost his footing and fell. I stamped on his face as I passed knowing that he would be despatched by the men behind. I heard his gurgle of death as I chopped through the shield of the man who stood before my axe. He stabbed at my chest with his sword. Had he aimed at my arm he may have hurt me but although the blade penetrated some links and I saw a tendril of blood seep out it was but a scratch. His brave attempt to hurt me cost him his life as my backswing struck his outstretched neck and his head bounced along the traitor's front rank.

Then I was face to face with Egbert who suddenly seemed quite small. He too had his axe out but I knew that he was not confident. The blade was clean whereas mine dripped blood and gore. His armour, for he was the first I had seen who had donned armour before fighting, was shining.

He had not fought this day and I had been fighting for hours. He should have had the advantage of being fresher but I knew that I was a warrior, a Housecarl and he was not.

He sneered, "Runt! "And swung his axe at me. I easily countered and smiled as the sliver of wood was sliced from the axe's haft.

"How embarrassing for you Egbert if you are killed this day by the runt!"

I swung my axe at his arm and he hurriedly changed his angle. Again, another sliver slipped from the ash and he took a step backwards. He looked in horror as though I might whittle the handle down to a toothpick. To me, it seemed as though we were alone fighting in limbo. There were other combats around us, for the wedge had lost cohesion as our enemies fell before us, but all I could see was Egbert. He was becoming afraid, I could see it in his eyes and he became impatient to end this duel which he had felt he would win easily. His impatience meant he made mistakes. Instead of the natural swing of the axe, in a figure of eight diagonally across the body, he made the cardinal error of a flat swing intended to decapitate me. It is the easiest blow to face for you drop your knees and lower your head. Even as I ducked, Death Bringer was slicing upwards. It ripped through his mail as though it were not there and tore into his stomach. For a brief moment, I saw his breakfast. His eyes, already losing life looked down to the entrails and guts pouring onto the ground and Egbert, my half brother died at my feet at the battle of Stamford Bridge.

The emotion of the moment, tiredness and the fact that our enemies moved swiftly away at the death of one of their leaders meant that we halted to regain our breath. Osbert slapped an arm across my back. "That was the finest axe work I have ever seen. It seemed to be part of you."

I looked at the blade, "Death Bringer is a fine weapon and it is now Brother Killer too."

Suddenly I heard a scream as Edward appeared from nowhere. He had a sword held in two hands and screamed at me. "Today the Runt will die!"

He swiped the sword two handed at one of my men who stood before me and I saw the blade cut deeply into his leg and the warrior fell to the ground. I just had time to drop my axe and swing my shield around as Edward aimed the next blow at me. I had seen the arc of his swing and anticipated the blow. It cracked off my shield but I could see that my brother had mistimed it and he had jarred his arm. I drew my sword and waved the others away. "He is mine, look to the rest and do not interfere. It is wyrd!" I grinned at him. "I hope that you have made peace with God, brother for you will be seeing him or the devil soon."

"You are the bastard's spawn and you will die."

His next blow I took on my shield and I leisurely hacked at his leg below the knee. I did not use my full power but the blood spurted. "That is for Aethelward."

I saw him almost cry and then he hacked at me again. The blow was better timed but I took it on my shield and sliced it into his mail shirt along his ribs with a side cut. The dark mark showed the blood. "And that is for Nanna."

He was screaming like a child and I heard Osbert say sadly, "Finish it, my lord."

His last swing was an overhead hack, aimed at my helmet and had he struck me he would have split my fine helmet but I was ready and my blade plunged into his chest, twisting as it entered. "And this is for my mother, for you were complicit in her death, killer of women." His face was close to mine and I watched the hatred and anger turn to shock as he knew that he was dying. I pushed him from my sword and he slid to the ground. Two of my brothers were now dead.

I took the time to look around the battlefield. I could see that Tostig and Hadrada were surrounded. To my right, Ridley had also halted and before us were the remnants of Egbert's men and the other traitors. Behind me, I could see that Osgar, Wolf and the others were struggling to finish off Tostig and Hadrada. The men fighting with the King and the Earl were the elite of the army and they did not die easily. "Ridley, keep after those traitors. Topcliffe! Wedge! Branton, get your archers. It is time for arrow work."

The men were bone-weary. They would struggle to lift their arms. I checked to see that the wedge was in formation. Branton appeared at my shoulder with Boar Splitter in his hand. "Thought you might need this lucky spear, my lord."

"Thank you, Branton." I pointed at Hadrada. "When you get the chance try for the King it might take the heart out of his men and save the lives of some of ours."

"It will be a pleasure, my lord."

"Topcliffe! Forward!"

As we marched forwards I looked to see where the Housecarls were struggling. I could see that Osgar and Wolf only had three warriors behind them. It seemed appropriate that we should aid my companions of the shield wall. "Osgar! Wolf! Wedge coming behind." Both men were engaged in deadly combat and could neither acknowledge us nor turn to see us. Our manoeuvre would rely on my timing. Branton, his archers and his slingers could see our point of arrival and they began to rain missiles on those behind, in the third and fourth tightly packed ranks. Had the warriors had armour the arrows would have been an inconvenience but without armour and using the shields to protect against the Housecarls it simply resulted in carnage. Wolf and Osgar moved forwards slightly as the pressure eased. I headed for the point between their shoulders. Knowing that I was arriving meant that when they felt my shield and saw Boar Splitter appear, they moved apart slightly and I stabbed forwards, my blade striking a shield and sliding up into the unprotected throat of a Norseman. Stepping forwards, I saw that it was Wolf and Osgar who were beside me.

"Just like old times eh Aelfraed."

"Aye, it is that. Now let us get this finished I have a thirst upon me."

It was indeed like old times and the fresh men helped to puncture the shield wall a little more. Wolf and Osgar were using their swords but they were using them like spears, pointing and stabbing over the edge of their shields. In contrast, the Norse shields were riddled with cut marks and I began to punch the boss of my shield against my opponents. I saw the look of horror on his face as he saw the cracks appear. I redoubled my efforts, all the time probing with Boar Splitter. With a sudden crack, a piece fell from the end of his shield and Wolf's blade slid through the gap to stab into his unprotected chest. We were close to Hadrada and I stabbed forwards to get closer to him. Suddenly something flew above my head and I saw one of Branton's goose tipped arrows strike him squarely in the throat. He stood transfixed for a moment and then crumpled to the ground as though the life had been sucked from him. There was a collective wail of despair as the most famous Viking of all time, the man who would later be called the Last Viking, succumbed not to a blade in single combat or even an axe, but an arrow from a lowly archer.

His men retreated around the body, protecting it with their shields. Their brave defence of their liege lord made our task even easier and soon we were despatching the badly wounded, who refused to give up their defence. Before I had time to check on my men I turned to see Sweyn stride up to Earl Tostig as he killed the last of the men who stood before them. Tostig, like my brother, was armoured and had not fought in the front rank. Like my brother, his blade was clean and he was facing an exhausted opponent. No man stirred to help Sweyn and yet I knew beyond all doubt that he would defeat the traitor. I could see the fear and resignation on his face. I could almost read the thoughts which said he should have accepted his half brother's offer instead he was fighting a warrior whom he knew could defeat him.

Sweyn's shield was around his back and he was wielding his axe. Tostig had his shield and a sword. It was an unfair fight and Tostig, who was an experienced warrior, should have been able to deal with the oldest warrior in the English ranks but he did not. The shield parry was half-hearted and the backswing of the axe caused sparks and pieces of metal to fly from the renegade's sword. Sweyn was pushing forwards and Tostig was struggling to keep his feet. Had he stood he might have had a chance but he was so busy watching his feet that he did not block the axe blow which broke his arm. The shield dropped, still attached to his arm by a leather strap. He desperately tried to raise the sword and block the axe but the blade slid along the sword and with no shield to stop it sliced into the neck of Earl Tostig. The momentum carried the blade through and the half-severed head fell to one side before dropping to the floor. As the rest of the army saw their leaders fall they began to flee.

I was just about to shout, '*After them,*' when I heard a wail from Branton. "My lord, behind us!"

I turned and saw Eystein Orri and the guards from the boats, fully armed and armoured racing towards the rear rank of the Housecarls. "Ridley, Ulf, turn! Shield wall!"

We had little time to ready ourselves other than to lock shields and prepare to meet what the Norse later called Orri's Storm. I do not know, but I believe that Orri must have seen his future father in law fall to Branton's arrow for they came at us with unbelievable fury. We barely had time to raise our shields. They were not in a cohesive mass and came at us piecemeal; none the less they were a handful. I heard a cry to my left of '*Coxold*' and knew that Ridley had seen our dilemma and was bringing the right flank to aid us. I hoped they would reach us in time for Sweyn and the Housecarls were almost spent. The first warrior to attack me had outrun Orri and he slashed at my spear with his sword. Sparks flew as the metal crashed. I punched at his shield and he spun around slightly. I was regretting my spear for, with his sword he could get in closer, but I knew that as soon as I dropped Boar Splitter, he would gut me. I had to close with him and I did something he did not expect. I stabbed down on his foot with the spear and pinned it to the ground. Pulling my dagger from behind my shield I pushed forwards so that he fell to the ground. I am a big man and heavy as well, our combined weight took us both downwards and his foot was ripped in two by my spear. As he opened his mouth to scream I rammed my dagger into his open mouth and he died. I leapt to my feet looking for my next opponent as I drew my own sword. Luckily for us and sadly for some of them, they had run from Riccall in mail armour carrying shield and axe on the hottest September day any of us could remember, as we watched some of them died on their feet as their hearts gave out but the rest still fought in fierce anger. They were brave and tough warriors and we had the hardest fighting of the whole day. It was like drunken men trying to fight each other wielding weapons which seemed inordinately heavy.

We were spread out more now and two warriors advanced on me. My fine helmet and mail marked me as a lord and I think they both sought glory. They were older men and they split up to come at me from two directions. The worst thing to do in that situation was to allow them to dictate the pace and I began the fight. I feinted at one while I punched the other with my shield. He had not expected that and tumbled over; before I could finish him off I felt a pain in my right leg and turned to see the first warrior twisting his sword as he pulled it out. The delay cost him his life as I sliced across his throat my own blade. I felt a blow to my back as the fallen warrior struck me and I fell to the ground. I rolled over and readied my sword only to see him loom over me with sword raised to finish me off. Branton's arrow struck him, as it had Hadrada in the throat, and he fell to the floor.

Branton and Osbert raced over to me. I looked at them in surprise. As they supported me I shook them away, "The wound to my leg is nothing."

Osbert took his hand from my back and showed it to me. It was sticky with blood, "The wound to your back is, my lord." His face filled with concern as he shouted, "Topcliffe!"

My men formed a defensive circle around me and the archers shot any who approached. Branton raced down to the river while Aedgart took the tunic from a dead warrior and tore it into strips. He quickly bound my leg tightly and I felt a burning as the effect of the wound grew. Branton came back with moss from a tree and I felt him and his brother pack the soft material along my back and then they bound strips of cloth around it.

Suddenly the wound felt cooler and I felt the water drip slowly down my back.

"The battle still goes on. Osbert and Aedgart take the lead and I will follow."

They both looked at me doubtfully, "While any remain, I will stand." Using Boar Splitter as a staff we made our way to where Eystein was engaged in combat with Ridley's men. The men of Coxold were struggling to stem the tide of fresh warriors. I patted Osbert on the shoulder, "Charge them." He looked at me. "Now!"

"Very well my lord, Topcliffe let us gut these Norse swine."

They charged forwards and I hobbled along afterwards. My archers shot their last few arrows into the melee but I noticed that Branton kept them close to me in a protective circle. I could see that Ridley was engaged in hand to hand combat with Orri. They were well matched but Ridley was using a one-handed axe, the one favoured by the Franks, and he was able to use his shield. Orri had a sword and I was in no doubt that even a tired Ridley would prevail. The Norwegian was a fine swordsman and I winced as I saw the backslash which opened Ridley's mail. The blood did not gush and I hoped that it was a flesh wound such as I had suffered. Ridley's axe began to pound relentlessly on the shield of the Norseman and I could see it splintering. When it went, it shattered and the blade continued through to slice off Eystein's hand and arm. He tried to carry on bravely but when Ridley countered his next blow with his shield he had no defence against the axe which sliced him through the middle. With him died the hopes of the Norse and we had finally won. I sank to my knees and smiled as Ridley hobbled over. Even as I opened my mouth to compliment on his victory, I fell forward and my world suddenly became black.

Chapter 14

I dreamt of Nanna and I fought a dragon to protect her; I was chased by my brothers each wielding an axe and I could not move fast enough to escape them; I found myself on a high mountain in Wales looking down on a host of Vikings and then I was falling, down and down. Suddenly I felt Nanna's hand and heard her voice coo, "Come back my love, come back" and the world seemed peaceful once more.

When I awoke, I expected to be in heaven. I looked up and saw wooden boards above my head which seemed a strange decoration for a celestial palace. Then I heard a voice next to me, a familiar voice, Aethelward's, "You are awake at last. We thought we had lost you."

I tried to raise myself up but a pain coursed through my body and I sank back, my eyes closed to ease the pain.

"You will still need to rest, nephew, for you nearly died."

I opened my eyes again and saw his face. As my eyes lowered I saw that his arm was bandaged too. "What happened? Where am I?"

"Before I start on that story there are some people who need to see you for they have been waiting for some days for this moment." He moved away and a door opened.

Suddenly there was a sea of familiar faces, Thomas and Sarah, Osbert, Branton and, of course, my faithful friend Ridley. My three comrades all sported wounds whilst Sarah was tearful. She reached out and touched my hands, "Thank the Lord for that. They are warm. They were so cold, my lord, that I thought you were dead." She kissed them, "I will bring you soup for we need to build up your strength."

Thomas smiled as she left, "She and Lord Aethelward have both been at your side for days my lord. It was, as my wife said, a hard time, for you looked like death. I am glad that you have returned to us and now I will leave you with your comrades."

Ridley and Osbert looked tearful. "What is the matter? Is there some bad news I do not yet know?"

Ridley shook his head, his voice sounding choked, "It is just that we feel we let you down. We are your men and we did not protect you."

I shook my head and smiled, I had feared that something had happened to Gytha, "My dear Ridley you are a lord and you have your own men."

He looked very seriously at me. "No master, I have a title but I will always be your man."

I turned to Branton and Osbert, "And you two have no reason to castigate yourselves. You fought as bravely as you could and the blow to my back was wyrd."

Osbert shook his head, "No my lord we should have stayed with you but the heat of the battle was upon me and my blade sang."

"That is because you are a warrior. And where is my other warrior, Aedgart?"

Osbert's face clouded over. "He fell protecting you my lord and died at Stamford. It was a good death."

I nodded. He had died as a warrior should with a blade in his hand. I was sad for his passing but pleased with the manner. Sarah and Thomas returned with a bowl of soup and some of her freshly baked bread. I suddenly realised that I was hungry. My comrades helped me to sit up but pain ripped through me and I winced.

"The wound will take time to heal properly, nephew. It went to the bone. But it is healing, slowly."

"Tell me all as I eat. What happened to Harold, my father and brother? Does Gytha know and what of the Normans?"

They all laughed at the usual torrent of questions that poured from my lips. "We could be here a long time then Aelfraed. Let me answer the questions in the correct order. King Harold has left for the south for we had a message that the Normans had landed. He promised to tell Gytha of your wound on the way and I sent those of your men who were fit enough to go with him and escort her back here." His face darkened, "As for the traitorous Edwin and Edgar." He rubbed his wounded arm. "I searched for them on the field and first I found Edwin. The craven coward begged for his life and swore allegiance to King Harold; as though anyone would trust the turncoat snake. I killed him where he cowered. My sister was avenged but your brother Edgar is every bit as dishonourable as your father and attacked me from behind. Luckily, he is as incompetent as he is sly and the blade merely pierced my arm. My sword took his head and we left them on the field for the birds and foxes to devour. You are now Lord of Medelai as well."

I had not thought that through. With the rest of my family dead, I was indeed master of one of the largest estates in Northumbria. "But I thought you were master?"

"No Aelfraed, I held it for a short time whilst Edwin and the others were traitors. No Harold insisted that it was yours. Fear not for me. The King has promised me estates of my own."

"And the King himself?"

"We finished off the remains of the invaders and pursued the survivors to Riccall. There were but twenty-four boats needed to take them back to Norway. I think the Norse threat is over. I do not think they will venture south again in our lifetime. The King then received the news of the Normans and hurried south to meet them."

"Wolf, Osgar and Ulf?"

Aethelward laughed. "They live. They would have come with us, were the need of England not greater."

"But we lost so many men. Will he have enough to face Duke William?"

Aethelward shrugged. "The Housecarls were intact but the forces of Mercia and Northumbria which Harold had counted upon were too weak to follow."

I suddenly realised what my uncle's presence meant; Harold did not have his strategos and the army did not have their lucky charm. I was distraught. Had their concern for me cost the King his throne? "Uncle, why did you not accompany the King? He will need your advice, now more so than ever."

"My wound was bad enough to keep me here anyway and I would have slowed them down. I suppose I could have followed but I felt my place was here with you for I was responsible for you fighting that day."

"You? How do you come to that conclusion?"

"Had I not trained you to be a warrior then you would have remained at Medelai and never fought. Now you would be the Thegn of Medelai without the wounds which cover your body."

"No uncle. If you had not come to Medelai and trained me then when Nanna died I would have left home to seek my fortune away from that nest of vipers."

"Besides I promised your mother that I would watch over you and I neglected that for many years. I was too wrapped up in the glory of combat. And now that you have finished your meal you need to rest. I will ride over to Medelai with Osbert and inform the Steward of his new master."

"It might be wise to leave Osbert there to keep an eye on that one for I trust him not and when I am well I will appoint another Steward whom I can trust."

"Your wounds have given you wisdom nephew."

I was tired and I lay back but sleep eluded me for a while as I absorbed all this new information that had come my way. I had thought that I had died; the fact that I breathed seemed a reprieve somehow and I wondered if wyrd had caused the bones to fall the way they had. Was it a new chance for me? Were Gytha and I about to embark on a happier time? I yearned for her next to me but, at the same time, I wished to be walking for she would fret and fuss at my present state. I realised that I did not know how many days it had been since the battle. Was she already on her way north? As I drifted into a deep sleep I resolved to heal myself faster.

The next day I received another visit from Ridley who had also been wounded. I had not had time to talk to him the previous day and I had not even noticed his wound. He told me that he had wanted to go with the Housecarls to fight the Normans but he had few men at arms left and his wound would have slowed him down. "When I saw you lying in that pool of blood, I thought you were dead. I became so angry I wanted to kill all of the Norse on my own. Later, when I saw how few of my faithful men of Coxold remained, I felt guilty that they had followed me and died because of my anger. This leadership is a double-edged blade is it not?"

"Aye old friend, life was easier when we were Housecarls."

"When I watched Wolf and Osgar march off with the King I wished I was with them. Does that make me a bad lord?"

"No Ridley for you are a warrior first and a lord second."

We talked for a long time about all that we had done until Sarah tut-tutted her way in and almost threw a grinning Ridley out. My Sarah was a force of nature alright.

I was on my feet two days later; much to the annoyance of Sarah who hovered nearby like a mother watching her bairn walk for the first time. I used Boar Splitter to help me but Thomas left to cut me a better one for Boar Splitter had suffered in the battle and needed repair. I would have to give it to Ralph to have the head reshaped and sharpened.

As I stepped out into the October sunlight my men at arms who remained and were practising with Branton gave a huge roar as they saw me. It did my heart good to see their loyalty. I wondered how many men had been sent to London for there looked to be remarkably few left.

I had learned from Aethelward that I had been unconscious for three days which meant that it was now five days since the battle. The wound on my back had become itchy which Aethelward took to be a good sign for it meant the wound was healing. I could not see that wound but each time Sarah dressed it and applied a fresh poultice, I heard the intake of breath as she viewed it. The concern on her face made me glad that I could not see it. The wound on my leg was angry and it too itched but, unlike my uncle's leg wound, it did not appear permanent and I exercised each day to make it stronger. I had adopted a hunched walk for it was easier on my back. My uncle and Sarah allowed this for a few days but then my uncle chastised me. "If you want to be a hunchbacked cripple for the rest of your days then continue to walk as you do but if you would lead your men again then straighten you back."

I gritted my teeth and slowly stretched. At first, I thought that I would do it painlessly but suddenly a sharp pain seemed to rip through my body as though I had been struck again. "Aargh!"

"There will be pain. Believe me, I know from my leg but the pain will lessen. You must persevere."

I was about to tell Aethelward that the pain was too much when Sarah said, quietly, "It will worry the Lady Gytha less if you walk with a straight back my lord. Your uncle is right although it pains me to see you so distressed."

With the thought of Gytha in my mind, I tried again. It was painful but I bore it knowing that the result would be that Gytha would be less worried and she had enough on her mind with the birth of our first child but a few months away.

"Come, Aelfraed, let us go to the river."

I hobbled after my uncle. Had Edward been alive how he would have mocked the two cripples and that thought helped me through the barrier of pain. Branton and my archers followed, intrigued. When we reached the river, I wondered why my uncle had brought me. "Take all your clothes off."

"But uncle it is cold!"

He laughed, "Are you a woman? I want you to take your clothes off and lie in the river."

I was puzzled. Branton and some of the archers had wandered over, partly to protect us and partly out of curiosity. "Why?"

"When I hurt my leg, some monks did this with my wound and it helped to heal me. I admit it was easier to put just one leg in the water but if you will try to fight two men at once this is the result."

If it had worked for my uncle, then I would try it for I was determined to be well again sooner rather than later. When I was naked, I felt foolish. There is something about a man being naked which makes him try to cover his manhood it was one of the things I had always wondered about berserkers- how could they have fought naked? I saw my men grin at my discomfort and heard my uncle say, "We have all got one, besides nephew, the moment you step into the water it will shrivel up and disappear inside your body so get on with it."

I stepped into the water which was flowing swiftly. I knew that this bank was quite shallow and relatively safe but even so the shock of the water on my feet was like a blow from a war hammer. Branton unstrung his bow and reached it out so that I could hold one end and balance better.

"Keep going until it is up to your knees!"

I glared at Aethelward. He had no idea just how cold it was! I obeyed him and faithful Branton also stepped into the water. When it reached my knees, I found that I could not feel my feet.

"Now sit down in the water!"

Sitting was an excruciating agony for I had to bend my back. That pain was replaced by the shock of my buttocks hitting the icy stream. It was as painful as the wound.

"Now lower yourself. Help him, Branton. Just keep your head above water and try to relax."

That was easier said than done but I managed to recline myself, grateful for Branton and the other archers who were either side of me. Branton managed to look sympathetically at me and nodded encouragingly. Strangely that helped and soon I found the pain from my back disappearing as my whole body became numb. I wondered how long I would have to stay there. I had no idea how long it was. It felt like an age but there was nothing to measure it by. Eventually, I heard my uncle, "Right lads help him up."

As we reached the bank he placed my tunic over my body and I felt a fire permeate my skin. It was a strange, although not unpleasant, sensation. I could see that my legs and body were blue; I had never seen anything like that before although when we were in the high passes of Wales amongst the snow I had seen warriors with blue fingers. As we walked back to the castle I found that I could move easier and the pain was not as bad as it had been hitherto. Once next to the fire I felt tired but better than I had since I had woken days earlier.

"Now if you do that every morning you will find that you will heal quicker."

"How does it work?" For work it did.

Aethelward shrugged, "I have no idea but as the monks taught it to me perhaps it comes from God."

Gytha reached home on St Paulinus' day, October the tenth. I was now walking much better for it was almost fourteen nights since the battle. One of the riders accompanying her had ridden hard to warn us so that the whole household was there to greet my bride. She was still riding despite the fact that she had a large bump which was my unborn child. She had a look of concern on her face which told me that she had interrogated my men and found out about my wounds. I tried to walk as easily as I could and made sure I did not use a stick. Branton hovered by my weaker right side, ready to support me should I falter.

I threw my arms around her and kissed her long and hard. "Oh, my love," she sobbed, "I heard you were almost killed."

I stepped back a little and opened my arms. "Do I look as though I am dead?"

"No, but I can see that you are drawn and thin. I know that Goody Sarah would have fed you well so there is a tale to tell here." She noticed Aethelward for the first time. "It is good to see you, my lord."

Sarah took charge. "The two of you get off your feet and get inside. I will bring some food for you. Now come on Branton help them into the warm." Thomas stood there with a look of pride and resignation as his wife told the lord and lady of the manor what to do. Shaking his head, he went to see to the horses.

Once we had been fed she demanded to see my wound. "But we have just eaten!"

"And Sarah insisted that we eat immediately but I have spent the last one hundred and ninety-one miles worrying about you my husband and I want to see the wound!"

I showed her my leg. She gasped. "There," I said, "nothing for you to worry about."

"No, my husband, show me your back!"

I cursed my soldiers and then relented. Gytha was a forceful woman and she was their mistress' they could not have denied her. I stripped off and turned. She gasped in horror and when I turned I saw her eyes were huge with tears. "It is healing." I reassured her.

"But how could you survive? It is enormous and runs down your back!"

I shrugged. "I have not seen it and I cannot judge but my uncle and Sarah are pleased with the progress and it hurts less every day." As I dressed I asked her, "And the child is he well?"

She giggled, "How do you know that it is a he? It may be a girl."

"I care not so long as it is healthy with the correct number of fingers and toes."

We both laughed and suddenly all tension was gone and we were as were before I had left to fight the Norse. We shared our mutual news. She was astounded to know that we now had two manors. "I have not learned how to manage one, let alone two."

"We will learn and we are lucky with Thomas and Sarah for they are invaluable. What of Harold and the Normans?"

Her face darkened. "I believe they had spies somewhere for they landed within a day or so of the King marching north. The Queen did her best and raised the fyrd and mobilised the local lords but without the King, there was no one to take charge. When he returned, it was as though a weight had gone from us but when I saw the pitiful state of the men, they were exhausted, then I feared for him. The Queen said that he was going down to the Lewis country for he knew that land well and she said he would fight, what was the word? Ah yes, that was the phrase, a defensive battle."

"Good, that is welcome news."

She looked puzzled. "Why is that good news? He will still have to fight."

"Yes, my love but the Normans have horses and can be mobile. They will find it hard to defeat him if he finds a good site, like a hill." I suddenly realised that if the King won then we would have to fight again. My face fell.

It was as though she could read my thoughts. "You will have to fight again will you not?"

"Aye, unless the King can totally destroy the Normans and even then the Duke will not leave for we are a rich prize which is worth fighting for. However, if Harold is defeated then he can come north where we have the might of Mercia and Northumbria to resist the invader. With Harold and Aethelward together again we can defeat Duke William. So long as Harold Godwinson is King then England shall live."

"But you are not ready to fight yet."

"No, but in the spring I will be and that is when we would be needed. So, I will be able to see the birth of my child and, perhaps I will not need to fight. However, we will prepare. I have already sent out instructions for Osbert and Branton to begin recruiting men to replace those who fell. Fortunately, we have much armour from the battlefield and we now have more money. We will be able to afford a better army and we will bloody the Norman's nose."

I could see that she was not convinced but then, why should she? She was not privy, as I was to the politics of power. I wondered if my whole life was preparing me for the challenge that we would now face.

A few days later, following much love and care from Gytha saw me fit enough to mount a horse. I had to use the mounting step which I had built for Gytha but it enabled me to sit astride my horse again. The true test would be when I tried to move. My experience in the water had shown me that some pain was necessary to move forward and I kicked hard on my horse. The jolting motion sent shock waves of pain up my spine. I gritted my teeth and rode in circles around the yard. To my immense relief, the pain did not worsen, it did not lessen either, but it was a pain I could live with. The following day Ridley, Aethelward and I rode to Medelai. I had a new Steward in mind, Thomas had recommended a farmer who had too many sons and would benefit from having an estate to run allowing his sons to continue their farming without conflict between them. The problem would be when I told Oswin of his fate. I took Ridley with me for he was Oswin's son and I did not wish to do anything behind his back.

Osbert had sent me daily messages about the estate and I knew that I would have no surprises there. What did shock me was the state of Oswin who appeared to have aged almost overnight. His hair was now pure white and he looked emaciated and old. I glanced over to Ridley and saw that he too was shocked by his father's appearance. It was now obvious to me that, even if I wanted to, I could not allow Oswin to remain in charge.

I dismounted with some difficulty and wondered how I would remount without a mounting step. That was a bridge I would have to cross later. "Oswin. You have heard the news of the lord and my brothers?"

"Yes, my lord."

"And you know that makes me the new lord of the manor?"

His eyes flashed anger, briefly and then he nodded, "Yes my lord."

"I believe that we need a change of Steward to take things forward." I softened my voice, "There has been a history Oswin and I would not wish to cause you pain. I will be sending over the new Steward on the morrow."

He nodded and said dully, "Yes my lord."

This was difficult; if he had been angry then it would have helped me but this dull acceptance was harder to deal with. "Have you anywhere to go?"

Before he could answer I heard Ridley say, "He can come with me and live at Coxold." Ridley had indeed grown up. I glanced at him and he nodded. "If you wish to come, father?"

It was the word 'father', I think which made the old man burst into tears. It took us all by surprise and being men we all looked away. Had Gytha or Sarah been there then they would have known what to do. "I would like that, Ridley, my son."

Later as we rode back to Topcliffe with Ridley and his father in a cart following, Aethelward turned to me. "You have grown nephew. That was well handled. I can see that my work here is done."

"You are leaving?"

"Aye, my wounds are healed and I will leave by the end of the week. King Harold will need all the advisers he can get."

"But I thought we would not be needed before the spring."

"Whatever happens when Harold and William meet the loser will not go home. If William wins then Harold will continue to fight and will need me. If Harold wins then the Duke cannot go home so long as there is a chance to capture this precious jewel of ours."

"I will tell Gytha that..."

He suddenly snapped, "You are not coming. Your wound would not enable you to fight. I do not need to fight, I am a strategos. You must build up your forces here so that when the King needs them you will be ready."

The storm abated and he smiled, I grinned back, "Yes my lord!"

Gytha too was upset when she heard that Aethelward was leaving but we threw a feast for him and invited Ridley, Osbert and Branton to say goodbye. Branton had been out hunting with his archers and brought a multitude of fine animals. Sarah had brewed a particularly potent ale and cooked up the last of the fruit which had fallen to make a pudding which was laced with honey and mead. It was a fine feast, all the better for the fact that we enjoyed it in our own home with friends. Gytha's face was a picture of happiness as she presided over her gaggle of warriors. Sarah fussed and fretted over her lady and the food while poor Thomas was rushed off his feet and ordered around by his wife. Had she been a man she would have been a Sweyn and we would all have feared him!

Perhaps it was the joyousness of the night that made the interruption so dramatic. One of the sentries rushed in just as we had finished the pudding, "My lord I am sorry but there is a messenger from the King!"

I waved away his apology, "Send him in Aidan."

I could see that Aethelward had suddenly sobered up and that the others looked puzzled. The rider who came in was muddied and bloodied. Aethelward recognised him immediately. "Aedgar of Coventry what news?"

His face was filled with anguish as he said, "King Harold is dead with all his Housecarls and many lords. Duke William and his Normans have won."

"Sarah, get this man some food. Sit down, sir, before you fall."

The man did so. "I have ridden all the way from London with the news and I fear that my horse will go no further." He greedily quaffed the ale and tore into the leg of the partridge. He told us the tale through his meal. "The King and his Housecarls were on the top of Senlac Hill, close by Hastings and the abbey. The Normans charged but could not even dint the shield wall and then the fyrd thought that the Normans were retreating and chased after them. They were slaughtered and then the Housecarls were surrounded. The King and his brothers died but the men refused to surrender and they died to a man."

Wolf, Osgar, Ulf and Sweyn and all our other comrades, dead! I looked at Aethelward. "What do we do?"

Aethelward waved the question away with an irritated flick of his wrist. "What of Ealdgyth and, Edgar the Aetheling?"

"They are safe and they are heading for Jorvik. The Queen has two young babes with her."

I saw the sympathy in Gytha's face. "Has a messenger also gone to Jorvik?"

"Yes, my lord. Those of us who were guarding the Queen were divided into guards for the Aetheling and messengers to spread the word north."

Aethelward looked at me. "I will need to visit the Earls tomorrow." To Aedgar he asked, "Where is the royal party now?"

He shrugged. "We rode hard but I would imagine that they would be at Lincoln."

"Aelfraed you will need to send Osbert and your men to protect the Queen."

"Of course." There was something else in his face which made me wonder for he had looked at me differently. I knew him well enough to know that he would not speak in public and I waited until we were alone.

He stood at the tower above the gate and looked south as though he could see the battle. I joined him. "All our friends…"

"Yes, Aelfraed but they died protecting their lord; they will be with him now in the halls of the heroes." It was interesting that the veneer of Christianity was just that for warriors, a thin layer that disappeared once they died in battle. He looked at me. "It is what I dreaded. If only Morcar and Edwin had been better warriors, then Harold could have stayed in the south and defeated William on the beaches."

"Yes uncle, but had you been here with them then they might have had advice which could have saved them."

"I agree Aelfraed, but I thought they had you and you could have advised them."

I was shocked. "But I am young and they would not have listened to me anyway. I did try."

"I know and I am not blaming you but the King and I hoped that your strength and wisdom, young as you are would have been enough. I am now worried that our two young Earls will not listen to me either."

"Oh, surely not! Everyone knows that you were the King's, right-hand man."

"Aye and the King is dead."

"What of the Aetheling?"

"He may be the son of Harold and a potential heir but he is still a boy. The two Earls will mould his destiny unless the Queen can use her influence with her brothers."

We stood in silence. My world had suddenly been turned upside down. I had met the Normans and they were a cruel race. The battle had been lost but there was a war to win. "Uncle, when the messenger gave his news you gave me a strange look. There is something you have yet to tell me is there not?"

He looked very sad and very old as he put his arm around my shoulder and drew me to him. "There is my sister son. Your father died at Senlac Hill. Your real father, not the snake who had your mother killed for laying with him."

Suddenly many things became clear; the way the Housecarls had accepted me, the ease with which I had joined them. "My father was a Housecarl?"

"No Aelfraed, your father was Harold Godwinson, King of England."

The End

Historical note

In Anglo-Saxon times a man swore an oath on his testicles as in 'to testify'. The assumption was if you lied, you had your testicles removed. Certainly, a compelling argument for speaking the truth! So, when Aelfraed swears his loyalty, it is more serious and binding than we might believe an oath to be. Harold did indeed capture and ultimately kill the only King of the Welsh by sailing to North Wales and defeating him. Cynan Ap Iago did regain his father's kingdom. I have no evidence that he resided at Gruffyd's court but it seemed a reasonable idea. King Harold did marry Ealdgyth soon afterwards but the way it has been described in the book is fiction.

The Archbishop of Canterbury was a Norman as were many of the senior churchmen but, as far as I know, there was no attempt on his life but to the Saxons, the Normans were the villains!

The events at the Battle of Fulford were as described. The two Earls placed immovable barriers on their flanks and that cost them the battle. They allowed Hadrada to claim the high ground and he fed in his troops piecemeal. The ones who arrived on the field first were lighter armed and less experienced warriors and Morcar defeated them but pushed on too much. When the better warriors arrived, they attacked the two Earls and both Earls fled to York. It is estimated that there were ten thousand warriors against the Earls' six thousand. The two Earls retreated to York and were besieged by Hadrada. I do not know who commanded the centre but it appears that whoever did, lasted a little longer than those on the flanks.

One aspect of the two battles, Stamford Bridge and Fulford which has always puzzled me is how close in time they were to each other. According to the Chronicles they were but five days apart and as it took Harold that length of time to reach the north then he must have set out before the battle which is why I created the scenario of a messenger heading south as soon as the Norse are sighted.

As far as I know, no one harried the Norse fleet but Aelfraed, our hero was in the right place at the right time and it is the sort of thing he would have done. As for his promotion to be a Thegn; before the Normans came then manors were given and taken by the king and his earls whenever they saw fit. William carried on, in the same way, rewarding his knights with the land occupied by the dead Thegns.

The battle of Stamford Bridge is also as described in the Anglo-Saxon Chronicles. The army of Harold did indeed find the Norse sunning themselves by the river and those on the west bank were slaughtered. Between one and three Norse warriors held off the English killing forty warriors. Some accounts have them as berserkers and I took this as my model for it explained how they could continue to fight even though outnumbered and wounded. Their sacrifice enabled the Norse to form a shield wall even though few had had time to put on their armour. The King did apparently offer Tostig his earldom and the offer he made to Hadrada is, word for word, what the Anglo-Saxon Chronicles at the time reported. Tostig and Hadrada were surrounded and the Norse king was killed with an arrow to the throat. How Tostig died we do not know. Eystein Orri did indeed run with his warriors all the way from Riccall- a heck of a feat! They were in full armour and many did indeed drop dead of exhaustion. Their charge was known as Orri's storm. The survivors only needed 24 boats and they returned to Orkney. Hadrada was called the Last of the Vikings and this was the last time they posed a threat to the western world.

After the battle, Harold heard that William had landed and raced south but he had lost so many lords and warriors that the army which faced William was a shadow of its former self and as they had marched over four hundred miles in a short time, they were exhausted. Even so, I still believe that had the fyrd not run then William would have been defeated for the Housecarls were a fearsome force.

Griff Hosker
December 2016

Other books by Griff Hosker

If you enjoyed reading this book, then why not read another one by the author?

Ancient History

The Sword of Cartimandua Series
(Germania and Britannia 50 A.D. – 128 A.D.)
Ulpius Felix- Roman Warrior (prequel)
The Sword of Cartimandua
The Horse Warriors
Invasion Caledonia
Roman Retreat
Revolt of the Red Witch
Druid's Gold
Trajan's Hunters
The Last Frontier
Hero of Rome
Roman Hawk
Roman Treachery
Roman Wall
Roman Courage

The Wolf Warrior series
(Britain in the late 6th Century)
Saxon Dawn
Saxon Revenge
Saxon England
Saxon Blood
Saxon Slayer
Saxon Slaughter
Saxon Bane
Saxon Fall: Rise of the Warlord
Saxon Throne
Saxon Sword

Medieval History

The Dragon Heart Series
Viking Slave
Viking Warrior
Viking Jarl
Viking Kingdom
Viking Wolf
Viking War
Viking Sword
Viking Wrath
Viking Raid
Viking Legend
Viking Vengeance
Viking Dragon
Viking Treasure
Viking Enemy
Viking Witch
Viking Blood
Viking Weregeld
Viking Storm
Viking Warband
Viking Shadow
Viking Legacy
Viking Clan
Viking Bravery

The Norman Genesis Series
Hrolf the Viking
Horseman
The Battle for a Home
Revenge of the Franks
The Land of the Northmen
Ragnvald Hrolfsson
Brothers in Blood
Lord of Rouen
Drekar in the Seine
Duke of Normandy
The Duke and the King

Danelaw
(England and Denmark in the 11th Century)
Dragon Sword
Oathsword

New World Series
Blood on the Blade
Across the Seas
The Savage Wilderness
The Bear and the Wolf
Erik The Navigator

The Vengeance Trail

The Reconquista Chronicles
Castilian Knight
El Campeador
The Lord of Valencia

The Aelfraed Series
(Britain and Byzantium 1050 A.D. - 1085 A.D.)
Housecarl
Outlaw
Varangian

**The Anarchy Series England
1120-1180**
English Knight
Knight of the Empress
Northern Knight
Baron of the North
Earl
King Henry's Champion
The King is Dead
Warlord of the North
Enemy at the Gate
The Fallen Crown
Warlord's War

Kingmaker
Henry II
Crusader
The Welsh Marches
Irish War
Poisonous Plots
The Princes' Revolt
Earl Marshal
The Perfect Knight

Border Knight
1182-1300
Sword for Hire
Return of the Knight
Baron's War
Magna Carta
Welsh Wars
Henry III
The Bloody Border
Baron's Crusade
Sentinel of the North
War in the West
Debt of Honour
The Blood of the Warlord (Feb 2022)

Sir John Hawkwood Series
France and Italy 1339- 1387
Crécy: The Age of the Archer
Man At Arms
The White Company

Lord Edward's Archer
Lord Edward's Archer
King in Waiting
An Archer's Crusade
Targets of Treachery
The Great Cause

Struggle for a Crown

1360- 1485
Blood on the Crown
To Murder A King
The Throne
King Henry IV
The Road to Agincourt
St Crispin's Day
The Battle For France
The Last Knight

Tales from the Sword I
(Short stories from the Medieval period)

Tudor Warrior series
England and Scotland in the late 145th and early 15th century
Tudor Warrior

Conquistador
England and America in the 16th Century
Conquistador

Modern History

The Napoleonic Horseman Series
Chasseur à Cheval
Napoleon's Guard
British Light Dragoon
Soldier Spy
1808: The Road to Coruña
Talavera
The Lines of Torres Vedras
Bloody Badajoz
The Road to France
Waterloo

The Lucky Jack American Civil War series
Rebel Raiders
Confederate Rangers
The Road to Gettysburg

The British Ace Series
1914
1915 Fokker Scourge
1916 Angels over the Somme
1917 Eagles Fall
1918 We will remember them
From Arctic Snow to Desert Sand
Wings over Persia

Combined Operations series
1940-1945
Commando
Raider
Behind Enemy Lines
Dieppe
Toehold in Europe
Sword Beach
Breakout
The Battle for Antwerp
King Tiger
Beyond the Rhine
Korea
Korean Winter

Tales from the Sword II
(Short stories from the Modern period)

Other Books
Great Granny's Ghost (Aimed at 9-14-year-old young people)

For more information on all of the books then please visit the author's
website at www.griffhosker.com where there is a link to contact him or
visit his Facebook page: GriffHosker at Sword Books